# Deadly Crush

Books by Maddie Day

*Country Store Mysteries*
FLIPPED FOR MURDER
GRILLED FOR MURDER
WHEN THE GRITS HIT THE FAN
BISCUITS AND SLASHED BROWNS
DEATH OVER EASY
STRANGLED EGGS AND HAM
NACHO AVERAGE MURDER
CANDY SLAIN MURDER
NO GRATER CRIME
BATTER OFF DEAD
FOUR LEAF CLEAVER
DEEP FRIED DEATH
CHRISTMAS COCOA MURDER
(with Carlene O'Connor and Alex Erickson)
CHRISTMAS SCARF MURDER
(with Carlene O'Connor and Peggy Ehrhart)

*Cozy Capers Book Group Mysteries*
MURDER ON CAPE COD
MURDER AT THE TAFFY SHOP
MURDER AT THE LOBSTAH SHACK
MURDER IN A CAPE COTTAGE
MURDER AT A CAPE BOOKSTORE
MURDER AT THE RUSTY ANCHOR

*Local Foods Mysteries*
A TINE TO LIVE, A TINE TO DIE
'TIL DIRT DO US PART
FARMED AND DANGEROUS
MURDER MOST FOWL
MULCH ADO ABOUT MURDER

*Cece Barton Mysteries*
MURDER UNCORKED
DEADLY CRUSH
CHRISTMAS MITTENS MURDER
(with Lee Hollis and Lynn Cahoon)

Published by Kensington Publishing Corp.

# Maddie Day

# Deadly Crush

Kensington Publishing Corp.
www.kensingtonbooks.com

KENSINGTON BOOKS are published by

Kensington Publishing Corp.
900 Third Avenue
New York, NY 10022

All Kensington titles, imprints, and distributed lines are available at special quantity discounts for bulk purchases for sales promotion, premiums, fund-raising, educational, or institutional use. Special book excerpts or customized printings can also be created to fit specific needs. For details, write or phone the office of the Kensington Special Sales Manager: Attn. Special Sales Department, Kensington Publishing Corp., 900 Third Avenue, New York, NY 10022. Phone: 1-800-221-2647.

Library of Congress Card Catalogue Number: 2024940937

KENSINGTON and the KENSINGTON COZIES teapot logo Reg. US Pat. & TM Off.

ISBN: 978-1-4967-4233-9
First Kensington Hardcover Edition: December 2024

ISBN: 978-1-4967-4235-3 (ebook)

10 9 8 7 6 5 4 3 2 1

Printed in the United States of America

For Ida Rose Maxwell-Russell, my sweet first grandchild
and the best baby girl in the known universe

# Acknowledgments

Thanks again to now-retired Cloverdale police chief Jason Ferguson, for answering more of my questions about small-town policing in Northern California. Continuing thanks to all the Reinhardts, my beloved San Francisco family, who feed me meals and information and let me stay in their beautiful Geyserville aerie.

I was remiss, in the acknowledgments in *Murder Uncorked*, not to give credit to Janet Catherine Johnston, a New England friend and speculative fiction author. She also happens to be an astrophysicist, teaches belly dancing, and holds a private pilot license. Thanks, Janet, for letting me channel a few of your many talents into Mooncat's character.

My town's historical organization, the Amesbury Carriage Museum, hosts a gala fundraiser and auction each year, to which I often donate the right to name a character in my next book. At last year's event, board member Pamela Fenner was the high bidder, and asked me to use the name of her late husband, Paul Fenner. In real life, they had lived in Northern California for many years, where Paul had become an amateur expert on wines and had made his own. Pam, I hope you love my version of Paul as the Colinas chief of police.

I modeled the Colinas Cat Rescue facility on our fabulous local Merrimack River Feline Rescue Society, where I have helped out in the past as well as adopted cats from. As far as I know, no MRFRS volunteers have ever been homicide victims.

The novel Cece reads about three generations of women on a wacky road trip to Graceland is *Graceland* by Nancy Crochiere and is a must-read.

As I was promoting *Murder Uncorked*, I met a woman who said her adult son was a person with Down syndrome, and that he was a voracious reader who loved all my cozies. I was so touched and impressed I had to give a reading habit to Mooncat's niece in this book. Thank you, Julie on Cape Cod, and I hope Brian enjoyed the books I signed for him.

Many thanks to Julie Pedroncelli St. John of Pedroncelli Vineyard for helping with a few realistic details (and for hosting my launch party for *Murder Uncorked*, book one in the series, when it came out). I'm also grateful that viticulturalist and Pedroncelli Winery vineyard manager Lance Blakeley took time out of his workday at the winery to answer my questions about lethal vineyard tools. Wine reviewer Jo Diaz helped with several details in this story.

Amy Glaser once again gave this book a close read and straightened me (and Cece) out in all kinds of ways.

This book took me a bit longer to write than usual. As I was closing in on the end of the first draft, my beloved first grandbaby was born three months early. My attention (rightly) went to sending out love, concern, and tiny baby clothes to my son and daughter-in-law, who sat with and cared for Ida Rose for more than a dozen weeks in the NICU half the country away. I'm happy to report that our little girl is home and thriving and the love of my life. Like any proud Gram, I'd be happy to bore you with pictures on my phone next time we meet.

Note to readers: The ideas and words in this novel were generated entirely by the author without contribution from an AI application. I wish I didn't have to include that statement, but you should know where your fiction comes from.

Thank you to my agent, John Talbot, and to my talented author pals, the Wicked Authors. Come visit us at WickedAuthors.com. I'm also part of Mystery Lovers' Kitchen, where you can find a fabulous author and her original recipe every day of the month.

I'm grateful to John Scognamiglio and Larissa Ackerman as

well as the rest of the expert team of Kensington publicists, artists, production staff, and salespeople. I also want to thank my talented graphics and social media helper, Jennifer McKee. You're the best.

To my sons John David and Allan and my daughters-in-law, Alexandra and Alison, to my sisters Janet and Barbara, to my dear Hugh: Bless you for your support and love, always. And thank you to all the enthusiastic readers, fans, librarians, and booksellers out there—I couldn't do it without you.

# CHAPTER 1

I drummed my fingers on the bar, about to panic.

January in the Alexander Valley north of San Francisco wasn't particularly warm. Today wasn't sunny, either, counter to most out-of-staters' image of California. A winter rain was forecast for later. I needed the lights and heat on, ASAP. Fifteen minutes before the Vino y Vida wine bar opened at one o'clock was no time for the electricity to still be off.

"What's wrong with you, Ian?" electrician Karl Meier snarled at his helper, who stood on a six-foot ladder. "I told you how to wrap that junction."

Karl's nephew, a skinny blond twenty-something with three piercings in each ear, ignored the verbal abuse and snipped off the piece of black electrical tape he'd been using.

I hoped the young guy knew what he was doing. Karl, neither skinny nor blond, had been the only electrician who responded to my queries for someone who could do the work.

I'd been the Vino y Vida manager here in the town of Colinas for almost a year, and our bottom line was healthy. It was about time for some upgrades to this popular destination housed in one of the antique adobe buildings that formed a cluster adjoining the historical museum. I wanted to start my low-level renovation by swapping out the old pendant—and petulant—light fixtures for new ones.

But Karl and Ian had arrived late. Their work proceeded slower than fine wine aging in oak barrels. Stocky, dark-haired Karl spent more time harassing the kid than working. The electrician didn't attempt to keep his voice down and he stepped outside for phone conversations half a dozen times. What ever happened to the work ethic, not to mention common kindness?

Despite the weather, or maybe because of it, I already had folks milling around on the sidewalk in front. They peered in the windows, eager to hoist a glass of one of the area's excellent vintages. The Alexander Valley here in northern Sonoma County was Napa's less well-known little sister. Many said our wines were better than Napa's, and I had to agree.

"Karl, I need to open." I crossed my arms over my chest. "And I can't function very well without electricity. I told you the job had to be finished before one o'clock."

He whirled. His already small eyes squinted and his mouth looked like he'd tasted something disgusting. But, as if he realized he'd been addressed by someone he needed to stay on good terms with in order to be paid for his work, he smoothed his expression.

"We're doing our best, Ms. Bart on." Karl spoke through his smile. "I'm sorry for the delay. Everything always takes longer in an old building, as I'm sure you're aware. Poor quality previous work, et cetera, et cetera. We'll be finished soon, and I know you'll be happy with the job."

I'd have been a lot happier if they'd been out of here half an hour ago. I'd uncorked and tasted today's wines, which were lined up on the bar. Glasses were sparkling and ready to go. The baskets of pretzels and rice crackers were filled. My card reader was fired up and ready, except running on a phone signal, not Wi-Fi. My starting cash was ready in the cash drawer. The too-quiet, too-cool air smelled of wine. It looked like I was going to have to open without power.

Karl turned away. "I'm tired of your incompetence, kid. Get down," he ordered Ian, his voice terse and tense. "I'll finish it the right way. Go get the rest of the lights out of their boxes. I assume you can do that without screwing up like you usually do."

Ian shrugged. Once down from the ladder and facing away from his uncle, he gave me a quick "What can you do?" look. He had the same small, deep blue eyes under a prominent brow as his uncle.

I felt bad for him. I should have listened to Jo Jarvin, my friend and the mechanic I used for Blue, my 1966 Mustang convertible. I'd called her earlier about dropping off my car this afternoon.

"You hired Karl?" Jo had asked, her voice rising. "Cece, I divorced the jerk for a reason."

"He was the only electrician around who was available."

"The man is a massive piece of, um, trash. He turns on the charm in public but insults and berates those he's ostensibly close to. Good luck, is all I can say."

Luck was all I could hope for at this point. That, and the wine bar lights working when we flipped the switch.

# CHAPTER 2

The guys were still working at two o'clock when my employee Mooncat Smith joined me behind the bar for her shift. I insisted they finish in the bar area first and clean up so I could pour and serve, but two of the tables were still off limits. Despite the weather, I'd seated several parties on the patio outside overlooking the Russian River. Both were groups of young people who said they didn't mind the cold, damp air.

"This isn't good," Mooncat murmured. The statuesque seventy-year-old had a fuchsia-colored ribbon woven into her long steel-gray braid, a ribbon that matched her flowing silk tunic, and she smelled faintly of lavender. She gazed at Karl's back as he reached up from the ladder to attach the last light.

"It isn't," I agreed. "And it'll be the last time I hire him to do any work in here."

"You told them we opened at one, I assume." She tied on one of our maroon half aprons.

"I did."

Karl twisted to look down at Ian, barking out an order and holding his hand out for a tool. Mooncat blinked.

"Don't tell me you hired Karl Meier." Her expression was grim.

"I'm afraid I did. Why, do you know him?"

A group of older women pushed through the door and approached the bar.

"I'll tell you later," Mooncat said in a low voice. "Just don't ask me to be nice to him."

"I promise. Can you check on the folks outside, please?" I smiled at the newcomers. "Welcome to Vino y Vida. Here's what we're pouring today." I described the Pedroncelli zinfandel and the other wines from valley vineyards as I wondered what Mooncat knew about Karl.

"What's the Winter Wine Road?" a white-haired woman asked. "We saw the poster."

"It's a fun event this weekend," I said. "Each person needs to buy a ticket, then you visit all the participating Alexander Valley wineries and take selfies. The first vineyard you go to gives you a glass for the day and a wine tote bag."

"Do they have buses or shuttles?" a trim blond woman asked.

"No, but the ticket for a designated driver is minimal," I said. "In fact, they won't accept big groups."

"There's only four of us," another one said. "We're all in a book group in Massachusetts."

"This trip must be a nice change of pace for you all." I thought of my friend Cam Flaherty, a farmer in the northeastern part of that state, who had given me tips about investigating a murder when I'd met her a little over a year ago at Christmastime. "And of weather."

"I'll say." The first woman tossed her head. "Although it's chilly here today, but at least it isn't snowing. Is your wine bar on the Winter Road?"

"No, but we'll be open all weekend."

In fact, my fraternal twin, Alicia, a longtime Colinas resident and successful real estate agent, told me to expect a lot of the overflow from the event. Allie said folks who didn't get enough tasting or who couldn't—or didn't want to—score tickets would stop in here for more wine. Extra business was fine with me.

I was glad for the tip. This was my first winter managing the wine bar, a job I'd started last spring after selling my house in Pasadena and moving up here to be closer to Allie and her family. I'd bought a sweet cottage, had a great next-door neighbor, and had made some friends. Plus, I loved hanging out with my twin nephews, Arthur and Franklin.

I'd also acquired a beau of sorts, the good-looking and mysterious Benjamin Cohen. He was as busy as I was, but we enjoyed each other's company and tried to carve out regular time to spend together.

Right now it was time to explain and pour local vintages.

By two thirty Karl approached me. Ian had carried out the ladder and toolbox and came back to sweep up bits of wire and detritus that the pair had left on the floor. He'd asked me for a rag to wipe off the tables they'd been working above.

"You're all set." Karl handed me a scribbled piece of paper. "Here's your invoice."

I stared at it but kept my hands on the bar. "I'd like a digital invoice. You have my email." What kind of business owner handwrote a bill on what looked like a piece of scrap paper? "Also, you haven't turned the power back on and tested the lights. Please do so before you leave."

He glowered for a moment before heading into the back room where the electrical box was. A second later, the cooler hummed into action. By the time I finished pouring a glass of a crisp unoaked chardonnay and set it on the polished redwood slab that was our bar, all the hanging lights glowed. Nothing shorted out or flickered. The guy might be a jerk, and a slow-moving one, but he seemed to know his profession.

He stepped back in. "Satisfied?"

"Thank you." I wasn't about to say more than that.

Mooncat approached, holding a tray of empty glasses. She set it down, her mouth pressed into a tense line.

"Hey there, Martha." Karl shifted into what he must think was his charm mode.

Uh-oh. He was aiming for trouble if he addressed her as Martha. Her parents had saddled her with the name, which she'd legally changed to Mooncat the day she turned eighteen. I knew she hated it.

"How's that niece of yours?" he asked.

"She's fine, as long as you stay away from her, Charlie." Her voice dripped with disdain. "And away from here, as far as I'm concerned."

*Charlie?*

He held up both palms. "Hey, hey, now. It was a simple question."

"Goodbye, Karl," I said.

Mooncat watched him leave. "That dude is so not my favorite person. He's bad news, Cece. Like, ultra-super ratso bad news."

# CHAPTER 3

I pulled Blue into the lot at JJ's Automotive at a little after five. The engine of my beloved ride was running rough. With such an old car, I always wanted to have problems attended to sooner rather than later.

Mooncat said she would hold down the fort at the wine bar while I ran the car over to JJ's at the edge of town. I'd have to hustle to walk back to Vino y Vida, but I could use more steps for the day, since I'd driven to work.

The sight of a bunch of very old cars in pristine condition always warmed my heart. Lined up along the side of the lot today were an early sixties VW Bug next to a late fifties Volvo sedan, both with rounded corners and tops. A long, big-finned black Cadillac was snuggled up to a turquoise-and-white Buick. The red '48 Chevy pickup that Jo drove to jump-start customers' dead batteries and pick up supplies was parked on the other side. I parked my vintage ride next to the Beetle.

"Hey, girl." Jo appeared in the open bay door, wiping her hands on a red rag. Her short platinum hair poked up all which way, as usual, and she wore her everyday uniform of work boots and dark blue work pants with a heavy metal band T-shirt. Today's featured Iron Maiden, with a long-sleeved waffle-weave shirt underneath for warmth.

"Hey, yourself." I handed her my spare car key, which I kept on a purple Alicia Halstead Properties key chain, one of Allie's giveaways. "Blue's feeling a little under the weather. Can you doctor her back to health?"

"You know it."

A golden retriever moseyed up, yawning.

"Hey, Ouro," I said, stroking his smooth head. "Were you having a siesta?"

"His life is one big siesta, punctuated with meals and the occasional burst of ball chasing." Jo gave the dog a fond look and stroked his head. She glanced up. "You want me to look at Blue now, or are you leaving her?"

"I need to get back to work. I'll leave her."

"Any sense of what the problem is?" Jo asked.

"Maybe the timing is off? I'm not sure. The engine sounds rough, and it's probably overdue for an oil change."

"But you haven't noticed leaks."

"No, thank goodness." A crack in the engine block would spell doom for my old girl.

"I'll do my usual once-over." Jo tilted her head. "Want a ride back?"

"I'd love one. Thanks."

"Give me a minute to close up."

I nodded. I'd rather hitch a ride in that glorious red truck than trudge in the twilight. I'd forgotten about the still-early sunset. The impending rain hadn't happened yet, but the clouds made the end of the day gloomy.

Jo disappeared into the back office. I gazed around the shop, which smelled of oil and rubber, exactly how a classic-car repair shop should smell. A big red tool cabinet held drawers full of wrenches, gauges, screwdrivers, and who knew what else. Shelves held oil filters and other small parts in their boxes. Larger tools hung from hooks on the wall. New tires in several sizes marched on end along a rack high on the wall.

A hydraulic lift filled the center of the shop. Now fully lowered to only a couple of inches above the smooth concrete floor, its four extensions stuck out like arms and legs in Vs. I'd seen Jo drive a car over the arms and position it. She used a lever on the wall to control the lift. She raised it until it almost carried the weight of the car, then squatted to make sure each arm support was where it needed to be to balance the vehicle evenly.

"Nobody wants a vintage automobile sliding off this thing," she'd said. "Me, least of all."

My mechanic only worked on cars with what she called analog engines—those made before computers were part of the package. Pistons and valves, spark plugs and a carburetor, plus a radiator and a few belts were pretty much all a vehicle needed, in Jo's opinion. And mine.

In a place like California, where undercarriages didn't rust out from salt applied to winter roads, vintage cars were plentiful. Given a competent caretaker like Jo, they could run forever.

I sometimes thought, if my life hadn't gone differently, I might have liked being a mechanic of simple combustion engines myself. But I'd dropped out of college to marry Greg. Daughter Zoe, now a sophomore at University of California, Davis, came along immediately after. I followed Greg's career instead of finding one of my own until his imploded. After his death eleven years ago, my sense of being a failure kept me from pursuing any meaningful work until now.

Jo, reemerging from the office door, interrupted my reveries. "Ready to roll?" A weathered canvas knapsack was slung over one shoulder as she closed the bay and turned the handle to lock the door. "*Ourinho, vem ca. Vamos para casa.*"

The dog trotted up and climbed into the middle of the red truck's wide bench seat. Jo's late mother had been from the Azores, and I was used to the Portuguese my friend sometimes sprinkled into her speech.

"Had your least favorite person in the bar today," I murmured as I clicked shut my lap belt, a safety feature Jo had added.

She shot me an alarmed glance.

"Yes, I know you warned me about Karl," I said.

Ouro gave a sharp bark.

"It's okay, buddy." Jo laid her hand on his head, then fired up the truck, which she always kept well tuned. "Ouro did not like my ex one bit. I should have listened to the dog from the beginning. He's a better judge of character than I am."

"That's pretty common, isn't it? I've heard dogs can tell what a person is like on a basic level."

"This one sure can."

"Anyway," I went on as the truck bumped over a pothole. "Karl and his helper were late and slow, but they seem to have done good work."

"He does know electrical systems." She pulled onto Manzanita, the main drag in town. "I have to give him that."

"But he's not much of a businessperson, and he was totally mean to his assistant."

"Also no surprise." She slowed for a stop sign, double-clutching to downshift. "Would you hire him again?"

"No way."

# CHAPTER 4

Two women traipsed into Vino y Vida at seven thirty that evening. Both looked taller than my five foot eight. One furled an umbrella, while the other shoved back the hood on a blue rain jacket. The predicted precipitation had begun shortly after Jo dropped me back at the wine bar. The fresh air the women swept in with them smelled like rain.

"Welcome to Vino y Vida," I called out from behind the bar and pointed. "We have coat hooks around the corner there." The wine bar included a small hallway that kept the doors to the restrooms discreetly out of sight, and I'd hung a line of hooks for coats, with a shelf above for hats.

A moment later they slid onto stools facing me. I blinked. These two women, about fifty, had nearly identical faces. One wore a blue fleece hoodie, the other a green fleece zip-up. Both had a hairline low on their brow, deep-set brown eyes, and locks as thick as mine. Green-fleece's dark hair, shot through with silver, was pulled back into a silver clip. The other woman's hair was cut to a half inch below her ears and had been professionally lightened and streaked. None of those differences could hide their similarity.

"I'm Cece Barton. Here's what we're pouring tonight." I gestured toward the whiteboard behind me, which listed Riesling, the unoaked chardonnay, a local petite syrah, a lovely zinfandel, and a dessert wine. "Have you been here before?"

The one in blue smiled. "No, oddly enough, considering how much we love wine. I'm Zara Choate, and this is my sister, Tara Pulanski." Zara pronounced her name to rhyme with "are a" but Tara sounded identical to "terra."

"And yes, we're identical twins," Tara said. "In case you hadn't noticed."

"Nice to meet you both." I returned the smile. "I'm a twin myself, but my sister Allie and I are fraternal."

"Allie Halstead?" Zara asked.

"The same," I said. "Pretty much everyone knows her."

"I haven't seen you around town, though." Tara studied me.

"I moved here less than a year ago."

"Cats are all that matters to her." Zara elbowed her sister. "Do you have any, Cece?"

"I do. Two. Are you a veterinarian?" I asked Tara.

"No. I'm the director of Colinas Cat Rescue. I hope yours are rescues."

"Both are, but they weren't adopted from your facility." Mittens, in fact, had adopted my nephews last winter at the weekly Colinas farmers market, but poor Arthur was so allergic they had to make a home in their shed for the kitty. When I moved north a few months later, I offered to take her. Both Arthur and Franklin knew they were always welcome to come over and play with the cat and with my kitty, Martin, whom I brought with me from Pasadena. "I've thought of calling to see if you need help at the shelter. Do you take volunteers?"

"Always," Tara said. "Thank you."

"Great. I'll be in touch." I'd been studying Zara. "Haven't I seen you at church?"

"Manzanita Congregational?" she asked. "Absolutely. Now I realize why you look familiar."

"I attend worship services most Sundays, but I usually don't stay for fellowship, and I'm not involved in any committees or Sunday school."

"That's okay. All are welcome."

"I appreciate that. Now, what would you both like to sip tonight?" I asked.

I poured the petite syrah for Tara and a Riesling for Zara, then headed over to a table of customers signaling for a second round. Mooncat came in from the back, where she'd been readying a mixed case of Zelma Vineyards varietals to ship. She headed to a table of six with our portable card reader to ring up their glasses.

Mooncat joined me behind the counter. "Zara, good to see you, girl. How's your shimmy coming?" She held out her arms and set her hips to undulate.

"Stop, now." Zara cast her gaze at the ceiling. To me she said, "I took Mooncat's belly dancing class last fall. Every time I see her she wants me to do stuff with my hips that they weren't made for."

"You're a female of the species," Mooncat said. "Of course they were made for it." She headed off to help a few more customers.

Zara shook her head and took a sip of wine. She rolled it in her mouth as if wanting to taste every aspect.

"Zara, what do you do for work?" I asked.

"I teach art at the community college, and I do my own art."

"Do you have any pieces at Acorn?" I gestured vaguely in the direction of one of the adobes nearby that housed an art gallery.

"I might soon. It's lovely in here, by the way." She waved her hand, encompassing the interior space. "You have a good eye."

Tara swiveled on her stool to survey the interior of Vino y Vida. "I like what you've done with it."

"Thank you," I said. "I can't take credit for all the decor, but it's nice, isn't it?" The gorgeous thick slab of polished redwood that served as a bar had always been here. This place had been a saloon in its earliest days over a century ago. The patio outside overlooking the Russian River was also preexisting. In the last ten months I'd freshened up the posters and artwork on the walls, made sure windows were clean in and out, and had given everything a fresh coat of off-white paint, including the bathrooms. The patio seating was wine barrels surrounded by stools, with a few low tables along the iron fence overlooking the water. It was all my doing.

"Years ago this place was a dump," Tara said. "The adobe was dissolving, the historical displays were dusty and broken, and nobody seemed to care if the buildings collapsed and slid into the water."

"That's awful." My bar cozied up with the Colinas History Museum on the long side of the L-shaped cluster. On the other side was a bocce court and benches overlooking the river. Forming the foot of the letter was the Acorn art gallery, which was owned and run by my friend Henry Cruvellier, and Alexander Books. "These antique adobes are treasures."

"That's why we mounted a fundraising campaign to preserve and rescue them." Tara lifted her chin and smoothed down the sleeves of her shirt.

"The town really got behind her. Finally." Zara tapped the edge of the bar. "Ask Allie. She'll remember."

"Awesome," Mooncat said.

I bobbed my head in agreement.

"The pendant lights are a nice touch," Zara added.

"Thanks," I said. "We had them installed earlier today."

"Karl hasn't been back to preen over his handiwork?" Mooncat asked me.

"Wait." Tara frowned. "Karl Meier is your electrician?"

"Not exactly," I said. "He did the job today, but I doubt I'll ask him back."

"Probably a good thing," Tara muttered.

"I'll say." Zara raised a single eyebrow.

"Did one of you have a bad experience with him?" I asked.

Zara pointed at Tara.

"Yes, but that's water under the bridge. I'm done with him, and good riddance too," Tara said. "I hope you were serious about volunteering, Cece. We're really short-handed."

"I'll see if I can work it into my schedule." I had a sudden pang of wondering if I'd agreed to an obligation I couldn't follow through on.

Tara's phone buzzed, and she turned away to attend to it.

I was just about to ask them what they meant about Karl when a group of about ten young men and women ambled in. They were laughing and enjoying themselves, and all had an outdoorsy look to them with fit bodies, sensible shoes, and ruddy faces. Maybe they were a running group or a hiking club. None appeared older than twenty-five, and some were possibly a lot younger.

"Excuse me," I said to the twins as I headed for the newcomers. I introduced myself. "Because of the rain, we're a little short on seats."

"If you don't mind, we can stand around the bar," one woman said.

"That's fine." I smiled. "I just need to check everyone's IDs. You don't have to tell me, but I hope you have a couple of designated drivers assigned."

"A hired party bus is waiting outside." A red-haired man, who turned out to be twenty-three, slung his arm over the first speaker's shoulders. "We're getting married Saturday." The pair beamed at each other.

"Congratulations." That called for complimentary glasses of an SOM sparkling wine for the bride and groom on the house. "Are you all a hiking club or something?"

"No," the bride answered. "We're hotshots."

I tilted my head. That seemed like an odd way to introduce oneself.

"She means we're wildfire fighters," Red Hair said. "On a hotshot crew."

"I see." I smiled. "Thanks for clarifying that."

"We have a whole month off and decided to grab the chance to have a wedding with all our crew around us," she said.

I looked up from the last driver's license. "That's such important work. Thank you for doing it." It was also dangerous work. Each one of them risked their lives every time they went out. All had proved to be over twenty-one, which must be a requirement for the job. "Come on over to the bar and I'll get you set up."

Zara and Tara left after one glass each. I was too busy to talk to either of them again, but when they paid, I told Tara I'd call about a good time to visit the shelter. Maybe then I could pick her brain about her negative experience with Karl.

# CHAPTER 5

My phone rang on the bedside table. It was barely seven thirty in the morning. I tended to be a night owl and hadn't slept until after midnight. I didn't have to be anywhere for hours. I usually arrived early to open Vino y Vida, but never six hours early.

The phone rang again, then stopped, probably after kicking into voice mail. I relaxed into my soft, warm pillow. I could grab another half hour of snooze time and deal with the caller later.

The cursed device began to ring anew.

"All right, already." Maybe it was Allie with an urgent child care request. The call could be from Zoe, wanting to talk through a paper or a feeling, except that never happened. Hey, there's always a first time, I told myself. Or Mooncat might have had one of her migraine headaches spring itself on her.

Letting out a sigh, I swung my legs over the edge of the bed and sat, jostling Martin, the larger of my two cats. Martin leapt down. On the rug, Mittens began to bathe herself. I grabbed the phone, which was still attached to the charger, and squinted at the display. This forty-three-year-old was going to need readers soon.

"Jo?" I said aloud to myself before I swiped the call into action. I hadn't a clue why she would be calling before she even opened her shop. "Jo? What's up?"

"Can you come to JJ's, Cece?" Her voice, already low, wobbled. "Like right now?"

"What's the matter?" I was wide awake now.

"I can't. I mean . . ." She went quiet. "Please?"

Whatever this was, it was serious. "Yes." I unplugged the phone. "Are you hurt? Do you need an ambulance?"

"I'm not hurt."

"It'll be ten or fifteen minutes. Sit tight, okay? Get away from danger." Whatever the danger might be.

"Thank you." She disconnected.

Just . . . wow. It wasn't a fire, surely. She said she wasn't hurt. I hoped she wasn't being threatened, especially by someone like Karl. But wouldn't she have mentioned that, or hinted at it? Perhaps she'd received a foreclosure notice. Maybe the crisis was a massive leak from the tank where she stored discarded oil. That would present an environmental hazard, which California was strict about, and therefore a huge cleanup hassle for Jo.

Whatever it was, I didn't have time to speculate. A friend needed me. I threw on stretchy pants and a sweatshirt. I swiped a toothbrush across my teeth and a brush through my hair. I pulled on tennies and a jacket and grabbed my phone and keys.

"Back in a flash, kitties," I told the two. Martin wove around my legs plaintively for his morning wet food. Mittens sat next to the food bowls and stared, ever haughtily.

"Hey, Ms. Mittens. Nobody's starving around here." Their dry food bowl was at least half full. They would both survive until I returned, accusatory looks and complaints notwithstanding. I hadn't taken time for coffee. They could certainly wait for breakfast.

I opened the connecting door to the garage. Which was empty of an automobile.

Of course it was. Jo had my car. I hurried to slide keys and phone into a cross-body bag, buckled on my helmet, and pedaled out on my new bike. Someone had hit me—on purpose—last fall as I crossed an intersection on my beloved yellow retro bicycle. The new model was equally as retro, with a wide, cushioned seat and upright handlebars, but electric green—although not an electric bike—and featured an even bigger basket to carry purchases home in.

It had taken me a while to feel safe riding again. Right now I had no choice. Walking would take too long. Ride share services so far hadn't really included Colinas on their radar. I'd summoned one before, but I had to wait an hour, not the five minutes I'd been used to in Pasadena or San Francisco.

Cycling it was, and as fast as I could safely go. At least the rain had stopped overnight.

# CHAPTER 6

Jo sat on the bench in front of her shop. She wore a heavy fleece sweatshirt zipped up to the neck. Her forearms rested on her knees, and her hands were clasped not in prayer but as if she didn't know what to do with them otherwise. Ouro's head was on his paws, but he lifted it when I wheeled up. Last night's gentle rain had moved through. The air was chilly with the sun barely up, but the sky was cloud-free.

The big bay door was shut, as was the service door to the office.

"I'm here." I levered down the kickstand and joined mechanic and dog.

Jo turned her head. She gazed up at me, her olive skin looking bleached, her eyes pained. "You know, Cece, after I married, I had a few rotten years there. But I thought my life was back on track again. Right? I mean, my business is thriving. I love what I do, and I'm good at it. I have friends, a great dog, my health, no appreciable debt."

"Absolutely. And I hear a 'but' coming."

"You can say that again."

I unclipped my helmet and hung it on a handlebar.

"I really appreciate your coming." After a moment, she exhaled a creaky breath and stood. "We'd better get this over with."

Ouro jumped up, gluing himself to Jo's leg.

"No." She pointed at the ground. "Lie down."

The dog whined.

"*Agora.*" Jo's tone and pointing were clear. She meant "Now."

He obeyed, assuming the Sphinx pose.

"Good boy. Stay." To me, she said, "He can't be in there."

Why not? My concern rising, I followed her through the office door, clicking it shut behind me. Jo moved into the garage proper, and I stepped in behind her. She moved to one side. My hand flew to my mouth as a noisy breath rushed in.

A man lay face down. He was pinned under the lift, except it wasn't lifted at all. "Pinned" wasn't the right word either. It was more like he'd been crushed. My brain was oddly keeping track of words. Words or not, this was murder. He couldn't have lain on the floor AND controlled the lever. The bouquet of the shop now included another smell, and it wasn't a pleasant one.

Dark stuff stained the floor under his head. That had to be blood. The thought roiled my stomach. But who was this guy? And why was he dead? Here, in Jo's shop, crushed under the center of her livelihood.

I wanted to look away. And yet . . . something about his dark hair made me keep my focus on the horrific sight.

Grabbing Jo's hand, I mustered my voice. "Is that Karl?"

Her eyes wide under a furrowed brow, she nodded. Once, slowly.

"Did you, um, touch him?" I whispered.

"He's cold, Cece. Karl is dead."

I shuddered. "I feel like I've never seen a dead person before." I hadn't even seen Daddy's body after the bus hit him. Mom had identified him and, according to his wishes, had him cremated. My grandfathers had been cremated, too, and one of my grandmothers. We didn't do open caskets in our family.

"That's why I called you." She tore her glance away from the corpse. "You solved that murder last fall. And wasn't there one the Christmas before that you worked on?"

"Yes. Kind of. Except those people were already dead and I didn't see their bodies."

"I need to call the police, don't I?" Jo asked.

"Absolutely." Why had she called me instead of 911 in the first place? "We should go outside." I scanned the garage. The back door was another wide roll-up door, which opened to the hill behind the shop. She often left it open when the weather was fine, but it had been closed yesterday when I dropped off Blue. "Is that door locked?"

"It should be." She swallowed and took a shaky step toward the back. "I'll check it."

"No," I said, grabbing her arm. "I do know one thing. We need to stay out of here. You can go around outside to test the lock. I'll come with you."

I glanced once more at the deadly lift and the crushed remains of Karl Meier. And then I saw something else. A big red adjustable wrench lay on the floor a few feet beyond Karl. Jo would never leave a tool on the floor like that. The handle of the wrench was over a foot long, and the jaws of the head gaped open.

The tool looked heavy enough to inflict real damage if it was used as a weapon. If it had been used to crack Karl on the head, for example.

# CHAPTER 7

As I waited on the bench in front of JJ's Automotive for the police to arrive, I realized with a shock that I had seen a dead body before. Of course I had. The shock of seeing a lifeless Karl must have blocked the memory.

I was the one who discovered my husband's cold corpse eleven years ago. I'd been out at my part-time job for the morning. When I came home, our modest Pasadena house was too quiet. It was Greg's day off. He'd said he wasn't going anywhere, and his car was in the driveway. I called for him. Silence. I opened the door to his den and screamed.

He'd been messing with his cursed gun, the one I hated and wished he didn't own. Cleaning it, loading it, I couldn't tell. What was clear was that it had gone off and killed him. It was a horrible sight, one nobody should ever have to see.

The authorities had ruled the death accidental. I've wondered since that day if Greg somehow caused the accident. He hadn't been happy with his life. Due to his own behavior, his fancy career with the State Department had gone down the tubes. He wasn't particularly happy with me, either, which was mutual.

Accidental death or not, I was more than glad our daughter, Zoe, then ten and at elementary school, hadn't discovered him. The two had been super close.

The aftershocks of his death still affected my relationship with her. I did my best to love and parent her solo, but she blamed me for losing her precious daddy. Still did. She somehow knew he and I hadn't been getting along. My only hope was that, with maturity and a longer-lens perspective, she would understand I had nothing to do with her loss.

Jo and Ouro came back around the corner of the building to the front at the same time bike cop Lee Norsegian pedaled up. I disconnected the call I'd left open at the request of the dispatcher and stood, the seat of my pants now damp from the rain-soaked bench.

Norsegian spoke into the mike near his shoulder as he dismounted.

"Officer," I said in greeting.

"Morning, Ms. Barton, Jo." He looked from Jo to me. "Which of you discovered the remains?" A still-pale Jo raised her hand.

"Did you also view the victim, Ms. Barton?"

"Please call me Cece. Yes, I did."

"Either of you go near him? Touch him?"

"I touched his face after I saw him there. He was cold." Jo's voice wobbled.

"That's all you touched?" Norsegian asked.

She nodded and sank onto the bench. Norsegian pointed at me.

"Jo asked me to come over," I said, hearing sirens in the distance. "All I did was step into the garage. I touched the outside door handle. I think that's it."

"Good." He stepped toward Ouro and held out the back of his hand.

The dog sniffed and seemed satisfied. Lee pulled a dog biscuit out of an outer pocket on his uniform cargo pants. After Ouro scarfed it down, he sat on the ground next to Jo, alert but calm.

"Good boy." Norsegian pulled on a pair of black stretchy gloves. "You folks stay out here. The detective and others are on their way."

"Yes, sir." I perched next to Jo. "You okay?" I murmured after he'd gone inside.

"Not really." She stroked Ouro's head as if comforting herself.

My own head was exploding with questions. How had Karl gotten into the shop? Who had lowered the lift on him, and how? Maybe he was hit and fell while the lift was raised, and his attacker decided to finish off the job.

Jo's shock at finding the body was way too fresh to pester her with questions. The police would do that soon enough. I only hoped she had a good alibi.

I hit on a safe topic. "You and the officer are on a first-name basis. How do you know each other?"

"He's four or five years older than me, but his little sister and I went to school together."

"Here in Colinas?"

"Yep."

A white SUV, with SONOMA COUNTY SHERIFF written in green on the side, pulled into the lot, and was followed by a black Colinas PD cruiser and an ambulance, both with their roof lights activated. The sirens stayed silent.

A slender man in khakis and a sport coat climbed out of the passenger side of the SUV. I recognized him. Jim Quan was the county sheriff's detective who'd worked on that troublesome case of murderous mittens before Christmas over a year ago. The more recent homicide investigation had been led by Kelly Daniell, also a Sonoma County detective. Maybe she was on a different urgent case.

I rose as Quan approached.

"Cece Barton?" He squinted at me through his wire-rimmed glasses. "What brings you here?"

Jo raised her head. "I asked her to come. After I . . ." She brought her fist to her mouth and sniffled.

Norsegian emerged from the garage. "It's as reported, sir. The victim is unresponsive, without respirations, and cold to the touch."

"Thank you, Norsegian," Quan said. "Please guard the door. Everyone stay right here. I'm going to take a look inside."

Norsegian stood in front of the door with feet apart and elbows out, hands behind his back. Quan returned, looking more somber than a few minutes ago.

A tall, lean man in a long-sleeved shirt with the Colinas Police Department logo on both sleeves approached us. "You got here fast, Quan." His smile seemed perfunctory. His brown hair was short and well tamed, and frown lines creased the skin between his brows. Four stars were pinned to each collar, and on his chest was a seven-pointed star-shaped badge reading *Chief of Police, Colinas, California.*

"Chief." Quan nodded without returning the man's smile. "I was in the area."

I hadn't met the chief before, which was surprising given that I'd been involved in a murder investigation last year. Our paths simply hadn't crossed.

"Who do we have here?" the chief asked Quan, instead of greeting us.

Quan faced Jo and me. "This is Colinas Police Chief Paul Fenner. Sir, meet Jo Jarvin, proprietor of JJ's Automotive, and Cecelia Barton, who says she was summoned by Ms. Jarvin."

*Says?* Yes, I said so. Because it was true. It sounded like the detective didn't believe me.

Fenner folded his arms. "Do you know the victim?" he asked Jo.

"He's my—"

"Excuse me, miss." Quan interrupted her, his palm out in a stop gesture. "Fenner, with all due respect, homicide investigations are the purview of the county sheriff's department, as I'm sure you're aware. My team will be questioning both Ms. Jarvin and Ms. Barton, separately." He stressed the last word.

Chief Fenner made a noise in his throat. "You let us know how we can assist in any way." He made another fake smile and didn't turn his gaze away from Quan.

When the detective didn't back down from the staring match,

the chief turned away. "You can get on with your job, Norsegian," he snapped at Lee. "Establish perimeter. Guard the doors. You know the drill." As if too busy to stay, he strode back to the cruiser and drove off.

Those two top dogs seemed to have a territoriality issue. I knew Quan was competent, which was all that mattered in a homicide investigation. While not warm and fuzzy in his manner, he was respectful and all business, unlike Chief Cold and Rude Fenner.

Quan seemed to let out a breath. The ambulance had been waiting, engine idling. He headed to the driver and conferred through the open window. I heard words like "wait" and "come back." In the end, they shut off the engine and stayed.

Jo, meanwhile, slumped with her eyes closed against the bench's back. Her arms were wrapped around her torso and Ouro's head was in her lap. She looked miserable. I perched next to her. We were friends but not confidants. We'd gone for hikes a few times, and once she'd invited me for coffee to the yurt she lived in. I cared about her but wasn't sure how much consoling she needed.

As always—so far—in my life, I was fearful of going too far, of offending her. I'd failed too often at almost everything, at least in my own eyes. I was working on my self-esteem and knew part of my history was being the lesser-accomplished twin. I loved Allie with all my heart. Her being a superstar at everything she touched hadn't been easy for dyslexic me. She never rubbed it in or made me feel bad about my lesser achievements. I knew my sad-sack attitude was entirely of my own doing, but that didn't make it any easier to vanquish.

# CHAPTER 8

A county sheriff's vehicle marked "Coroner/Sheriff" pulled in a few minutes later.

"Please move away from the building," Quan instructed Jo and me. "My team needs full access to the crime scene."

Jo winced at the words but stood and trudged a few yards away, Ouro at her side. I went with her.

"Are there keys or a code we'll need to access any of the doors?" he asked her.

"No," she said. "Once you're inside, you turn the bay door handle vertically to unlock it."

"Come with me, please." He ushered the mechanic to the front seat of the vehicle he'd come in. Ouro climbed in with her. Quan leaned in and spoke with her for a moment, then shut the door with a soft thud and returned to me. "I need to ask you a few questions."

"That's fine." I hadn't had even a sip of coffee yet today. I hoped this questioning wouldn't last long.

"How do you know Ms. Jarvin?" he asked without preamble.

I pointed to Blue. "That's my car. I brought it to her for an oil change after I moved to Colinas last year. It's a 1966, and that's the era of cars she works on."

"Do you socialize with her?"

"A little. Not much."

"Please tell me about this morning."

"She called me at about seven thirty. She sounded upset and asked me to come over here right away. She didn't say why."

"Was she inside or outside when you arrived?"

"Out front with her dog," I said.

"How did she seem?"

The detective wasn't taking notes or recording our conversation. He must have a great memory.

"Pale. Upset. Shaky."

"Please go on," Quan said.

I pictured the scene. "I followed her inside. We entered through the office and stepped inside the garage proper. It was, well, you went in. It was like something from a horror movie." I hugged myself. "Awful."

"Did you know the victim?"

"He was Karl Meier, Jo's ex-husband. He did some electrical work in my wine bar yesterday. That's the only way I knew him."

"You both recognized him."

"Yes."

"How long had they been divorced?" He tilted his head.

"About three years, I think. The split happened before I knew her."

"Did you ask Ms. Jarvin how he got in there? Did you ask if she'd killed him?"

My mouth drew down. "No! Of course not. She didn't murder Karl. Jo had no reason to. She'd finally gotten apart from him, legally divorced, no financial arrangements, as far as I know. She has a great business. And to crush a man under your own lift? No way."

Seriously. Who wants to bring their car to a vintage automotive shop where someone has been murdered with part of the equipment? For Jo to kill Karl that way would be lunacy. Killing him by any method would be, but especially that one.

A Sonoma County sheriff's minivan labeled CSI UNIT pulled up. A Colinas patrol officer approached us, hovering a couple of yards away as if reluctant to interrupt.

"That'll be all for now, Ms. Barton," Quan said. "Thank you for the information." He handed me his card. "I might need to speak with you further. Please be in touch if you think of anything else, and we'd appreciate it if you stayed local for the time being."

"I have a wine bar to manage, Detective. I'm not going anywhere. Where's Kelly Daniell, by the way?"

He tilted his head. "She's out on maternity leave." He gave a single nod. "That's right, she had the case you were involved in last fall."

"She did."

"I hope you're not going to make a practice of intruding on murder investigations, Ms. Barton." His voice turned steely.

"Don't worry. I have no intention of doing that."

"Please refrain from speaking to anyone about the details of what you witnessed this morning." He turned away to speak to the officer but then faced me again. "And don't discuss it with Ms. Jarvin, either."

"Yes, sir." The dude had read my mind. I'd planned to retrieve my bicycle and walk it over to the SUV. I wanted to tell Jo to call me later if she needed to talk. Well, I still could. Nothing wrong with offering my support to a friend. I made my way to the bicycle, glad I'd parked it in front of Blue and hadn't leaned it against the shop wall, which was now marked out-of-bounds by yellow police tape.

Quan beat me to Jo. He was climbing into the driver's seat by the time I retrieved the bike and clipped on my helmet.

*Darn.* I'd have to text her, instead. She must be a wreck. Discovering Karl like that and having to close her business for a few days, at the least. Worst of all, being grilled by a county sheriff's detective.

# CHAPTER 9

Allie brought two steaming mugs of coffee to her kitchen table by the window and set one down in front of me. The sun streaming in through the eastern-facing window lit up the oak grain of the big farm table, the center of activity in this warm and welcoming family.

"I'm glad you decided to come here instead of going straight home." She sat across from me. Shorter than my five foot eight by two inches, her hair was blond to my thick honey-colored mop, and her blue eyes also differed from my gray-green ones. She clearly hadn't been out today and wasn't going anywhere any time soon. My only sister was always well coiffed and nicely dressed in public. Right now, our soft pants and sweatshirts with messy hair matched, but we'd never been mistaken for identical twins.

"Same here. Your house was more or less on the way home from Jo's shop." I sipped the aromatic coffee. "Mmm. I needed this so bad. And I knew you'd be itching to hear the news." I selected a cheese Danish from the plate she'd set out between us.

"I am. I read on the community group that something happened, and I heard the sirens earlier, although not a lot of them."

I swallowed my mouthful of sweet deliciousness. "There was no rush. Jo found her ex-husband dead in her shop."

"Whoa. Seriously?"

"Yes."

"And she called you before the police?"

"She did, although she didn't say why she wanted me to come, only that it was urgent. Odd, right?" I took another bite of pastry. It wasn't my usual healthy breakfast, but I was ravenous.

"I'll say. Who's the ex?"

I washed down the bite with more coffee. "Karl Meier. Do you know him?"

"That's unfortunate." Her lips curled as if she'd tasted wine turned to vinegar by a leaky cork. "He's, I mean, was bad news."

"You had dealings with him." I ran my fingers along the smooth grain of the table.

"Cee. I sell homes. Houses need electrical work. Yes, I'd dealt with him, but not for more than one job."

"He did some work for me yesterday at the wine bar. I didn't know about your experience with the guy, or I wouldn't have hired him. Even while he was there I'd already decided not to use him again."

"Good choice." She raised her impeccably arched eyebrows, then took a sip from her mug.

I sipped too. "Thanks for this, Al. I dashed out without one sip of coffee in me."

"For you, anything." She grinned. "Although the pastries are a day old. The agency's meet-and-greet coffee hour wasn't well attended yesterday." Once a week the real estate agency Allie had founded sponsored a casual midmorning event for prospective home buyers and sellers to drop in and meet Allie and the other agents who worked with her.

"But this Danish tastes fresh and crisp."

"There's no pastry a toaster oven can't freshen up." She helped herself to a chocolate croissant. "Have you told Benjamin what happened?"

"Not yet. I'm sure he's at work." I met the man I was now seeing in October. For a while during that homicide investigation, I thought Benjamin Cohen might have been the villain. He'd been a guest in Allie's B&B and had begun courting me. Despite being handsome and fit and gentle, he was secretive and not forthcoming about his work. Still, as I hadn't dated anyone for ten years, the attention was flattering. I was more than relieved to learn he'd been helping the police and wasn't a target of their suspicion.

"So, how did Karl die?" Allie asked.

I pictured the horrible scene and shuddered. Allie reached out a hand and covered mine.

"It's okay. You don't have to talk about it."

"It was really awful," I said. "You know, I never saw the victims last fall or the December before."

"Making Karl's the first body you'd encountered since Greg."

"Right." I swallowed. "Anyway, the detective asked me not to talk about the details."

"Kelly?"

"No, it's Jim Quan, the one from the mittens homicide."

"Yuck." Allie wrinkled her nose. "The detective who thought I'd killed that poor person."

"Among other suspects, yes."

"I mean, who murders someone over a civic disagreement? If that were the case, the population around here would be a lot smaller."

I smiled at her.

"You really can't tell me what happened?" She leaned closer over the table and whispered, "I won't tell a soul. Promise."

"Pinkie swear?" Surely my wombmate could keep the secret, which would probably leak out from some other source soon enough.

"Pinkie swear." She linked her pinkie finger with mine and squeezed.

"Okay." Somehow the feel of her finger, of her smooth skin, soothed me. We'd been pinkie swearing since at least kindergarten. "I don't want to land on Quan's bad side."

She straightened the first three fingers of her right hand and held it up. "Girl Scout's honor."

Allie had excelled at scouting, which our mom urged us both to participate in, earning the Gold Award in high school. I liked camping and horseback riding, but I had trouble with the written part of the badge process. I professed not to care about working toward scouting honors, when really I didn't want one more area where I felt I was competing with—and losing to—my twin. To be clear, she never lorded it over me and always offered her help. Except those offers had actually made me feel worse about her successes.

"Okay, okay." I took in a deep breath and let it out. "Somebody crushed Karl under the lift in Jo Jarvin's shop."

She gasped and stared at me. She opened her mouth to speak and then shut it.

"Yes. It's too horrible for words," I continued. "He was lying on the garage floor. The lift had been lowered onto him until it couldn't go any lower."

"But how . . . ? I mean, he wouldn't just lie down, right?"

"I don't know. In the moment, I couldn't ask Jo what she thought. I saw some blood near his head."

"So maybe he was shot and dragged there," she murmured.

"Or whacked on the head. Same effect. Because nobody lies down on the floor under an automotive lift voluntarily. This wasn't some teenage video challenge gone viral." I occasionally read about a poor kid who had taken a dare he or she shouldn't have, or whose body hadn't reacted like everyone else's. At least my Zoe never got into trouble with that kind of thing while she was in high school. Now, as a mostly serious college student, the danger had hopefully passed.

"How grisly would that be?" Allie shook her head. "I'm glad my kiddos aren't into that TikTok stuff yet."

"Good. Anyway, Karl's death couldn't have been suicide under any scenario I can imagine," I added.

Allie sat back and crossed her arms over her chest as her brows pulled together. I knew from our more than four decades together that she was putting her brain to work on this.

I drained my coffee.

"So," she began. "You don't think Jo would have murdered Karl, right?"

I repeated what I said to Quan. "No reason at all."

"But somebody wanted to make it look like she had."

"I hadn't thought of that. Yes. Stage the killing in her shop. But who? And how did they get in there?" I glanced at the Disney clock on the wall. When Allie and Fuller had renovated their Victorian home and expanded the kitchen, she'd decorated the space with style. It was chic without being cold, with clean lines, bright colors, and not a trace of kitsch. Except for the analog wall clock featuring cartoon characters. The boys adored it, and I appreciated that my twin was loving enough to allow a silly clock in her designer space.

Except right now the clock read ten thirty.

"I need to go get ready for work," I said. "Thanks for breakfast and the open ear."

"I'm always here, Cee."

"Just remember our pinkie swear." I stood.

She grinned again. "Cross my heart and hope to . . . help you solve this bugger."

I kissed her soft cheek and grabbed my bag. We agreed long ago to revise the end of that childhood mantra. Hoping to die was never a good thing.

# CHAPTER 10

"Thanks for filling in on a Friday, Dane," I said to my usual weekend employee at two that afternoon.

Sounding barely alive, Mooncat called to say she was down for the count with one of her occasional migraine headaches. I phoned Dane Larsen, who started working for me a couple of months ago. A visual artist, she said she needed more income after she and her husband split up. I was happy to have more help.

Henry showed Dane's paintings in his gallery, and I loved one so much I bought it to hang in here. It was a closeup of an outdoor table at a vineyard. Two people held wineglasses and clasped each other's free hand. All the picture showed were age-spotted, lined, and wrinkled hands; the wineglasses; and green vines stretching over the hills behind.

"No problem, Cece. I can always use more hours." Dane ran the soft dish towel around a glass fresh out of the dishwasher and held it up to the light to make sure it was clear of spots. Her blunt-cut nails were never entirely free of paint. I didn't care. I knew her hands were clean.

Only two small tables held wine sippers right now, but Fridays were usually busy. Having two of us on the job was more than necessary.

A couple of men came in and slid onto stools at the bar. These weren't silver-haired retiree tourists or hip high-tech workers from San Francisco. My customers wore work jeans and sturdy boots. One, who looked like he might be one of the many talented among farmers in the valley, had on a plaid flannel shirt, and the other sported a denim work shirt.

"Welcome, gentlemen," I said. "What can I pour for you today?"

Denim Shirt glanced at the whiteboard. "I'll have a glass of the AVV organic cab, please." His thick, dark hair was still shower-wet from the looks of it.

"The pinot gris for me, ma'am. We were pruning those grapes elsewhere yesterday." His smile was warm and lit up his eyes.

"Coming right up." I set down both glasses. "Where do you work pruning?"

"At Holt," Plaid Shirt said. "My name's Tom Phang, and this is Felipe Diaz."

"I'm Cece Barton, manager here. Nice to meet you both."

"We like to come taste the fruits of our line of work," Felipe said. "Well, from a year or two ago."

"Don't they give you bottles to take home?" I asked.

"Sometimes." Tom made a face. "But it's fun to get out, and we can't prune when the vines are wet with rain."

"I understand there was a murder in town." Felipe lowered his voice. "Is it true?"

Tom's expression turned somber. "We heard it was Meier, the electrician."

Dane, who had been listening, stepped closer.

"Sadly, it's true," I said. "Was it on the news?"

"Yes, but not the name," Tom said. "One of the guys told us that."

How had the news gotten out about Karl's identity? Surely the police wouldn't have released it until they'd notified Ian and any other relatives. I was positive Allie hadn't leaked the name.

"Are you talking about Karl Meier?" Dane asked.

"Yes, ma'am," Felipe said. "He did some work out at Zelma, where my brother is employed. I'm afraid the deceased, may the sainted Maria watch over his soul, was not kind to the workers."

"No, Karl wasn't a kind person by any stretch of the imagination." Dane's nostrils flared. She turned away.

She must have had a run-in with him. Was there anyone around who thought Karl was a decent person? I wasn't sure.

"Enjoy your wine, fellows." I moved down the bar next to Dane. "You hadn't heard about his murder?" I kept my voice soft.

She gave a snort. "I'm your classic clueless artist with my head in the clouds. I never hear news until it's old."

"It sounds like you had a bad experience with Karl."

"Did I ever." She shook her head. "I'll tell you later if we get a chance."

"Sounds like a plan." I glanced around. "I'll be in the back room doing some labeling. Give me a shout when things get busy." I headed into the back room.

I used to shudder when I had to work in here. I'd been attacked in this very room last fall. I had my arms full of bottles after hours and backed in through the swinging doors. It hadn't been easy, but I managed to overwhelm the killer. Now I entered face first, just in case.

I sat at the worktable with a case of Twomey Cellars sauvignon blanc and a stack of our adhesive-backed stickers. We had an agreement with several wineries to sell their bottles. Our Vino y Vida sticker was printed with our logo, two Vs cradling a round-bowled glass of wine. It read "Tasted at Vino y Vida, Colinas, California."

But first I pulled out my phone. I always switched it to Do Not Disturb while I was working, with exceptions set for Zoe, Allie, and my mom. I had text messages from Jo and Allie. And one that made me smile, from Mr. Benjamin Cohen himself. I opened his first.

**Little bird told me of disturbing discovery this AM. You okay? Thinking of you. XXOO.**

The dude was sweetness personified. Being a consultant to various law enforcement agencies, naturally he would have heard. And being him, he'd be worried about my feelings. I shot back a reply.

**I'm fine. Thanks for asking. I left Blue at JJ's yesterday, so I'm probably sans car for a few. I'll manage.**

He wrote back that I should hit him up for a ride at a moment's notice, which made me smile. I thanked him. I sent another text.

**Looking forward to Sun. XXOO**

We had a date for Sunday midday and beyond. Farmers market, lunch, a stroll, and whatever else transpired.

*Good. Me too. Call me any time.*

I sent him a thumbs-up icon and sat back. Was I fine? I seemed to be. True, witnessing Karl dead under the lift had been horrifying, but I had no emotional connection to him. My work wasn't threatened by his murder. If anything, I was intrigued by who could have killed him, and how. But maybe I should worry that I didn't feel more shaken up.

Jo had been unmistakably shaken by her discovery, and her business might be at risk. I opened her text.

**Sorry about your car. Can't get to it till they give me back my shop.**

As expected, but her message was the sign of a responsible business owner. Jo had had a terrible experience that affected her livelihood as well as her heart on some level, I was sure. And she was worrying on my behalf about not being able to work on Blue. I truly didn't care. I could always rent a car if I absolutely needed to leave town. Otherwise, Allie or Benjamin were around, or I might be able to borrow my neighbor's car.

I'd gone after our grisly viewing to find comfort with Allie. Did Jo have a good friend or sister to talk through her discovery—and her feelings—with? I didn't know.

She'd sent the text an hour ago. I tapped out a reply.

**No worries. No urgent need for it. You okay?**

I waited, but my phone stayed quiet. I checked Allie's message.

**Hope you're OK. Can you hang with boys tomorrow 10-noon? I have a volunteer stint for the Winter Wine Road. Fuller's busy.**

A chance to play with my favorite kiddos when both their parents had to be elsewhere? You bet I could. I thumbed a reply.

**Yes. Will be there by 9:40 but have to leave by 12:30 to open VyV.**

**K. XO**

I stashed the phone. I'd better get to my labeling. I was the boss, but I didn't want Dane to think I was slacking off back here.

# CHAPTER 11

I waited inside near the door at Edie's Diner at five thirty. The air smelled heavenly of fried food, Mexican spices, and meat on the grill. I didn't eat meat but I loved smelling it cooking. The soundtrack in here was a low buzz of conversation punctuated by clinks of flatware on dishware, plus sizzling popping coming from the pass-through window to the kitchen.

Proprietor—and friend—Ed Ramirez was busy taking orders at the other end of the long counter. The popular retro diner, all chrome with red-topped stools and red benches in the booths, was nearly full but didn't have anyone waiting to be seated. I'd called in takeout dinner orders for Dane and me. Meatball sub for her, shrimp quesadilla for me.

The sign above the door always made me smile. The same as the sign outside, it read, GOOD EATS AT EDIE'S DINER. GOD BLESS AMERICA AND EDIE'S DINER TOO! The eats were beyond good, and who couldn't use a blessing from above?

Ed bustled over in his red Edie's polo shirt adorned with a white half apron. A big man of about sixty with hardly any white in his full head of dark hair, he'd left the pressure of the New York publishing business and moved home with his husband, the owner of the Acorn art gallery, to be closer to his aging mother. Ed had said buying, renovating, and running the diner brought him more joy than publishing bestsellers ever did.

"*Mija*, your dinner is almost ready." He bussed my cheek, then shifted to a whisper. "We heard about what happened. How are you?"

Gotta love a small town. "I'm fine, thanks. I'm not sure how Jo is, though."

His thick eyebrows rose as he gestured with his thumb. "She's in the last booth. Ask her yourself."

I hesitated. I'd ordered takeout so Dane and I could both keep working. I needed to get back to the wine bar as soon as I was handed the food.

"I'll bring your bag when it's ready," Ed said. "She's alone and might need to see a familiar face."

"Okay. Thank you." I headed down the aisle to where Jo sat with her back to the rest of the diner. I slid in across from her on the smooth leatherette seat. "Just wanted to say hi."

She cradled a mostly empty pint glass of beer between her hands. A plate holding half a fish taco and a smattering of black beans was pushed away. "Hi."

"How are you?"

"Let's just say I've been better." A black ball cap bearing the orange Giants logo covered her hair, and a black sweater covered her shirt. "They had me to go to the police station, and they asked questions for, like, hours. It wrecked me, Cece."

"That's no fun. But they let you go. They can't have any evidence against you, right?" They couldn't. Still, grilling Jo for a long time didn't sound good.

"Of course not. But they kept pressing me on how Karl got into the garage. On the details of our divorce. On any contact I'd had with the jerk since. All of it."

"I'm really sorry you had to go through any of that," I said.

"And they wanted to take my fingerprints. I pushed back. I mean, my fingerprints are all over everything in there! They said it was only to rule them out."

"Did you let them?"

"Yeah." She lifted a shoulder. "I didn't kill Karl."

"Obviously." I cleared my throat. "I'm no expert here, Jo, but maybe you need to contact a lawyer."

Her eyes widened into brown pools. "Seriously?"

"Yes. To take care of your interests as an innocent person."

Jo was almost thirty, nearly a decade older than my Zoe. She had a successful business and worked hard, and I liked her spirit. But sometimes I felt our age difference. Right then I wanted to go all mom on her and make sure her rights were protected. Or maybe it wasn't momming but merely being a slightly wiser, older friend. Or perhaps it was because I was ultra cautious about going all mom on my own daughter, who had bristled for years at being given any kind of advice. She still did.

"Geez," Jo said. "I had a lawyer when Karl and I made it official. It was what they call a collaborative divorce, but she was a divorce lawyer. I wouldn't know who to call in a case like this. Maybe Dad knows someone, but he's been in Seattle for a while now."

Once Jo was twenty-one and had become adept at her father's trade, he had given her the business and moved to Seattle to become a saltwater fisherman. She told me he'd been deeply affected by her mom's death from cancer when Jo was fifteen, and he'd needed new surroundings.

"Let me see if Allie has a name," I said. "She'll know someone, for sure."

"The thing is, I don't have a lot of money to throw around." Jo drained her glass. "Especially if my shop has to stay closed for a while."

"I hear you. I'll see what I can find out."

Ed approached with a white handled paper bag. I stood and came around the table, laying a hand on Jo's shoulder. She and I had never been on a hugging basis, and I didn't want to presume to change that. But I cared about her and wanted to be sure she knew.

"I'm sure the authorities will let you resume business by Monday," I murmured. "Call me anytime, okay?"

She laid her hand atop mine for a moment. "Thanks, Cece. I appreciate it."

Outside the diner, I slung the bag's handles over my forearm and shot Allie a text about needing the name of a good criminal lawyer for Jo ASAP, and preferably one at a low cost. Allie knew everybody in town. I had every confidence she would come through.

The official wheels of justice were turning. It wasn't hidden knowledge that actual justice wasn't always the result. A lot depended on the thoroughness of the police involved, the cleverness of the real perpetrator, the judge, and maybe even that obnoxious Colinas chief of police. Yes, Jo needed a competent lawyer on her side, and soon.

# CHAPTER 12

Vino y Vida was buzzing that evening. A chilly Friday night in winter brought out the after-dinner crowd and then some. This was my first January managing the place, and I hadn't known what to expect. I was grateful Dane had filled in for Mooncat, because tonight we needed all our hands and feet to keep up. I'd have been toast here alone.

Fifty-five degrees was chilly for Californians. It must have felt balmy to tourists from northern places like Maine, Minnesota, and Michigan, not to mention Manitoba. We had all of them in one room.

Two middle-aged couples stopped me as I passed by with a tray of empty glasses. They said they were here from St. Paul celebrating one couple's fortieth wedding anniversary.

"We heard some poor man was found murdered in the most horrible of ways," one woman said. "Is it true?"

"I'm sorry to say it is," I said.

"Should we be afraid?" the other woman asked. "They haven't caught the killer. We planned to stay through until Tuesday, and we love the darling B&B we're staying in. But maybe we should leave." She raised her penciled-on eyebrows.

"Are you in the Victorian at the other end of town?" I asked.

"Yes," the first woman said. "We love it, and the nicest lady runs it."

*Bingo.* "Allie is my twin sister. Anyway, you're safe here in Colinas. We have an excellent police department and county detectives are on the case. You don't have to worry." I had no basis to assert that. May it be so. I would also shoot Allie a word tomorrow morning to be as reassuring as possible with these guests. She never lacked for business, but nobody wanted our town to be known as the modern day Cabot Cove.

Locals also added to the crowd. Henry Cruvellier and Ed drifted in around eight thirty and grabbed the only two open seats in the place, which were at the bar. Both men had become my good friends in the past year.

Henry leaned over the bar for a kiss. He was fashionable, as always, in a black wool turtleneck sweater, gray houndstooth slacks, and a silvery blazer, all of which made his short white hair and white Vandyke beard almost glow.

"We have to stop meeting like this." Ed winked.

"I know." I smiled at them. "Twice in one day."

"You're busy tonight." Henry crossed one leg over the other at the knee.

"Yes. It's apparently the place to be," I said. "Have you guys been out to dinner?"

"We have," Ed said. "That new fish place in Healdsburg is excellent."

"Very elegant presentation, and the seafood is fresh and delicately seasoned," Henry said. "Highly recommend." He caught sight of Dane. "Ah, my favorite local artist. I thought she worked here only on weekends."

I explained about Mooncat being indisposed. "We're so busy, I'm totally glad Dane could sub in. What can I get you to drink? It's all on the board."

"Give us a minute?" Ed asked.

"Take as long as you need." I hied off to clear a table, take an order for refills, and answer a question that was blessedly not about murder.

When I returned, Dane and Henry had their heads together. Ed had struck up a conversation with the two women next to him, who said they were here from the other Portland. On the West Coast, if you said Portland, most people assumed you were talking about the city six hundred miles north of here in Oregon, not the one three thousand miles away in Maine.

Each man had a glass in front of him. Dane must have poured for them. I stepped behind the bar. All the current customers had been served and seemed happy for the moment. I could grab a couple of minutes to see what my friends knew. Ed turned away from his neighbor. Henry and Dane glanced up.

"Dane," I murmured. "This afternoon it sounded like you had some history with Karl. Care to share?"

"Okay. You all know my daughter."

I nodded. Serena had waited tables at Ed's diner in the fall, and I'd also met her here in the bar having a glass of wine with her grandfather.

"She was friends with Ian, Karl's nephew, even though she's a few years older," Dane began in barely more than a whisper. "She mentored him in art at the high school when she was a senior and he was a freshman. Ian lived with Karl, and more than once Serena heard him being really mean to the kid. Once she tried to intervene."

That would have been five or six years ago, while Jo was still married to Karl. I wondered how having a teen in the house affected their marriage and when he'd come to live with his uncle.

"What happened?" Henry kept his voice equally low.

"Karl tried to come down hard on her," Dane said. "But my girl wasn't having it. She dished it right back. I felt bad for Ian."

"He's an adult now," I said. "He was in here working for Karl yesterday. Do you know if he still lives with him?"

"I think he moved out to share a house with a group of friends," Ed said.

"I don't blame him. I hope he does okay, now that he's basically alone in the world," Dane said. "I'll have to let Sere know what happened."

Henry held up a finger. "Karl also did some work for me. I wish you'd asked me about him, Cece, before hiring him."

"Darn," I said. "I should have. You had a bad experience with Karl?"

"I did." Henry took a dainty sip of his port. "He overcharged for work that needed to be completely redone. Frankly, I didn't understand how he stayed in business."

Ed gave him a fond look. "But you didn't want to report the guy."

"That could have led to recriminations, including the man coming after me. You know how it is these days. Civility and respect have become extinct for some people." He squared his shoulders. "I let it go, but I knew I'd never hire him again."

"That was my resolve, too," I said. "Except it came true in a different way than I'd ever imagined."

Business picked up again. Dane and I both were fully occupied with serving, taking card payments, and cleaning up until nine, half an hour before closing time, when the place grew quiet again. Three tables and two bar sippers besides Ed and Henry were our only customers.

"I'm going to turn the sign on the door to 'Closed,'" I said to Dane.

"Fine with me."

I headed for the door, which pushed open before I got to it. A smile split my face, and it wasn't because of the prospect of ending this long, fraught day early.

Benjamin, my handsome beau of the last three months, stood in the doorway, smiling as broadly as I was. "Wondered if you'd like a ride home after you close."

"Hello, favorite man," I said. "Do come in. I'd love a ride in a little while."

We exchanged a quick kiss before he joined Henry and Ed at the bar. He asked for a small port to keep them company.

I raised my voice, addressing the room. "Folks, last call. We close at nine thirty, but if you want one more quick glass, this is the time."

The hands of all the customers in the house went up. This wouldn't be an early night, but it was good for business. I didn't care anymore. I had a ride with my man, a visit, and some canoodling, if not a sleepover. I would take all of it.

# CHAPTER 13

When I'd eased myself into seeing Benjamin last fall, when I'd allowed myself the idea of romance, he was the first man I'd dated in the decade since my husband's death. During that time, I'd wanted to focus on Zoe, my job, and holding our lives together.

These days my daughter didn't want my focus. She was thriving quite nicely at college without me. I was settled in a new place and doing well at my work, which made me happy with the direction my life was taking. Maybe being content with myself for the first time in possibly ever was all it took to let the universe know I might like to loop a decent man into the mix.

I'd been more than wary of Benjamin at first. He'd been a visitor to town, staying in Allie's B&B for a few weeks. But he'd shown himself to be honest and caring. He knew how to take care of himself and wasn't looking for anyone to do that for him. He was a runner who didn't mind braving hills and rattlesnakes. And the man was more than adept at showing his feelings in the most delightful of ways after the bedroom door closed.

By now he was more than a visitor. He'd been living in Seattle when we met, but after his visit to Colinas for his job, he'd decided to stay. Allie had found an Arts and Crafts bungalow for him to buy several months ago.

I sometimes wondered why I hadn't met him in college instead of Greg, but that way lies insanity.

Once we were home and I fed the cats, I poured two fingers of cognac into a small snifter for my ride and me. I joined Benjamin on the couch, snuggling into his proffered arm. As always, the man smelled faintly of herbal shampoo, tonight with the addition of some kind of aftershave.

Martin jumped up to join us. He eyed my lap, but in the end stepped over it and curled up on Benjamin, who was fast becoming his favorite adult male human.

"Cheers." Benjamin held up his glass and clinked it with mine.

I swirled, sniffed, and sipped. "That hits the spot." The rich amber drink went down warm and smooth.

"I should think so." He squeezed my shoulder. "You've had quite the day, Cece."

"That's for sure." I touched his knee. "Do you already know all the details about Karl's death?" My guy sometimes worked as a cyber-consultant for the police, and I didn't know what he'd already heard.

"I'm not currently working with the authorities. All I know is that I saw an alert about a body being found and your name was mentioned."

I knew not to ask him where he was currently employed. He didn't like to talk about his work, and that was really the only pink flag in our relationship—pink, not red. Greg had been secretive about way too much. I had a gut feeling I could trust Benjamin in a way I never could my late husband.

"It was bad." I took a deep breath and recounted what Jo showed me this morning. "Did you know Karl at all?"

"Karl Meier? Electrician?"

I nodded.

"I got a quote from him for some electrical work I wanted done at my new place." Benjamin shook his head slowly. "The price was way above a couple of other quotes, and I didn't like his manner. Something about him made me not trust that he'd do quality work on time. I hired someone else."

"Sounds like him. Henry told me this evening that Karl did shoddy work for him, too, which he had to have replaced. And Dane said Karl treated his nephew terribly, something I witnessed yesterday."

Benjamin set his glass, which he'd barely touched, on the end table and stroked Martin's back. "The man was difficult, no question. But so are a lot of other people. Who would take their dislike so far as to murder someone?"

That was definitely the question of the week. I sat with my thoughts, cradling my glass in my hands. Who indeed?

He squeezed my shoulder, interrupting my reverie. "I'm going to have to get going, Cece."

*Wait, what?* "You just got here. You're not staying?" I twisted to gaze at him.

"I can't, I'm sorry. My son's going to be in the city for work, and tomorrow is the only day he has free. I told him I would pick him up at SFO when his flight from Seattle gets in at eight in the morning."

"Oh." I tried not to show my dismay. No wonder he hadn't finished his drink. He had to drive home and get up early tomorrow.

"Off you go, kitty." Benjamin tried to pick up Martin, but the cat wasn't having it. He yowled his refusal.

"Just stand up," I said. "He'll jump off." Martin was a big tabby and an indoor cat, at that. He was a bit too sedentary and didn't like being told to move once he'd gotten comfortable.

Benjamin began to rise. The cat jumped. The human leaned over to kiss me, a gesture I returned without my usual enthusiasm.

"I've disappointed you," he murmured.

"You have, but I'm a mature woman. I'll get over it." I stood. I wasn't about to beg him to stay.

"I'm looking forward to Sunday." He shrugged into his baby-soft leather jacket.

"Me too. Have fun with your son." I locked the door after him. I was a big girl. Years beyond being an actual girl. But did one ever get over old patterns of feeling rejected and wanting more? I'd love to meet his kids, but I hesitated to suggest it. His son had recently started a job in hi-tech in Seattle, and his daughter was in her last year of college in Boston. He knew Allie, her husband, and the boys, but he hadn't met Zoe. Yet. Maybe we weren't at that stage of our relationship yet.

I sat on the couch again and finished my cognac. Eying his, I thought, why not? I still had some thinking to do tonight.

# CHAPTER 14

By eight the next morning I was in a fleece hoodie, coffee in hand, wandering around my garden out back. The valley fog was a deep blanket, but it wasn't as thick as it sometimes can get, and it intensified the scents of herbs and other growing things. I set down my travel mug and pulled a few weeds from the two-foot-high raised beds I'd built. I grabbed the garden scissors and clipped off a few outer leaves of dark green kale for my smoothie, then harvested several stalks of parsley to go with it.

"Knock, knock," came a voice at the gate between my house and my neighbor's, followed by actual knocking.

I hurried over to the gate and turned the lock. "Come through, please."

Richard Flora ambled in, wearing his usual loose gardening trousers with a canvas jacket against the weather. A navy Greek captain's cap covered his head.

"How are you this fine morning, Cece?" Smile lines crinkled around his eyes.

"I'm fine. How are you?"

"Feeling spry today, miracle of miracles. That's not always guaranteed at ninety, don't you know."

"Come sit with me." I led the way along the mulched path between the beds to my patio, part of which had a roof to provide shade and shelter from the elements.

I wished I'd offered him my arm. He stumbled a little but regained his balance. The last thing I wanted was for him to fall and hurt himself on my watch, or anywhere for that matter.

"I understand you played a role in the unfortunate discovery yesterday morning," he began after we were seated.

"It's true. I'm not even going to ask how you know."

"I have my sources." He stretched out his legs, looking amused.

Of course he had his sources. He had a career as a journalist when he lived in San Francisco. He and his late wife had built the house next to mine as a vacation home. They'd retired to live in Colinas full-time twenty-five years ago, and he'd been a widower for about a decade.

Richard wasn't someone to sit back and stay home in his retirement, though. I was sure he'd had his hand in various town organizations and committees.

"It must have been quite the shock to you," he went on. "Finding Meier like that. And to Jo."

"She was the one who discovered him. Jo had the real shock. She phoned and asked me to come over. I think she wanted company before the police came. But yes, it was a disturbing sight to say the least."

"I should say. I wonder if the police will think she carried out the deed."

"I hope not, but it did happen in her shop, and she was the ex-wife." I sipped my coffee. "I'm sure she's on the list. Have you heard of any arrests or news about the case? I haven't looked yet this morning."

"No, more's the pity. And you know how television news is. All sensational gab with no substance. They play footage of well-styled young women and men speaking in dramatic voices in front of JJ's Automotive, except they have no news to share."

I smiled at the image he drew.

"I suppose Jo isn't happy about the coverage." He tilted his head. "Have you spoken with her since?"

"I saw her at the diner yesterday when I was picking up my dinner. She wasn't happy with the amount of questioning the police made her go through. I did encourage her to find a criminal lawyer." I realized I hadn't heard back from Allie about a name. "Would you happen to know of someone good? Jo's worried about money, but I think she's going to need the protection."

"I might have a name in my Rolodex. I'll look when I'm back home."

"Thanks, my friend. You really do know everyone. I imagine you also knew Karl."

"Not well," he said. "I tutored his nephew one year. I believe he was in eighth grade, and the lad was struggling with the reading and writing required for his English class. It's a difficult age for any child, and Ian's mother's death really set him back."

"That's sad. Was she Karl's sister?"

"Yes."

"How old was he when she died?"

"Ten, I believe," Richard said.

"That's how old Zoe was when her father died. It's a hard age to have to go through such trauma."

"Indeed. Ian's mom had been a single mother, and the father was not involved. Karl was generous to take the boy in."

"Ian must have been part of the package when Jo married Karl," I mused, more to myself than to him.

"Yes. I don't believe it was a happy household, from what I've seen and heard."

"Karl didn't treat Ian well at all while they were working in Vino y Vida Thursday."

"The man was not content with himself." Richard wagged his head. "As a result, many others did not enjoy his company."

"Someone took their dislike a step too far."

"Indeed, they did." He surveyed the yard. "Say, your winter garden is looking good."

"Thanks."

We shifted into talking about growing greens, what seeds we

planned to start for our spring gardens, and how to identify a tiny beetle that had been riddling my arugula leaves with pinholes. When he said he had to be getting home, I escorted him to the gate.

I always kept it locked now. Someone had tried to get into the back of my house via that gate last October. They hadn't succeeded, but Richard's yard had open access to the street along the other side of his house. As a woman living by myself, that horrified me. I trusted Richard completely. Others who might creep around and into my private space, not so much.

I had things to accomplish as well. I still needed to do my Pilates routine, shower, eat, and bike to Allie's to hang with my little pals.

# CHAPTER 15

"Where are you going to be working?" I asked Allie after riding over to her classic Queen Anne home.

"At Holt Vineyards." She leaned toward the hall mirror and applied lipstick. "Out on Las Marias Road."

"I don't know that one."

She blotted her lips with a tissue, grabbed her purse, and selected her keys off a rack. "This is the first year they've participated in the Wine Road. I'll bring home a bottle and we can share it sometime."

"Did you get my text last night about a lawyer for Jo?"

"I did, but then life got busy. I'm sorry. We always do pizza and a family movie on Friday nights, and I forgot. I'll find one this afternoon, I promise."

"Thanks."

"How's she doing, anyway? Poor Jo." Allie spoke to herself in the mirror as she fiddled with her hair.

"Not great. I hope getting her some legal advice will help."

"It should. Listen, I have to fly." She turned away and called up the stairs. "Boys? Auntie Cece's here, and I'm leaving. Be good."

Arthur slid down the railing, his blond curls flying, clad in his usual athletic pants and a long-sleeved LA Galaxy T-shirt. Franklin, in jeans and a Harry Potter sweatshirt, trotted down after him, book in hand.

"Bye, Mama," Franklin said.

"See ya, Mom. Auntie Cee!" Arthur threw himself at me, wrapping his arms around my waist.

Allie slipped out the door.

"Hi, Auntie Cee." A big smile split Franklin's face.

Studious Franklin was a mini version of his father, Fuller, with skin and hair darker than his brother's. Blond wild-boy Arthur was a near clone of Allie. I hugged both of them.

"Hey, geysers," I said. "What's the news across the nation?"

"There was a magnitude four point five earthquake in Los Angeles overnight." Franklin took my question literally, as he often did.

"That's too bad," I said. "I'm glad it wasn't worse."

"I thought you were going to say, 'What's the plan, Stan?' like you usually do," Arthur said.

I laughed. "I figured you would each propose a completely different plan. That's why I changed it up. How about we go sit at the kitchen table? You can each share a piece of personal news, and then we can play Uno."

"I wanted to play outside," Arthur protested.

"And I was hoping we could play chess," Franklin said. "I learned two new gambits in Chess Club."

"Chess would leave out Artie, and the fog outside hasn't lifted yet," I said. "You both love Uno."

"Okay. Can we bake after that?" Arthur loved to bake, especially when it was something sweet.

"Only if you have all the stuff for cheese crackers." I tried to honor Allie's attempts to keep him off sweets, which only made him more active.

"We do." Franklin nodded. "Cheddar cheese and Rice Krispies were on Mama's shopping list yesterday."

"Perfect. Let's go sit and share our news." I led the way to the table where Allie and I had sat yesterday morning.

"I'll get the cards." Arthur ran to the family room.

Once he was back, he described the latest level he'd achieved in *Minecraft*. Franklin told me about the biography of Fannie Lou Hamer he was reading.

"Are you guys excited about your birthday next week?" I asked.

Arthur nodded with all the enthusiasm of an almost eleven-year-old. "We're going to have a totally awesome party."

"On Thursday, your actual birthday?"

"No." Franklin sighed. "It has to be on Saturday, a week from today. You're invited."

"Good," I said. "I'll get somebody else to work for me that day. Hang on a sec while I send myself a reminder." I tapped a note into my phone. I always tried to stay off the device when I was with my nephews so I could give them all my attention.

"What's your personal news, Auntie Cee?" Franklin asked. "I overheard Mama and Daddy talking about someone who died yesterday. Mama said your name but I couldn't hear any more after that."

*Whoa.* I didn't want to go there, but I couldn't not answer the kid.

"Well, my friend Jo found a person in her shop who had died overnight."

"She's the one who fixes Blue, right?" Arthur asked.

"Yes. She asked me to come over, because she was feeling kind of upset about her discovery."

"So you saw the corpse." Franklin's eyes went wide. "What was the state of rigor?"

The kid read constantly at a level far above his grade in school. He consequently had a wide range of knowledge and the vocabulary to talk about it. I shouldn't have been surprised he knew about rigor mortis, but I was. He probably knew more than I did. The extent of my knowledge came solely from crime fiction novels and shows.

"I don't really want to talk about what I saw, honey." I kept my voice gentle. "I am trying to be a good friend to Jo."

"Okay." Franklin pointed at Arthur. "It's your turn to deal. I dealt first last time we played."

We played. We baked. We headed outside to play tetherball after the fog lifted, which it usually did by late morning.

Allie often moaned about the workload of having two children the same age, but a parent couldn't ask for better kids. They were bright, inquisitive, sweet, and generally well-behaved and respectful. They had two parents who loved them and who also maintained a level of discipline, something all kids need. The boys fought sometimes, as any siblings do, but they took care of each other too.

Their lives stood in stark contrast to Ian's. He'd had a single mom, who died when he was ten, and an absent father. The uncle who took him in seemed far from loving. Ian had trouble in school. He worked for his uncle who didn't treat him any better as an adult.

I wondered what Ian would do now. Maybe he would continue working as an electrician. He might inherit his uncle's estate, if he was Karl's closest relative. I wasn't aware if Karl had other children. I knew he and Jo hadn't had any together.

"Ha! Gotcha," Arthur chortled as the ball wrapped all around the pole, shaking me out of my reverie.

"You weren't paying attention, Auntie Cee," Franklin said.

"You're right, I wasn't." I, the tetherball champion in my Davis childhood neighborhood, had been doing some proverbial wool-gathering. I smiled at the kids. "Congratulations, Artie."

# CHAPTER 16

I was ready to open Vino y Vida by ten minutes before one o'clock. Today's wines were uncorked, and pretzels were ready in bowls, as well as the gluten-free crackers in other bowls. The place was strictly a wine bar, and those were the only foods we served, although I'd been considering adding other provisions. My customers would welcome local cheese, olives, grapes, and hard salami, and the prep would be minimal.

Allie had arrived home in time. Before I left, she whispered she'd learned something at the winery, something I would want to know, but the boys were all over her. We didn't have a minute to talk, plus I had to get going.

"I'll call you later." She made the thumb-and-pinkie phone gesture at her ear.

I was itching to know what she'd found out. By her tone, it was about Karl's murder. What kind of news could she have picked up at a winery during a busy event?

I wondered where Dane was. She was supposed to start her Saturday shift at one. She hadn't called, and I hoped she was okay. Managing alone on one of our busiest days was going to be tricky. I wouldn't ping her until one fifteen. She might have run into Wine Road traffic or had some other delay. If she wasn't going to make it, though, I was stuck. My third employee, Dev

Vedantam, had already asked for the day off, and Mooncat's migraines usually had a two- or three-day ramp-down until she felt better.

I checked the time. I still had a minute to shoot Jo a quick text.

**Checking in, wondering how you are. I'm at Vino y Vida until nine thirty. Stop in if you can.**

Should I ask her if Karl had other kids? What about siblings beyond the sister who died? *Nah.* Not in a text. If she came by, I'd ask in person. Karl's next of kin mattered if he had any kind of an estate. The potential to inherit money and property was a well-known homicide motive, at least in fiction. I had no idea if it was in real life.

Jo didn't reply right away. A crowd was forming on the sidewalk out front, with more than one person peering in through the front windows. Might as well get to it.

I unlocked the door. "Welcome to Vino y Vida. Sit wherever you like, and I'll get your pour order as soon as I can. The patio overlooking the river is open and now that the fog has lifted, it's really nice out there." And it was. The day had turned out to be a sunny, if brisk, winter Saturday.

Seniors, young people, and a big group of fifty-somethings surged in. I got to work.

Three men about my age or younger came in. Two perched at the bar, while one stayed standing in the third point of their triangle.

"Be with you in a minute," I called to them as I carried a tray of four full glasses out to the patio. Where in the world was Dane?

I finally got back to the bar. "What can I pour for you today?"

"I'll have the pinot noir, please," one with a shaved head said in a resonant baritone.

I took orders from a dark-haired man, and one with a short crop of red curls, gelled in what I assumed was a fashionable style. All three wore the kind of jeans that looked like a European cut. Their shirttails were untucked, and they sported various sorts of hip leather shoes. This must be the current business casual style.

As I turned my back to uncork a bottle of pinot noir, they resumed their conversation.

"It should be easy to acquire," one said. "The town has to be hurting for money. Who isn't?"

"It's a great location for condos with the river right outside," another said.

"Walking distance to downtown too," the third voice chimed in. "Part of it, really, but at the end, so it's quiet."

I blinked. They were talking about buying property from a town and putting in condos. This town? *My* property? I didn't own the Vino y Vida building, but I managed the business and it was a popular destination. The town, under the umbrella of the historical society, owned the whole row of antique adobes. What a ridiculous notion, that the Colinas government would sell it to these dudes to make into luxury housing.

It was a fabulous location—for us. As the guy said, our cluster sat at the end of Manzanita Boulevard's popular shopping district, which was blessedly free of chain stores. Our three businesses here and the historical museum were easy to access but quiet. And the setting was lovely.

The town always needed money. The schools were overdue for renovations, and the ball fields needed upkeep. Anyone navigating the downtown sidewalks knew they were in terrible repair. But to make a buck on our cherished and significant historical buildings? That would be a travesty of the worst order.

I took in a calming breath and let it out before turning back and pouring their wine.

"Are you all here for the Wine Road?" I asked as if I hadn't heard a word of their conversation.

"No," Redhead said. "We're on a kind of work junket."

"What kind of work do you do?" I pressed.

Shaved Head pulled out a business card and slid it across to me. "We're a development company." He seemed to exchange a glance with the other two.

I glanced at the card, which bore a Sonoma address.

"If you hear of any nice properties for sale up here, please let me know." He extended a well-manicured hand. "I'm Gareth Rockwell."

I reciprocated with putting my fist out for a bump. I didn't shake hands at work.

"Allie Halstead is the agent you want to talk to," I said. "She'll find you something." And it wouldn't be here.

Gareth took out a phone and tapped in a note to himself. He spelled Halstead. "Is that correct?"

"Yes," I said. "She's probably listed as Alicia."

"Thanks."

"Enjoy your wine, gentlemen." I turned away.

This Rockwell character had better not consider trying to acquire our property. I'd sic Allie on him whether he contacted her or not. He'd never know what hit him.

# CHAPTER 17

Dane had blown in at around two o'clock, apologizing up one side and down the next. I didn't have time to listen to her excuses.

"Apron up, wash your hands, and help," I said. "We can talk later." I needed reliable help. If she was going to flake out on me, I might need to look elsewhere for a third employee.

That is, if the property wasn't sold out from under us. The developers sipping as part of their little junket had left a few minutes before Dane arrived. None of them had pressed me any further about properties for sale. *Good.*

A group of eight women with Southern accents bustled in, bringing the smell of fresh air mixed with their cologne. One approached me.

"We're so dang disappointed," she said. "We got us a little tour bus and everything, but we can't get into the Wine Road. We was all looking forward to it."

"It's true, they can't accommodate groups of over four people, but you can taste some excellent wines here." I eyed two empty four-tops. "I'll make up a table for you there. It overlooks the Russian River."

"Why, that's so sweet of you, hon. Do you have those cute carry bags and all?"

"We do sell Vino y Vida two-bottle bags. But if you buy a case, I include a bag as a gift."

She scrunched up her nose. "That's a heck of a lot of bottles to carry home on the airplane."

"I can ship them to you, ma'am."

Her expression brightened. "That's real kind of you, doll." She turned to her friends. "Girls, we found our perfect place after all. Gladys, be a Georgia peach and go tell the driver we'll be here for a couple few hours, would you please?"

We had a lull at about three thirty. I grabbed a quick facilities break, then brought a new bag of mini-pretzels to the front. Dane was unloading the dishwasher and glanced up at me.

"I really am sorry I was late, Cece," she began. "I'm a ditzy artist, and I was so absorbed in my painting I lost track of time. Then traffic was horrendous when I had to cross Vineyard."

"It's the Winter Wine Road. That's why we've been so busy." I took a deep breath. I had to gear up for scolding someone older than I, a position I didn't want to be in. Still, it had to be done if I wanted to continue being successful at this business. "But I'd like you to decide if your job here is a priority for you. I need reliable help."

"I know. And it is a priority. I've already decided to begin setting a timer for two hours before I have to be here. That will remind me to stop, get cleaned up, and have plenty of time to start my shift on time."

"Okay. That sounds like a plan." I surveyed the wine bar space. All was still quiet. Nobody had their hand up needing service. And Karl's killer was still wandering around out there. "Question for you."

"Ask me anything."

"Yesterday you spoke about Karl Meier not being a kind person. Did you personally have a bad experience with him?"

"You could say that." The corners of her mouth turned down. "Maybe I should have said he wasn't an honest person, although mean enters into it. After my husband and I split up in November, I decided to spruce up my studio, which is in the oldest part of our house and had almost no outlets. I hired Karl to do the work. Based on how he treated Ian, I shouldn't have hired him in the first place. Karl did sloppy, shoddy work, and I ended up having to hire someone else to fix it."

"Did you confront Karl about it?"

"Yes, and he was incredibly rude to me. I know he's dead, but he was a complete sleazeball. In my opinion, the world is well rid of him."

The door opened. This might be the end of our conversation, depending on who came in. But it wasn't a customer unless Detective Jim Quan was here to sip on his day off. By the stern expression on his face, it looked like he was working.

He approached the bar. "Ms. Barton."

"Are you here with news that you have a suspect in custody?" I asked.

"No." He addressed Dane. "Are you Dane Larsen, ma'am?"

"Yes." She dragged out the word. "And you are?"

"Sonoma County Deputy Sheriff Detective Jim Quan. I'd like a word with you, please."

Her already pale face went even whiter. "Okay. I guess." The glass she held began to shake.

"Let me take that." I gently took it from her hand.

"What's it about?" Dane's voice shook in unison with her hand.

Quan ignored her question. "Is there somewhere private Ms. Larsen and I can speak?" he asked me.

"You can use the back room," I said.

"Thank you." He looked at Dane and gestured toward the back. "Ma'am?"

She cast me a terrified look, but she laid down the cloth she'd been using to polish the clean wine glasses and preceded him through the door to our workroom.

I wanted an answer to her question about why he needed to speak to her as much as she did. I was going to have to wait.

# CHAPTER 18

When Dane emerged, she slid behind the bar. "It's your turn at bat," she muttered. "He's waiting for you."

"Me?"

"Yep."

"Are you okay?" I asked.

"Not really."

"You'll need to manage alone out here for a few minutes."

She nodded, picked up an empty tray, and headed for a vacated table. I made my way into the back and sat across from Quan at our work table.

The space was lined with sturdy shelves holding cases of wine. Extra glassware and bags of pretzels and rice crackers were in a cabinet. Shipping tape, scissors, fine-point markers, and stick-on mailing labels were on a table. An employee restroom was tucked into one corner of the room. A mini-kitchen area held a coffee machine, a sink, and a small microwave atop a dorm-sized refrigerator. The space was small, but I'd made some changes after I took over the manager job and set it up with an eye to efficiency. It worked well for us.

"How long has Dane Larsen been working for you?" Quan folded his hands on the table.

"She started in mid-December, so only about a month. Why?"

"Did you run any kind of background check on her? Get references from prior employers?"

"No. Should I have?" I asked.

He stonewalled me again. "Do you have any knowledge of her whereabouts Thursday night?"

I blinked. "No. We don't hang out socially. She works for me. I have no idea where she was." I had an idea why he was asking. Now I was worried that Dane had some hidden criminal past or something.

He unfolded his hands and drummed his fingers on the table. "All right. How about yourself?"

"What about me?"

"I understand you might have had a difficult relationship with the victim."

*What?* "I didn't have any relationship with him. I hired him to do some work for me on Thursday. That was the first and only time I met him."

"Where were you between the hours of eleven Thursday night and five Friday morning?"

"I was home."

"Can anyone vouch for that being true?"

"Only my cats." I crossed my arms.

"Did you have a key to the automotive shop?"

"Of course not. Why would I?"

He didn't respond, not that I expected him to. Again, he wasn't taking notes or recording our conversation. That was some memory he had.

"What would I have discovered if I had run a background check on Dane?" I asked. "Should I not have hired her?"

"I can't say."

Can't or won't? Same result.

"Do you have any knowledge of where Jo Jarvin was on Thursday night?" he asked.

"No. But seriously, sir. She had no reason in the known universe to kill Karl, in her shop or anywhere."

"Somebody did." His erect posture sagged. "Do you know of anyone else who clashed with Meier or bore a deep-seated grudge against him? I have to confess this investigation is already running into a lot of dead ends and stone walls."

*Whoa.* Was he asking for my help? "Well, a pair of sisters were in here recently, a Tara Pulanski and Zara something or other. I happened to mention that Karl had changed the lighting over the tables and neither seemed to care for him. I don't know anything beyond that."

He pulled out his phone and tapped into it. "What was the last name again?"

I repeated it. "She's apparently the director of the Colinas cat rescue place." I cast about for Zara's last name until I remembered it. "Zara Choate is her twin and is an artist. She also teaches art." It occurred to me that Dane might know her.

"Anyone else?"

"Karl treated his adult nephew Ian quite harshly while they were working here. I believe he'd been Ian's guardian after the boy's mother, Karl's sister, died about a decade ago." I decided on the spot not to relay what Richard had told me. The police could dig up Ian and Karl's relationship if they hadn't already.

"So noted. Is that it?"

"Yes." Or was there something else? Mooncat told Karl to stay away from her niece. We'd gotten busy that day, and I'd never found out why. I wasn't about to unleash Quan on my best employee—or her niece—especially not while Mooncat was suffering from a migraine.

Then there was whatever Allie had alluded to. That would have to wait, as well.

Dane popped her head in. "I'm sorry to interrupt, but a tour bus just rolled up. You'll need to help ASAP."

"Thanks, Dane." I stood. "That's going to have to be all for now, Detective."

He rose too but waited to speak until Dane disappeared into the front again. "Thank you for being forthcoming. I hope you will share any additional pertinent information you might run across."

"I will. Are you parked in the police station for the duration?"

Kelly Daniell, the detective in the previous case, had been given the use of an office in the Colinas PD as a courtesy while the investigation had been ongoing. The county sheriff's department facility was in Santa Rosa, which was over twenty miles south of here.

"I am."

"If you ever get time off, you can always stop in for a glass of wine."

"Thank you," he said. "I don't drink wine."

Maybe he didn't drink alcohol at all. Either way, it was none of my business. I followed him into the front and watched him slip out the door against the tide of thirsty customers making their way in.

"That was interesting, to say the least," I murmured to Dane as I washed my hands at our sink behind the bar.

"If you can call being grilled by the police interesting." She removed the dish towel she'd slung over her shoulder. "Dishwasher's empty. I'm going to go check on the patio."

I headed over and greeted the newcomers, who milled around and looked for empty seats.

"Welcome to Vino y Vida. I won't be able to sit you all together."

A woman with a no-nonsense cap of steel-gray hair smiled. "That won't be necessary." The first word sounded like "zat" and her diction was clipped and precise.

"Where are you all here from?"

"Vee are from Germany." Except the name of the country came out like "Chermany."

I realized others were conversing in that language, which I'd studied for only two years in high school.

"Welcome," I said. "You can sit anywhere that's open, and I think there are some empty tables out on the patio if you don't mind the temperature."

A tall man joined us. "As long as you think it's safe here." His accent was more British than German, but I could hear traces of his mother tongue. "We understand you have a recent and as yet unsolved homicide in your town."

"We do, but you're quite safe, sir. We have an excellent police department being assisted by the county sheriff's detective. Nothing to worry about."

I turned away, crossing my fingers. I desperately hoped that was true.

# CHAPTER 19

By five thirty, the tour bus had departed and so had all the other customers, in search of dinner, most likely. Dane headed out for her own dinner break, while I zapped a glass container of an eggplant parmesan I'd made earlier in the week.

I dragged a stool around behind the bar to eat. I was glad for the uncharacteristic quiet. It could get noisy in here when we were at capacity.

As the door opened, I glanced up. I might have to eat fast. But the newcomer was Jo, not a group of tourists in search of wine tasting.

After I swallowed my mouthful, I said, "Come and sit with me. I'm grabbing a bite of dinner."

She approached slowly, as if hesitant. I'd rarely seen her out of her work clothes, but today she wore a long blue sweater and black leggings with rainbow-colored socks and black leather tennies. She shrugged out of a nicely weathered denim jacket.

"Can I pour you some wine?" I asked. "On the house."

"I'd love a glass of something red and hearty, thank you. It's kind of bone-chilling out there."

I poured a glass of a robust red blend and slid it across to her. "Where's Ouro?"

"He's out in the van." Besides the truck, she also drove a VW van only a few years newer than my Blue. "I wanted to tell you the cops are done with the shop. Told me an hour ago. I'll get your 'Stang tuned up in the morning."

"Thank you. It must be a relief to get your business back." I took another bite of my casserole.

"I'll say."

I set down my fork. "Before I forget, you asked me about the name of a criminal lawyer. Allie texted me somebody she knows, and Richard left me a voice mail with a name. I'll forward Allie's message to you and add Richard's info in a text. I hope it helps."

"Thank you." She grimaced. "I'd be a lot more relieved if Karl's murderer were locked up. And there's a big wrench I don't think I'll ever use again, if I even get it back."

"Was that what Karl was hit on the head with?" I pictured the tool lying near Karl's body that morning.

"Yes. It's heavy, and if you got a good swing with it . . ." She shrunk into her shoulders.

"I saw that wrench on the floor."

"I'm sorry I had to wreck your morning." She sampled the wine, then took another sip. "Ooh, this is perfect, Cece."

"Quan was in here questioning me this afternoon. He also talked with Dane Larsen, who works for me on weekends."

"Dane's the artist?" she asked. "I've heard of her work."

"Yes. I've been thinking about how Karl and whoever killed him got into your shop. Are the locks easy to jimmy or something? I didn't see a broken window or anything."

"No, the lock wasn't forced. Windows were fine." Her posture slumped. "Karl still had a key to the place from when we were together."

"Ah." I left it at that. She'd tell me more if she wanted to.

Jo sipped again. "He didn't care about the business, and I don't think he particularly liked me spending so much time on it after Dad left. But one time there was something that came up, and it seemed like a good idea to make a copy of the key for him so I wasn't the only person who could get in. Except I never asked for the key back."

"He must have arranged to meet someone he knew at the shop."

"You mean the person who killed him." She winced.

"Sorry, thinking out loud here." I cast about for a reason. "But why meet them at your shop? Right? I mean, he owned a house."

"Yes, a crappy ranch house. I never liked it, even though it's on a nice piece of land. But he already owned it and insisted I move in with him and Ian. Ian always resented me."

"He wanted Karl to himself?" I asked.

"Maybe. He was pretty messed up all around, having lost his mom."

"I gather Karl kept the house in your divorce."

"He did," Jo said. "California's a community property state. I didn't want the place. I kept my business and bought a small piece of land and a yurt."

"I understand he was living in the house alone. I heard Ian had moved out to live with friends."

"Oh? I'm pretty sure the kid still lives there."

I had another thought. "Jo, was Karl's car there yesterday morning? At JJ's?"

"No. The detective asked me the same question. The only vehicles were the ones I was working on and my own."

"So the murderer picked up Karl, took him to the shop, and left after he was dead." A shudder ran through me. What if the lift had been lowered onto Karl before he was dead? Would he have woken up and cried out for help? Struggled to get free? The image was awful. It was possible no one would ever know exactly what transpired. I took the last bite of my supper.

"Okay if I have some of those?" Jo pointed to the bowl of pretzels at the other end of the bar.

"Mmm." I nodded but kept my mouthful of food firmly closed.

"Ian asked me to have dinner with him tonight," she said. "But not until seven. And I seem to have gotten my appetite back. Must be the red wine." She smiled and popped in a couple of salty, crunchy pretzels.

"But you said Ian resented you and that you hadn't gotten along when you were married to Karl."

"He did, and we didn't. But Karl was, like, his last living relative."

"Ian must have gone through a lot with his mother dying." I took a sip of my water. "My daughter certainly did, losing her dad at the same age."

"Absolutely. I mean, not that Karl was a very kind guardian, but he did take Ian in. I give him credit for that."

"I'm sure it's a shock to Ian that Karl's dead. And Ian's older now. He's not a child anymore. Maybe he's gotten over his youth angst."

"Maybe. We'll see. I haven't spoken to him in a few years."

"Where are you eating?" I asked.

"He wanted to meet at Hoppy's."

"Hoppy Hills? Ian must be twenty-one to be able to eat at a brewpub."

"His twenty-first birthday was last week." Jo's smile was wistful. "I really, really wanted to help parent him when we were together. Not to replace his mom, but to be a kind of auntie and counter the way Karl treated him. Except the kid pushed me away at every turn."

"I'm sorry to hear that." I was about to ask her—gently—what she ever saw in Karl. Instead the door opened and what looked like a bachelorette party of young women strutted in on high-heeled boots. "Stay as long as you want," I told Jo. "I'm back on the job."

"Thanks."

I tucked my container under the counter, swiped a napkin across my mouth, and called out a greeting to the newcomers. My brain, however, wanted that question answered. Why had Jo ever married Karl? I wasn't sure why I hadn't asked it before.

# CHAPTER 20

I turned the sign to CLOSED and locked the front door to Vino y Vida at nine thirty. Dane and I ran ourselves ragged all evening. I used to keep the wine bar open until ten, but nobody needed to be sipping wine that late, and I didn't like having to stay and clean up until ten thirty. I tended to announce last call at nine.

Dane was clearing tables that still had glassware on them. I began readying the bottles that were half full or more to be saved for tomorrow.

"Do you want any partials to take home?" I asked her. "Or a glass now?" We didn't keep the wine when the bottle was under half full. If no employee wanted it, I drained it into a container for a local vinegar maker or took it home myself.

"I'll grab half a glass now, thanks. But I don't need any to take home."

I emptied one bottle of cabernet sauvignon into a glass for her and drained the rest of the chardonnay into one for me. I carried the other bottles into the back and preserved them by pumping in argon gas and sealing the bottles. I came back to the front to find Dane reading something on her phone.

She glanced up and quickly stashed the phone in her pants pocket before picking up the rag she'd abandoned. She had nothing to look guilty about. I didn't care if she checked her texts or whatever after we closed. I fit glass after glass into the dishwasher.

"Is that it except for our glasses?" I asked.

"Let me check outside one more time." She grabbed the rag and disappeared out the door to the patio.

I took a sip, the cool white going down smooth, then wiped down the bar top from one end to the other. I grabbed a dry cloth and polished the beautiful surface. I tossed all the open pretzels in the compost container and wiped out the baskets, stacking them ready for tomorrow. Even though people primarily paid with cards, we had a fair number of cash purchases, so I carried the till to the back and locked it in the safe.

Where was Dane? We still needed to sweep the floor, check the restrooms, turn on the dishwasher, and do all the other small tasks before I could switch off the lights. Helping clean up was part of her job. She'd arrived late this afternoon. I hoped she wasn't also flaking out on the job at this end.

I was about to head out to the patio when she came back in, one hand holding two glasses and the rag, the other gripping the rims of three. She brought them straight to the dishwasher without meeting my gaze. I grabbed the broom and headed to the far corner of the space.

"Let's wait to start the dishwasher until we can add our own empty glasses, okay?" I asked.

"Sure." She picked up the rag. "I'll finish the tables."

"So," I began when our trajectories grew closer. "I haven't had a chance to ask you why the detective wanted to speak with you earlier today."

She pressed her lips closed and rubbed the table with extra vigor.

Her silence made sense. I hadn't actually asked her a question. "What did he want?"

"Probably the same information he wanted from you. Where I was Thursday night. Could anyone attest to that. Did I kill Karl. Standard stuff." She straightened. "I'll go tidy up the restrooms."

I knew a "I don't want to talk about it" reaction when I saw one. Fine. She was hiding something from me, but I clearly wasn't going to find out what it was tonight.

After the room was swept, I washed my hands, finished my wine, and added the glass to the dishwasher. I stuck in a detergent pod while I was there. Dane emerged and handed me her empty glass.

"Restrooms are all set. Okay if I take off now?" she asked.

"That's fine. Please don't be late tomorrow. You and Dev have the shift."

"I won't." She grabbed her long wool coat off the hook, a garment that looked like she might have picked it up in a thrift shop, and faced the door. She turned back, her mouth open.

I waited. Had she changed her mind about sharing?

"Sorry I was late, Cece. It won't happen again." She made her way to the door.

"Thanks," I called after her.

Maybe I'd learn later what made Quan want to grill her. Or maybe I'd never find out.

I double-checked that the front door was locked, then shrugged into my yellow bicycling jacket with the reflective stripes, switched off the lights except the small one behind the bar, and locked the back door behind me. Lights activated front, back, on my arm, and on my helmet, I pedaled for home. Carefully, since it was thoroughly dark, but I went as fast as I could go.

I was ready to put my feet up, have a snack and a drink, and not think about homicide until at least tomorrow.

# CHAPTER 21

Eight thirty the next morning found me happily digging into a stack of orange-flavored buckwheat pancakes at the Edie's Diner counter. I didn't know if heaven would feature smells, but if it did, the air had to smell like this.

The weather was dry but cool, so I'd slipped on a pale green cowl-necked sweater with patterned leggings and low comfy boots. Green was a color I'd been inclined to wear for years. When person after person tells you the color looks good on you, it's a natural choice.

Ed served the pancakes, a special on today's menu, with a choice of maple syrup, orange blossom honey, or vanilla yogurt. I went for the honey and yogurt combo.

From here I was headed to church services at Manzanita Congregational. While not raised in any church, as an adult I found the hour of worship and the hymns comforting. Going to church provided a respite from the outside world.

I was going to meet Benjamin at the farmers market after that, and I wanted to fuel up for my morning. Making pancakes for one at home wasn't anywhere near as interesting as the ones Ed dreamed up to serve.

"Mmm, so good," I told Ed when he approached. "And they're super light."

"Thanks, *mija*. Separating the egg whites and beating them until they're fluffy is key for that."

"I think you should put these on the regular menu."

"I could, except I probably won't. The egg white thing is a lot more work for the kitchen." He smoothed down his half apron. "But I'm glad you like them."

I took a sip of coffee, hot and dark with a little cream. Perfection in a mug.

"Listen." Ed glanced around, then leaned over the counter. "I want to help, you know, with what you're looking into."

He already knew me too well. "I'm not exactly the lead investigator, you know."

"But you and Jo are friends, and you saw the deceased." He kept his voice low and soft. "Neither you or I think Jo's the bad guy here—but somebody is."

"Exactly." I thought back on who'd expressed displeasure with Karl besides Dane. "You and Henry have cats, don't you?"

"We do. We got the sweetest kitties after we moved back here. It's funny. One kitty is pure white and the other is all black, but the rescue place said they're brother and sister from the same litter."

"Do you know Tara Pulanski?" I asked. "She's the director of Colinas Cat Rescue."

"Sure. She and her sister often come in to eat."

"She seems to have had some kind of unpleasant history with Karl. I want to go talk to her, maybe tomorrow."

"I'll come with you." His eyes lit up. "Do you have Mondays off?"

"Yes. You?"

"Absolutely. Henry would have a royal fit if I didn't. He closes the gallery on Mondays and Tuesdays, so that's our weekend."

"Let's go tomorrow after lunch." I wrinkled my nose. "On second thought, I'll call the place in the morning and make sure she'll be in."

"Good idea." He straightened. "Let me know. For now, enjoy your breakfast, hon."

I stayed, savoring my breakfast at a leisurely pace. Worship didn't begin until ten o'clock, and the church was only a couple of blocks from here. I listened to conversations others in the diner were having.

A couple was arguing about where to go on vacation. A child seemed to be offering a book report to his encouraging parents, or maybe it was a movie review. Either way, no detail was omitted.

I'd long had a superpower of being able to isolate conversations from the flood of background noise. Maybe it came from being an introverted child who'd had trouble reading. I would sit with a book open, but the story went so slowly I became distracted by what others were saying in the library or at school.

I'd finally been taught some skills to maneuver around my dyslexia, but even as an adult I often amused myself on airplanes and in public places by doing focused listening. I supposed I was an aural voyeur. Except it didn't hurt anyone, and what I heard was often an intriguing peek into the lives of strangers.

Amid the clink of silverware on porcelain and the sounds of meat sizzling on the grill emanating from the pass-through window, a man's voice poked through. The deep tone sounded familiar. I aimed my laser listening in that direction.

"The agent wanted to steer us away from the adobes. I told her no way. That's the property we want. Anyway, I'm going to meet her at noon and pretend I'm interested in these other places she claims have great potential."

I swore under my breath. That had to be Gareth Rockwell, the developer I'd met in Vino y Vida yesterday. Maybe it was Allie who was going to show him alternatives.

Laying down my fork, I twisted left and right, arching my back, tilting my head, pretending I was stretching my head and neck. Well, I was stretching, and more. When I glanced over my shoulder to the right, sure enough. The back of a shaved head sat alone in a booth for two a few booths down the aisle, phone to his ear.

I faced front again, still listening.

"Uh huh." Gareth nodded. "Yes, I will." He lifted his mug and drained it. "Sure. I'll be in touch." He jabbed at the phone.

I forked in my last bite of pancake. I still didn't know what Allie had learned at the Holt winery yesterday. I had to give her a heads-up about Gareth and his nefarious plans to destroy my beloved wine bar and the other businesses. At least, I thought that was his plan.

Huh. When Dane's ex-husband ran the historical museum and oversaw operations of the other adobes in our cluster, he called monthly managers' meetings. We hadn't had that in a while. The current overseer didn't seem to care what we did. Maybe it fell to me to organize an opposition to a potential threat.

"No wine with breakfast?" a deep voice behind me asked.

Startled, I whipped my head around. Gareth stood smirking at me.

"Good morning," I said. "I don't normally drink in the morning. You?"

"No, but I could make an exception for a lovely lady like yourself."

*Ick.* I mustered an insincere smile. "No, thanks. Enjoy your day." I turned back to my coffee. I could almost feel his shrug.

I needed to talk to Allie, and soon.

# CHAPTER 22

"Hello, Alicia Halstead's phone," a child's voice said.

"Frankie?" I paced along the side of Edie's building. I'd called Allie the minute I got outside.

"Yes, Auntie Cee. Mommy still isn't downstairs, but her phone is. And our pancakes are ready."

Noises of Arthur's and Fuller's voices were faint in the background. The boys loved to make Sunday breakfast with their dad when he was home.

"Okay, thanks," I said. "Will you please ask her to call me?"

"I will," Franklin said. "Oh, wait. Here she is. Mommy, it's Auntie Cee."

"Thanks, sweetie," Allie said. "One second, Cece."

A door clicked shut and the background grew quiet.

"What's up?" Allie was breathless. "Sorry, I'm trying to do too much at once, as usual. Brushing up on a prospective property, doing my hair, listening to a podcast."

"I feel bad for asking, but can you spare me a minute?"

"Go. My guys are used to me having crazy weekends."

"These men came into the wine bar yesterday," I began. "They're real estate developers and are looking at property from around here."

"Let me guess. They're out of Sonoma."

"Yes." I sank onto the bench in front of the diner. "Dude named Gareth gave me his card yesterday. I had breakfast at Edie's just now, and I overheard him telling someone on the phone he was meeting a real estate agent at noon. Is that you?"

"It is," Allie said. "He expressed interest in buying your cluster of adobes, which is ridiculous. For one thing, the town owns them, and they aren't for sale."

"Exactly. The guy is persistent and kind of slimy, despite his hip shaved head and business casual clothes."

Allie laughed. "I haven't seen him yet, but I know the type. Anyway, you have nothing to worry about, sis. I'll talk him out of the idea."

"Thank you, Al. That's a big relief."

"What do you have on for the rest of the day?" she asked.

"Church, then I'm meeting Benjamin at the farmers market and spending the rest of the day with him. We'll probably cook dinner together at his place."

"Ooh, girl! You really know how to do romance." She snickered.

"Hey, I think it'll be fun." I cleared my throat. "But quick, can you tell me what you learned at the vineyard yesterday? You didn't want to tell me around the kiddos."

"Right. I met Wesley Holt, the owner, while I was there. Cee, he reminded me in a weird way of Karl. They have different names, so they can't be brothers. But—"

"Mama!" Artie's voice intruded. "The pancakes are getting cold, and we can't eat without you."

"I'm coming, sugar," she said to him. "Sorry, Cece. Let's catch up tonight or tomorrow morning, okay?"

"You're on. Probably tomorrow."

She disconnected. A fat crow grabbed a crust of bread off the pavement and flew into the nearest tree. A cloud scudded by, and a heavy truck clunked through a pothole in the road. I checked the time. It was only nine thirty. I still had half an hour until services began and only a five-minute walk. I stood and moseyed along the sidewalk, hands in the pockets of my coat.

Wesley Holt sounded like a mystery man. I was pretty sure I'd never met him. Holt Winery wasn't one Vino y Vida had a buying relationship with. And why would he remind Allie of Karl?

I mentally shrugged. I had run into people in my life who brought to mind a different person. They happened to have a voice like someone else I knew, or shared some quirk of how their mouth was shaped or their hairline. That one small feature might remind me of a past friend, a beloved aunt, a television personality. It didn't mean they were related.

On the other hand, Wesley could be Karl's cousin. Both surnames sounded Germanic, and their first names could also be. I might need to make a business jaunt out to the winery tomorrow to discuss serving his wines in Vino y Vida. I could do a bit of sleuthing, at least if Jo finished getting Blue in good running order.

Poor Jo. Yesterday she seemed to have gotten over the worst of the shock of finding her ex-husband murdered. But having the authorities considering her as a potential suspect couldn't be easy. Allie and I both endured that over the past year. The experience was no fun.

I wondered how Jo's dinner with Ian went last night. They'd both had major problems with Karl. Their shared meal couldn't have been a mutual grieving session, unless it was. After a person died, one sometimes remembered their good side more than their bad.

I'd adored my father, and he'd been a sweet man. But his forgetful, disorganized, inattentive brain had caused problems for our family, for Mom most of all. It had fallen to her to keep the household running while holding down a demanding academic position at the University of California, Davis.

Daddy's being lost in his thoughts had prevented him from achieving the success as a novelist he'd dreamed of having. It had also caused his death. Stepping in front of a city bus he hadn't noticed had ended his life. Since then, the family—Allie, Mom, and me—had done our best to remember him only for his positive qualities.

Speaking of inattention, I now stood in front of the church, and it was ten before the hour. I might as well head in. A spot in a quiet back pew for a few minutes of meditation would do me a world of good.

# CHAPTER 23

I wasn't able to leave my thoughts behind during the worship service. I usually left church feeling more centered and peaceful than when I'd come in, but not today. Images of a dead man and concerns about Jo had dominated, plus mental wonderings about who had pulled that lever to lower the lift floated through my mind.

The sermon, predictably, had been about forgiveness. Forgiving others for misdeeds both major and minor. The minister also spoke of forgiving oneself. She had a point. I'd been hard on myself for most of my life, focusing on my shortcomings instead of my successes, on where I'd failed instead of who I'd shown love to. I was working on that one.

Fellowship, consisting of coffee, tea, muffins, and coffee cake, was held in the adjoining hall. In the six months since I'd been coming here on Sunday mornings, I rarely stayed for the socializing. But today I wanted to hit the restroom before meeting Benjamin at the farmers market, and the facilities were on the far side of the fellowship hall. I shrugged into my coat and waded through the buzz of conversation.

I wove my way through the room, nodding at those who chose to make eye contact. On the closest wall was a framed poster of the Serenity Prayer, a must for a room that hosted AA meetings several times a week. A banner reading BE THE CHURCH listed ways to embody the life and spirit of Jesus. Sunday school classes were held upstairs, but a corner of this room included colorful mats, a few soft toys, and a small bookshelf full of children's reading material.

When I emerged from the restroom, I pointed myself to the door leading to the outside.

"Cece?" a woman's voice called.

I glanced over to see Zara Choate, one of the twins who'd been in the wine bar the other night. She smiled and gave me a little wave. I approached where she sat alone at a small table with a paper hot cup. One small plate held half a muffin and the other a fat square of coffee cake.

"Zara, right?" I asked.

"Yes. It's good to see you." Her dark hair was loose on her shoulders today, with a small clip holding it back from her forehead, and she wore a maroon sweater that lit up her Mediterranean skin.

"Likewise." I smiled.

"I love your coat," she said.

I ran a hand down my swingy retro coat, which was both warm and cute. Hip length in purple fleece, it had a round collar, three big buttons, and deep pockets.

"Thanks," I said. "I do too. I found it for a steal at a consignment shop in Healdsburg."

"Even better." She gestured at the other chair. "Please join me."

I thought for a brief moment. I didn't have to meet Benjamin for another half hour. "I will, thanks." I sat and unbuttoned the coat but kept it on. "Does Tara worship here, as well?"

"Her?" Zara scoffed. "She's an atheist or an agnostic or a Buddhist, depending on the day. She also went through a Bahá'í phase. Nothing so pedestrian as Protestant services for my twin."

"We each find what suits us, I guess. Did you grow up Congregationalist?"

"We did, over in Sebastopol." She slid the coffee cake across the table toward me. "Help yourself. I grabbed it for my friend, but she got called off to a committee meeting."

"Thanks. You and Tara both live in Colinas now?" I took a bite of the pastry, which was rich and buttery and a perfect post-church snack, with sweet peach slices layered under a cinnamon crumb topping.

"Yes. I moved to Colinas first." She sipped her coffee. "After her divorce, Tara followed me here from Sonoma and founded the cat shelter. How about you?"

"I moved up from Pasadena last spring." Now I wished I'd grabbed coffee.

"Listen." Zara leaned closer. "I heard you were on the scene when a dude was murdered in that auto shop, JJ's. That must have been horrible for you." Her deep-set brown eyes were intense.

"It wasn't pleasant."

"I know one isn't supposed to say such things about the dead, but Karl Meier was a total jerk. You should hear Tara talk about him."

My attention perked up. "She mentioned something to that effect when you both were in the wine bar. Can you be specific?"

"He volunteered at her shelter. The man apparently loved kitties with a passion. He would do all the dirty work, changing litter and wrangling the ill-tempered cats, so he could have time to cuddle and play with them."

I remembered that Dane's ex-husband—also a bit of a jerk—had volunteered there.

"So, what was the problem?" I asked.

"It was the way he treated his fellow volunteers. And Tara, herself." She shook her head. "He was rude, demeaning, and cold, like he was Mr. Superior."

"But Tara kept him on because he was valuable to the center?"

"I guess." She raised a shoulder and dropped it. "Do you think the owner of JJ's killed Meier? Jo Jarvin? I mean, how else could he have gotten in there?"

*Ugh.* Any scraps of peace I'd gained from worship flew out the window. "I'm sure Jo is innocent, Zara. The county sheriff and city police are investigating the death." I stood.

"Wait a sec. Is Jarvin a friend of yours?"

"She is."

"Sorry, I had no idea." She held up both palms. "I didn't mean to offend you."

"No offense. But I have to get going to meet a friend." I slung my bag over my shoulder. "Thanks for the coffee cake."

"See you around."

I headed out. She hadn't offended me exactly. I was glad I hadn't reacted with anger, but her question bothered me. It shouldn't. Lots of people, apparently including Jim Quan, were wondering the same thing. I doubted anybody in the general public knew Karl still had a key to JJ's. It was natural for people like Zara to think an ex-wife was the likely villain.

What I wanted to know was what Karl and his killer had argued about. Most important, who had the murderer been?

# CHAPTER 24

"How was your day with your son?" I asked Benjamin after we began our stroll through the bustling farmers market in the public park. I'd met him at the park's sculpture garden a few minutes before noon, as we'd agreed.

He didn't respond for a moment. "It was fine. I haven't told you that my relationship with Max has been somewhat fraught. I'm trying to heal it, which is one reason I wanted to spend the time with him yesterday."

"And was it? Healing?"

"Not entirely." He grimaced and touched my arm, pausing in front of a booth selling varieties of pistachio nuts in many flavors grown a bit farther south of here. "The thing is, he still resents that his mother and I split up. It was a mutual decision between us, but my son blames me. I was the one who moved out of the family home, and life was harder for all of us after that."

Benjamin opening up to me about his divorce and his son was new. "How did your daughter take it?"

"She has a way of seeing the truth. She stayed supportive of both her mom and me."

"You're lucky."

He slung his arm over my shoulders. "I know you and Zoe haven't had an easy path."

"No, we haven't." I picked up a bag of chili-lemon pistachios. "These are her favorites." I handed the vendor six dollars and thanked him. "Shall we move on?" I didn't want to hash over my personal woes in a public marketplace. We could come back to our relationship with our children later.

We strolled past a flower display and a non-organic vegetable farmer who sold pears and pineapples, among other produce. Neither were in season around here. The market rule was supposed to be only food produced locally. Maybe the market manager was more lax in the colder months.

I kind of hoped to chat with Sam the Cheese Man, who was usually a market regular. He also happened to be Dane's father. But he was nowhere to be found. Perhaps he was off on a winter vacation to parts tropical.

In the slot where Sam usually sold delicious hard and soft cheeses was a booth vending wine. Little paper cups sat half full of reds and whites in front of a sign reading, PF VINEYARDS TASTING. OVER 21. The banner at the back proclaimed, PF VINEYARDS with purple and green vines twining around the words. I'd never heard of that winery. Maybe it was new.

A tall man behind the display table turned toward us. I blinked. It was the Colinas chief of police. Quan had called him "Fenner" that morning at Jo's shop. Chief Fenner sold wine? Did he make it too? I couldn't remember his first name, but he looked softer, more congenial in this setting.

Benjamin smiled and stepped forward, extending his hand. "Paul. I see you took my advice."

Fenner smiled in return. "You were right, Cohen. Our wine is good enough to sell. I've moved a case already in the first hour here." He pumped Benjamin's hand.

My brain was reeling a little. Benjamin was on a first-name basis with the town's head police officer. Who made his own wine. Which was good enough people wanted to buy it.

"Do you know Cece Barton?" Benjamin asked Fenner. "Cece, this is Paul Fenner."

"Good morning, sir," I said.

The chief gave me a second look. "Cece and I met on Friday morning under less than felicitous circumstances. But, please, at the market I'm Paul."

"You're a weekend winemaker, Paul?" I asked.

"Yes, along with my lovely wife, Pamela. She's both the brains and the beauty behind the operation."

"Cece manages Vino y Vida here in town." Benjamin's voice projected pride. "She could offer your vintages at the wine bar."

"Oh?" Paul cocked his head. "I suppose, although I doubt we produce enough volume to provide you with what you need."

"Take a taste," Benjamin urged me, gesturing at the cups. "It's quite good."

I swirled one of the reds in my mouth before swallowing. "This is quite nice." I discussed the varietal with Paul. "It's a lot of work to manage a vineyard," I added.

"It is, which is why we only grow that one grape and buy the rest."

"Solving a homicide is a lot of work too," I said. "I haven't heard that anyone is in custody yet. Do you have news you can share on that front?"

Paul lifted his square chin. The guy had to be at least six foot six, so the gesture seemed unnecessary. I already had to gaze upward to see his face.

"Nothing I can share, no," he said.

"Is the case mostly Quan's responsibility?" I asked.

Paul looked down at me, his dark brows meeting in the middle under a straight, low hairline. "I'd rather not discuss work matters in this setting, if you don't mind. I'm here as a wine vendor, not an officer of the peace."

"I understand. The thing is, Paul, Jo Jarvin is my friend." I returned the chief's gaze, also not smiling. "She says she's still being questioned, but she never would have killed Karl or anyone else."

Paul opened his mouth, then closed it, pressing his lips together.

Benjamin, who had been following our back and forth, cleared his throat. "I'll take one of each, please, my friend."

A tune performed by fiddle and banjo wafted over from across the park. A couple strolled by holding paper boats full of the delectable tamales sold by the Tia Tamale food truck. A tamale was always a treat I indulged in to mark the end of market shopping. The fresh citrus scent of the orange, yellow, and green orbs at the next booth filled the air. All of it lured me away.

Benjamin handed cash to Paul and received a two-bottle PF Vineyards wine tote full of his purchase. Benjamin thanked him.

"Nice to meet you under better circumstances, Paul." I mustered a smile. "Sorry for bringing up business." Allie was always telling me I apologized too much, but the chief was right. This wasn't the place to discuss police matters.

"Have a good day, you two." Paul turned to face a new customer. "What can I offer you to taste?"

We moved on to the citrus farmer, where I picked up two pink grapefruits and a half dozen blood oranges. Benjamin snagged a few lemons and limes.

"How are you on a first-name basis with Paul Fenner?" I asked him as we strolled on.

"I consulted on a case for the Colinas PD." He shrugged. "After it was over, we got to talking about wine. The guy knows his stuff despite being an amateur."

I tucked my arm through his and squeezed. "You are a man of many talents and even more mysteries."

"I thought you liked it that way." He shot me a mischievous glance.

I reached up and kissed his cheek. I'd prefer fewer mysteries, but I wasn't complaining. Not at all.

# CHAPTER 25

Benjamin and I were nearing the end of our circuit of the market. He'd bought a boule of fresh sourdough and a bottle of Alexander Valley Winery olive oil, plus a bag of carrots, a bunch of scallions, and a pound of mixed mushrooms. I'd picked up a square of walnut fudge, a bag of mesclun greens, and a round of herbed chèvre from a different cheese person. The greens were for my house, and I planned to bring the cheese and fudge to Benjamin's as a contribution to the dinner he'd offered to make.

My stomach was growling for my tamale, but my phone rang before I could do anything about it. I dug it out of my purse and touched Benjamin's arm to indicate I was stopping. The caller ID was Jo. Let this not be bad news.

"Your car's all set, Cece," she began without preamble.

*Whew.* "Thanks. How long will you be there today?"

"Not long. I'm finishing an oil change, and then I'm clearing out."

"Okay. I doubt I can get over there in time," I said.

Benjamin signaled to me that he was getting in line for the tamale truck, and I gave him a thumbs-up.

"Do you want me to leave the Mustang unlocked with the key under the floor mat like we've done in the past?" Jo asked. "You could pick it up anytime today."

"No. I don't think so." Under the circumstances, more security was better than less. "I can get it tomorrow."

"That's fine. I plan to go for a hike this afternoon, just me and my dog. He won't pester me with questions about murder or give me accusing looks like I'm the bad guy. I'll be here my usual hours tomorrow."

"Great. I'll either bike over or get a ride." I glanced around, but nobody seemed to be listening. "Are you okay?"

"Been better, but I'll manage. See you *amanha*." She disconnected with the Portuguese word for "tomorrow."

I'd been about to ask her how her dinner with Ian went, except she clearly didn't want to talk about anything associated with Karl's murder. I didn't blame her for a minute. A long hike with Ouro would be a good thing. She and I could chat tomorrow. *Amanha*.

Benjamin was still at the end of a dozen hungry shoppers lined up for tamales when I joined him.

"That was Jo," I said. "They gave her access to her shop, and she finished the work on Blue."

"Do you need a ride over there?"

"No, she's leaving. I'll pick it up in the morning." I surveyed the tamale menu, which never changed. The cheese-and-bean filling was my only option since they didn't offer a fish tamale. Come to think of it, that didn't sound very good, despite how yummy fish tacos were. Otherwise, it was beef, pork, or chicken, none of which I'd eaten for years. The veggie tamale was delicious, though. I could eat one every day.

"Well, hello there, neighbor," a man said from behind me.

I turned. "Richard, what a pleasure. Here to grab lunch?" I smiled.

"Yes, times five." He beamed. "The ROMEO club chose tamales for lunch."

I wrinkled my nose. "You're in a club of all Romeos?" Richard had a lady friend in San Francisco, but a group of them, possibly all as old as he?

He laughed. "It stands for Retired Old Men Who Eat Out. Some of us have been retired longer than others. It sounds better than OFWNBTD." He pronounced each letter.

"I'm stumped."

"Old Farts With Nothing Better To Do." He winked. "They're all over at a picnic table under the trees."

Benjamin turned and was taking in our conversation.

"Richard, you remember Benjamin Cohen," I said.

"Indeed I do," Richard said.

"Hello, Richard." Benjamin extended his hand. "I like that second name a lot."

Richard shook hands. "I'd invite you to join but you are neither old nor with nothing to do, if that isn't too many negatives."

"Is Pete cooking today?" I asked him. His great-nephew sometimes cooked for Ed at Edie's but he'd filled in here in the fall and said he was saving up to buy the business.

"No, he's off at a culinary workshop in San Diego, I believe."

The line inched forward. As Benjamin gave Tia our order, Richard tapped me on the shoulder.

"Stop by and see me in the morning, will you?" he asked.

"You bet. But is it—"

He interrupted me by holding a finger to his lips. "Yes, it's about that. Not here."

"Gotcha. Thanks."

A white-haired friend joined Richard to help carry their lunch. Benjamin and I said goodbye and took our tamales to a bench on the edge of the park. I enjoyed my weekly taste of heaven even as I wondered what gossip about the homicide my neighbor knew.

# CHAPTER 26

Being two healthy forty-somethings, Benjamin and I enjoyed an interlude of afternoon delight after he drove us to his house.

Now at three thirty, we sat relaxed and pink-cheeked on the southwest-facing deck behind his Arts and Crafts bungalow. It was a three-bedroom home across town from where I lived, with a wide overhang shading the front porch. A large dormer in the back expanded the second-floor space without ruining the historical appearance of the front.

Despite the structure being over a hundred years old, it was in great shape. The previous owner had done extensive renovations to bring necessary systems up to code but kept the antique character of the house. The work Benjamin did before moving in was all minor and cosmetic.

The winter sun was just enough to warm us, plus we each held a mug of steaming hot mulled cider to which he'd added a glug of locally distilled rum. The aroma alone relaxed me.

"I really like your new design touches inside." I stretched out my legs. "Where did you manage to find the rug and blanket, along with matching pillows?" He'd scattered pillows in peach and dusty blue on his cream-colored sofa. The blanket across the back was in a geometric design that picked up those colors plus a sandy yellow and a pale green. An area rug coordinated with all of it. "They look like they came straight from New Mexico."

"That's because they did. They're the real thing." He smiled. "I bought them in Santa Fe and brought them back."

I scrunched up my nose. "When was that?"

"Remember the trip I took right after the New Year?"

I nodded. He'd said that it was for work, and I hadn't inquired where he'd be. Based on previous trips he'd taken, I knew he didn't like to talk about his job. Or sometimes wasn't allowed to.

"I was consulting in Santa Fe and Los Alamos," he murmured. "I did a little shopping before I came home."

Los Alamos was the top-security research center where they'd produced the first atom bombs during World War II. Who knew what they were working on now, or how he was involved. I didn't ask.

"And you went by car rather than flying," I said.

"Correct. I decided to load up the vehicle before I left there." He drove a compact SUV, and his driving alone would have left plenty of room for a few pieces of home decor.

I sipped my spiked cider. A thin cry from the sky made me look up. A hawk circled, soaring against the pale blue using its acute eyesight to search for dinner, for prey. Karl had been somebody's prey, and it was creepy to think of that person now searching for their next victim.

"A kiss for your thoughts?" He nudged my knee with his.

"The kiss, yes. I don't want to ruin our afternoon with my thoughts." I mustered a smile. "What's on the dinner menu, and how can I help?"

He gazed at me for a moment. "I thought I'd make a creamy carrot soup, my special mushroom-cheese tart, and a hand-tossed Caesar salad. You can be my sous chef if you'd like."

"Sounds yummy."

"But I'm pretty sure you were thinking about Meier's murder. Am I right?"

I let out a sigh. "Yes."

"I get that you don't want to dwell on it or spoil our time together by digging into dark topics," he said. "But I heard something you might be interested in."

"About the murder?"

He bobbed his head. "Kind of. About the victim, at any rate."

I sat up straight. "Okay. Give."

"First things first." Benjamin grinned and pointed to his lips as he leaned toward me.

"All right, although your cause and effect is all messed up." I kissed him. If the kiss lasted longer than strictly necessary, who was counting? "Now, what do you know?"

He drank from his mug, then cradled it with both hands as he crossed his denim-clad legs at the ankle. "Well, I heard Meier might have gotten in a little too deep with some unsavory characters."

"What do you mean? Like the mob?"

"Not sure. One of my contacts mentioned it."

"Is the mob even a thing anymore?" I asked.

He turned his head to face me. "Of course it is."

"It's a valid question." I flipped my hands open. "I mean, they're in New York, right?"

A slow smile spread over his face. "You are such a Californian. Have you ever seen those maps that depict New York City as taking up half the continent? You, Cece Barton, would draw the reverse. The Golden State would be enormous, and everything east of the Rockies would be about an inch wide."

"It's all I know. Plus Japan."

"Which is farther west from here despite people calling it part of the Far East. My point is made."

His smile was so fond I couldn't object. Then I remembered how this had all started.

"So, tell me more," I said. "Who are these unsavory characters?"

He opened his mouth. My phone rang in my pocket. I left it alone.

"Go on," I urged. "I'll get that later." I was dying to hear what he'd learned.

The phone rang again.

"Just answer it," he said. "I'm not going anywhere."

"Okay. One sec." I pulled it out to see Zoe's name on the messages. It rang again. This time I jabbed it on. I hoped she wasn't in trouble. Hadn't been hurt.

"Honey, are you okay?" My voice was breathless.

"Mama, where are you?"

I couldn't tell if her tone was anguished or breathless. "I'm at Benjamin's. Where are you?"

"At home. At your house. Why aren't you here?"

"You are? Did you tell me you were coming?"

"No, but . . ." Her voice trailed off. "Can you come home?"

I thought of asking her more questions. I thought of saying no.

"Yes. I'll come as soon as I can." I glanced up at Benjamin with a question in my eyes.

He nodded.

"Hang tight. I'll be right there." I disconnected. "I am so, so sorry. It sounds like Zoe's in some kind of trouble. And you know she almost never—" I clapped my hand to my mouth as my eyes welled.

"She almost never asks for your help." He rose. "I know. Your girl comes first, which is as it should be. I'll run you home." He held out his hand to help me up.

"Thank you." I gave him a quick hug, then hurried inside to grab my shoes, bag, and coat.

Thoughts of the unsavory characters didn't exactly fly out of my mind, but this wasn't the time to dig into that topic. Not at all.

# CHAPTER 27

After Benjamin dropped me off, I nearly ran to the house. I slowed when I saw my mother's dark blue car parked in the driveway. Was Mom here too?

The front door opened as I reached for the handle. My tall, willowy daughter stood in the doorway.

"Are you all right?" I held out my arms.

She pulled a frowny smile. "I'm fine." She extracted herself from my embrace quickly, as she always did.

I followed her inside and made sure the door locked behind me. A half-empty bottle of beer sat on the dining table next to an open laptop. Her device, not mine.

"I'm delighted you're here," I said slowly, picking my words with care. "Did your Gran come, too?"

"No, but she let me borrow her car." She boosted her purple-tinted hair into a messy bun, sliding a hair elastic off her wrist to secure it.

"I thought you sounded a little, um, frantic when you called. Are you sure everything is okay?"

"Yes, Mom." She ran her finger through the condensation on the green glass of the bottle without looking up. "Well, sort of."

"What's going on, sweetie?"

She met my gaze with her father's brown eyes, bigger and more luminous than my green ones. "Get yourself a drink. This could take a while."

*Yes, ma'am.* When I stood, both cats came running, with Martin proclaiming it was the dinner hour. It was a little early, but while I was in the kitchen, I scooped the wet food into their individual dishes, then brought a glass of IPA to the table. I hadn't had a beer straight out of the bottle since I was her age. My Scorpio baby had turned twenty-one in November.

"Cheers." I raised the glass to her.

She clinked her bottle. "So, were you going to tell me about this dude in town who was murdered?"

"How did you know about that?"

"Mom. Ever hear about something called news?"

"Is that why you came?" I cocked my head.

"I'm worried, okay? I mean, it's not like Colinas is a very big town, Mom." She glanced away again.

I started to cite the yadda-yadda about how competent the detective and police were but cut that off before I got going. It felt like she had something else going on, and platitudes served neither of us.

"I know. I appreciate your concern." I sipped my beer.

"Are you, like, investigating again?" she asked. "I read that you were there when the body was found."

"I'm interested, naturally. My friend Jo, the mechanic, found the corpse. She called me before she called the police, which was odd, but I understand. She was scared and nervous. The thing is, the police wonder if she killed Karl."

"She knew him?" Zoe's voice rose in surprise mixed with horror.

"Unfortunately, he was her ex-husband."

"Eww."

"I'm sure she didn't murder him," I said.

"Did you also know him?"

"I'd met him only the day before." I told her about the electri-

cal work. "So, yes, I am looking into the murder a little. But safely."
I smiled at her. "How are things at school?"

"Fine. OMG, Mom. I am so loving my weather internship at
the TV station." She went on to tell me about shadowing a local
television meteorologist.

My only child's dream was to become a weather scientist, and
she was pursuing it with a passion. More power to her. May she
have all the success I hadn't yet had in more than twice her years.

"That's great, honey. I want to hear all about it." I smiled.
"How long can you stay? I have tomorrow off. Maybe we can—"

"I have to get Gran's car back tonight." Her fingers got busy
on the laptop's keyboard.

I blew out a breath, but quietly. She never stayed long enough
for us to grow closer. I always held out hope that one day in the
future, she would. That we would.

"Can you at least stay for dinner?" I expected her to decline
the invitation. She had a two-hour drive back, and the sun was already setting now at five o'clock.

"Sure."

Her quick, matter-of-fact response warmed my heart.

Zoe focused intently at the screen for a minute, then lifted her
gaze to me. "You know I'm minoring in Japanese, right?"

"Yes. I think that's great."

"I'm applying to go there next year for my study abroad. I was
poking around looking into anything I could find about Daddy's
job in Tokyo."

*Uh-oh.* Zoe had been a baby growing into toddlerhood when
we'd lived in Japan's largest city. She'd seized on that personal
history after she began studying at Davis and loved all she'd been
learning about Japanese culture and language.

What I'd never told her was her father's own history. How his
career with the diplomatic service had imploded because of what
he'd done, the reason we'd had to leave the country abruptly.

"Oh?" I tried to keep my voice casual.

"Yeah. I really had to dig. Was he fired, Mom?" She wrinkled her brow and scrunched up her nose. "I saw one thing about how the State Department accepted his resignation halfway through his posting and wished him well in his next endeavor. No thanking him for his service, no lauding him. What happened?"

I studied my beer glass. I inhaled the hoppy aroma and took a swig.

"What?" she pressed. "I deserve to know."

"You absolutely do. You're an adult. Let me start by saying I never wanted to . . ." *Gah.* I didn't know how put it. *Simply tell the truth, Cecelia.* I remember my own father saying that to me many times. I took a deep breath. "I never wanted to speak poorly of Greg to you. I didn't want to mar your memories of your father or make you think worse of him."

"But there's reason to, apparently."

"He had some issues. He was let go from the job in Japan because he had an affair with Nomoko, the woman who was his local counterpart. That kind of relationship was strictly and explicitly forbidden, in writing. After we returned to California and settled in Pasadena, Greg got a job with an import-export business, but he continued to have serial affairs."

Her jaw dropped. "What a flaming jerk."

I smiled sadly. "I'm sorry, Zo. I never wanted you to know."

"Why didn't you leave him?" Zoe sounded astonished. "How could you, like, even put up with that?"

"I had to think of you, honey. You two were so close." I lifted my chin. "And money was in the equation. I never had a well-paying career. I didn't know how I would swing a house and childcare and all the rest on my small paychecks. We were barely making it on two incomes."

"Man. I never had a clue."

I wasn't sure she'd have been able to hear it if I'd told her before now. Teenagers were rightfully and biologically self-absorbed. Maturity had a lot going for it.

Zoe drained her beer and stood. "I'm getting another one. You?"

I reached for her arm. "Honey, you have to drive back."

She set her fists on her waist. "I'll go early in the morning. We need to keep talking."

I gazed up at this brilliant, prickly, beautiful girl of mine. A no-nonsense woman with a mind of her own and a kind heart, exactly as I raised her.

"Awesome." I rose. "Let's rustle up some dinner together while we talk." That old parallel play thing might work in our favor.

# CHAPTER 28

I forked in my last bite of the frittata we'd cobbled together out of potatoes, kale, eggs, and cheese, plus herbs I'd snipped from out back. I sipped from the pinot noir in my glass and counted my blessings to have shared a meal with my daughter. Candles brought a warm glow. Cats peacefully snoozed nearby, and not a harsh word had been spoken. If this change in our dealings with each other stuck, I was a lucky woman.

"That was good, Mom." Zoe took her own sip.

"Thanks. Sorry about no salad. I forgot to grab the greens I bought at the market before I left Benjamin's."

"No apologies. We had kale and green herbs, both from your garden. How's it going with the boyfriend, anyway?"

"He's good," I said.

"I mean, how's the relationship going? You know, you and him."

I sat with that for a moment. For Zoe to take an interest in what was going on in my life was so new I thought it might give me whiplash. It was as if turning twenty-one had flipped a switch in her emotional brain. I wouldn't argue with that.

"I think it's going well," I began. "I'm taking it slowly and care-fully. But I like him, a lot, and he's so far proving to be pretty much everything I'd want in a partner. Kind, affectionate, self-sufficient. And I trust him."

"He's not too hard on the eyes, either." She gave me a wicked smile.

"Not a bit."

Zoe swirled the wine in her glass. "Why didn't you date after Daddy died?"

I reeled but kept going. "You had such a tough time with his death. I didn't want my attention to you diluted by the complications of a relationship." I swallowed. "Since we're being honest, here's another reason. I had lost all trust in your father. It's seriously taken me this long to attempt to trust a man again and feel safe bringing someone into my life."

She nodded, staring into her glass.

Time to get off this dark subject. "How about you, honey? Any love life going on?"

She glanced up with a smile playing on her lips. "Maybe. There's someone in my physics lab I kind of like. We've been hanging out a bit."

"Ooh. What's his name?"

"Mom! You can't assume it's a man."

She was right. "My bad. What's their name?"

"Nah. You had it the first time. Henry. He's kind of geeky, but in a really cute way, and he loves all the important things as much as I do." She ticked them off on her fingers. "Stinky cheese. Horror flicks. Owls. Contra dancing." She pulled her mouth to the side. "Well, he's still getting up to speed on that last one. He'd rather be playing the music than dancing to it."

"I'm happy for you, honey. Do you have a picture of him?"

"Yeah." She smiled to herself as she scrolled through her phone to find one of the two of them.

Taller than Zoe's five foot ten by a couple of inches, Henry was skinny and wore both a goofy grin and a cone-shaped New Year's Eve hat. His arm was slung around Zoe's. Her smile couldn't have been more adoring. My heart was that of a grateful mother. She hadn't dated at all in high school. I couldn't be more happy that she'd found a sweetheart.

"That's a darling picture of both of you. Bring him home some-time," I said.

"I might." She stood and picked up her plate, then reached for mine.

"I'll clean up. You want to set up the Scrabble board?" We'd agreed on a game after dinner.

"Sure."

By the time the dishwasher was humming and the counters were wiped clean, Zoe sat at the dining table staring at her laptop, no game in sight.

"You have to see this." She beckoned.

I pulled up a chair next to her.

"I thought I'd try to dig into this Meier dude." She pointed at the screen. "He was into some bad juju when he was younger."

"Oh?" I wasn't seeing what she was, but I realized I'd never followed up with Mooncat about when she'd referred to him as Charlie. "Like what?"

"It seems he made a bad investment, or one he couldn't afford. He was busted for not paying back taxes and for defaulting on a loan."

"What did he invest in?"

Zoe studied the screen. Her fingers flew. She studied it again. She sat back, pulling the covered elastic out of her long brown hair and onto her wrist, shaking out her hair. It was thick like mine but a rich dark color like Greg's had been, except hers fea-tured reddish highlights where it wasn't purple.

I gazed at my girl and reached over to stroke the curl on her near shoulder. "Your hair looks so pretty down like that." I stopped myself from mom-saying she should wear it that way more often. I pulled my hand back, in case the move had annoyed her.

She gave me an affectionate side-eye, then twisted her locks back into a knot and reapplied the elastic. She pointed at the screen.

"See?" she asked. "Meier tried to buy a winery. Dude probably had no wine education, no idea what was involved."

I squinted at the screen.

"What, the old lady needs reading glasses now?" Zoe asked, but her tone was warm, not cutting.

"Ugh. I probably do. What winery was it? One around here?"

"Yeah, it's somewhere in the Alexander Valley. The winery was Ridley Vineyards, on Las Marias Road. Do you know the winery?"

"I don't, other than that it's outside of town. That road is how you get from here to the town of Las Marias."

"Makes sense," she said.

"So, Karl had financial issues and tax problems, but he must have been cleared of them. I mean, he had a functioning electrician's business."

"He must have figured out how to sort things out." She shut the laptop, stood, and kissed the top of my head. "How about that Scrabble?" She headed into the bedroom I always kept ready for her, which is where I stored the board games.

If this thawing, or maybe it was a new closeness, kept up, I was going to have some figuring out of my own to do. Not worrying about her possible negative reaction to me showing my love, for starters. I would gladly take it.

# CHAPTER 29

The house was empty when I awoke at seven thirty. Zoe left a note on the kitchen table that said she took off at five o'clock to return Gran's car and get to an early class. She'd ended it with a sweet caution.

*Be careful, Mama. Love you.*

My eyes welled with tears. Happy ones. Until last fall, she hadn't said she loved me since before Greg had died. I didn't care what had caused this change in attitude, although I wondered if being happy in love herself had broken through the block she had about me. I thanked whatever romance gods had brought her and Henry together.

The fact that the dude loved owls must be the cherry on top for Zoe. It was Greg who taught her about the nocturnal birds. Together father and daughter had studied the calls and habitats of owls everywhere, especially the ones found in the foothills of the San Gabriel Mountains, a short drive from our Pasadena home.

I shook off my memories and read a text from Benjamin.

**Hope you had a lovely visit with Z and that all is well. If she went home, interest you in a postponed dinner tonight?**

That sounded nice. What good was a day off if one didn't make good use of it? I texted back my acceptance and thanks.

"Yes, kitty-cats, you can have your breakfast." I smiled down at

Martin, who wove himself around my ankles as he bitterly wailed about the empty treat dish. Mittens, on the other hand, sat in front of her wet food dish, haughty as she waited. No begging for that girl.

Cats fed and coffee made, I pulled on yoga pants and made sure I was minimally decent—which meant donning a heavy fleece over my sleep shirt so I could forgo a bra—and headed out to the garden with a travel mug full of all-important java. The sun was only now peeking over the trees behind my back wall. The air was brisk, but at least it wasn't raining.

I knocked on the gate. "Richard, are you there?"

He didn't answer.

I knocked again. "Hello? Neighbor?"

The only response was a metallic clatter and a few choice swear words. I hurried to open the gate. In the far corner of the garden that filled Richard's yard, twice the size of mine, was his octagonal writing shed, the one labeled JOURNALISTE. He was on hands and knees in front of it, reaching for the door handle. I set down my mug and rushed over.

"Let me help you." I braced my knees and extended both hands to him.

"Cecelia. Thank you."

Between us, we got him to his feet. A shovel and a pitchfork lay on the ground. He dusted off his knees, elbow, and hands.

"Good Lord." Wearing a disgusted look, he shook his head. "What a fool I am."

"Are you all right? What happened?"

"I wanted to dig up that Canyon Snow iris to divide it. I got myself all bolloxed up in the tools. When I began to fall, the famously poor reflexes of the elderly refused to come to my rescue."

I didn't dare suggest he might want to hire someone younger—much younger—to help with jobs like that. Richard was singularly prickly when it came to his cherished garden. For the most part, he managed. But this situation could have ended up with a much worse outcome.

"You can leave it for now, right?" I asked. "Let's go sit."

"Splendid idea, my dear. I might even accept the loan of your arm." His smile was as broad and warm as ever, but his voice shook.

I extended my elbow. Once he was seated in his favorite chair on the patio, I retrieved my coffee and joined him.

"What is new in your world, neighbor?" he asked. "Did your lovely mother come to visit?"

"You remember her car?"

"I might be woefully wobbly, but the old memory is intact." He pointed at his head.

"Actually, Zoe borrowed Mom's car and came to check up on me." I sipped my still-warm brew. "We had a quite nice visit, in fact."

"I'm glad to hear it. I suppose she's old enough now to see a different way to relate to her mother."

"That seems to be the case, thank goodness." I'd told him in the past a little of my sorrow at not having a close relationship with my daughter.

"I expect you have a few questions for me regarding the murder." He folded his hands on his lap, his voice now steadier.

"I do. For starters, do you know the Ridley winery on Las Marias Road?"

"The former Ridley winery, you mean."

I waited for him to elaborate. Two little California quail ran along the top of the fence. One stopped and called out its three-note call, repeated three times. It ran farther, stopped, and sang out again. Those birds always made me smile.

"Wesley Holt bought it a few years ago," he said. "The place had been, shall we say, in disrepair. Vines poorly tended, the building run-down and uninviting. To his credit, Holt has done a wonder at renovating and refurbishing all of it, and his recent vintages are more than drinkable."

"They sponsored a stop on the Wine Road on the weekend. Allie volunteered at Holt."

"You should bring your sister by for a glass of wine some afternoon. She's a lovely person."

"I will." I cradled my lidded mug and frowned. "She said Wesley reminded her of Karl Meier somehow. Do you know of any relationship between them? Are they cousins or something?"

He tilted his head. "Nothing definite, no."

"Huh. Last evening Zoe dug into the internet and found that Karl had tried to buy the winery when it was still Ridley. He failed in several ways and got into trouble for his efforts."

"I'm not surprised in the least." Richard tented his fingers.

Maybe the two men didn't know each other. Or maybe they were rivals, even enemies. I hoped Wesley hadn't been the one to end Karl's life. My thoughts moved on to others who had expressed dislike of the victim.

"Richard, what do you **know about** Tara Pulanski?"

"The cat rescue director. She does good work, has lived in town for some years now."

"I've heard Tara intensely disliked Karl."

"Can't help you there." His gaze traveled to a flash of blue in the scrub oak beyond his wall. He pointed. "Western bluebird."

"Pretty." Maybe he commented on the bird to get me off the topic of homicide. I didn't blame him. The morning was pleasant and he was ninety. Who wanted to spend precious hours dwelling on murder?

# CHAPTER 30

Ten o'clock found me at Allie's again, coffee in front of both of us at her kitchen table for a visit. She'd offered to run me over to JJ's to get my car after we caught up with each other. I'd paused my walk over at the Exchange Bakery and Gourmet Provisions to pick up a half dozen croissants and Danish pastries.

"Mmm, flaky," Allie mumbled around a mouthful of croissant.

I sipped from my mug and rolled the coffee on my tongue. "Cardamom? Nice."

"Yeah. I had it that way at a fancy coffee shop in Healdsburg and loved it. Makes the coffee taste exotic, doesn't it?"

"Yep. Kind of Middle Eastern, maybe Turkish. Do you sprinkle in the powered spice?" I asked.

"No. I add a cardamom pod to the beans when I grind them. The flavor's a lot better that way."

"I like it. So, how'd your real estate meet-up with the developer go yesterday?"

"Gareth Rockwell? He's your typical overambitious type. I'm pretty sure I thoroughly discouraged him from trying to acquire the adobes, although I can't promise anything." She brought her brows together. "I think there was something up with him and Karl Meier."

"Seriously?"

"Yes. In fact, he asked me to show him Karl's house."

"Wow," I said. "But the guy just died. His estate won't be settled for a while, will it?"

"It won't. I drove Gareth by the property and asked how he knew the address."

"What did he say?" I asked.

"Something or other vague. I never did find out."

"He knew Karl's name was linked with that house." I frowned.

"He did."

"That's so strange. What kind of house is it?"

"It's kind of a plain-wrap 1960s ranch, but it's up in the hills and happens to have a stunning, unobstructed view of the valley," Allie said. "And get this. It sits on two full acres of land."

"Huh. So the house could be added to, and maybe the acreage allows for another unit or two to be added."

"Exactly."

"I wonder if Karl owed Gareth money for some reason." I tore off a piece of the cheese Danish on my plate and popped it into my mouth.

"Could be. This afternoon I'm going to dig into the deed on the property and see if I can find out what the situation is." She drummed her fingers on the table.

"You mean, Gareth might already own a share of the house?"

"I doubt it, but stranger things have happened. To change the subject, how was your date yesterday?"

"Cut short, but for a good reason." I filled her in on Zoe's surprise visit. "We haven't had such a sweet, conflict-free visit since she was ten."

"Since before Greg died. You told her about his affairs, but did you two also talk about how he died?"

"No. She didn't ask, and I didn't want to go there. She heard enough bad things about him for one evening. I'm glad I was the one to find him and not her."

"Totally."

"Will you tell me more about Wesley Holt?" I asked. "You mentioned him in connection with Karl."

"Right." She snapped her fingers. "I told you he reminded me of Karl. At one point the lights in the Holt tasting room flickered and went off for a few seconds. They came back on, but he was mad. He had to wait for the Wi-Fi router to reboot for sales to work, plus he had to reset the clocks and all. He kind of stormed in cursing out the electrician who'd done the original work."

"Did you ask who it was?"

"Cee." She gazed over the tops of her new red-rimmed reading glasses. "Who am I? Of course I asked."

"And of course it was Karl."

She nodded.

"I assume Holt knew that Karl was dead," I said.

"I tried to slip him a word about how maligning a dead man out loud made him look bad to customers." She lifted her eyebrows. "He was too mad to hear it."

"The winery hasn't been open very long, has it?"

"Three years? Four, maybe."

"Last night Zoe dug into the internet and learned that Karl had tried to buy the place when it was called Ridley."

"I remember that," Allie said. "He had no idea what he was doing and ended up going under. All he was left with were debts he couldn't pay."

"He must have already been an electrician," I mused. "Maybe that's when he did the defective wiring work."

"Probably." She glanced at the clock at the same time as her phone dinged. "Okay, sister of mine. Time to run you over to JJ's. I have a meeting in half an hour."

I carried my mug and plate to the sink. "Save the pastries for the boys."

"Thanks for bringing them."

"Anytime. Double birthday party next weekend, yes?"

"Heaven help us, yes." Allie cast a helpless glance at me. "With eleven other kids. You have to promise to ply me with whiskey the minute the last one leaves. Or maybe before it's over."

"Can you believe the twins are turning eleven?"

"Not for a minute." She grabbed her purse and keys. "How did that even happen?"

I slung on my own bag, carrying my jacket in my hand. "Hey, we turned eleven and the world didn't stop. It'll be fine, Al."

# Chapter 31

After Allie dropped me at JJ's, I glanced into the open doors of the garage. A green fifties Chrysler was up on the lift inside, and in the bay next to it sat a white late-sixties VW Bug with the door to the rear engine compartment raised. I didn't look too hard, but it appeared the floor under the lift had been cleaned of Karl's blood. *Good.*

I waited on the bench out front while two women conferred with Jo in the office. A man fired up a mid-seventies Jaguar sedan and drove away. Blue, the top up and secured, waited in one of the parking spaces to the side of the building. The winter sun was trying to gain strength as the new year slid toward the spring equinox, but the days weren't much longer yet. I was glad for my jeans, sweater, and jacket.

At least Jo didn't seem to be hurting for business. A man being murdered in her shop hadn't scared away these customers. *Also good.*

A few minutes later, the women emerged. At least twenty years older than I was, they had similar short hairstyles—one with white hair and the other slate gray—and wore sensible shoes. The shorter one headed with a gimp in her step to a modern hybrid parked at the end of the row of cars.

"Thanks, Josie," the taller woman said before she sauntered to the hybrid.

Jo followed them out.

"Josie?" I stood. "I thought you went by Jo."

"They were friends of my mom. Known me since I was in diapers." She gave me a wry smile. "But you have to watch out with nicknames. Almost nobody gets to call me Josie. Once a diminutive nickname like that catches on, it's all over."

"Isn't Jo a nickname?"

"Yes. My given name is Josefina, but I like to be called Jo, and that's that." She tossed her head toward the office. "Come on in." She handed me the work slip, which totaled up the parts and labor.

"No problems with the car?" I dug a credit card out of my bag.

"Not a one. I adjusted a belt here, a spark plug gap there. She's running as smooth as melted chocolate." She pointed to the card reader on the desk.

"Thank you so much for getting to it." I tapped the card, and our business was completed. Except I wasn't done.

"How are you feeling?" I asked as I stashed the card.

Her shoulders slumped. "I've certainly been better. Still, it feels great to be working. And nobody seems scared off by what happened. If anything, the phone has been ringing, like, off the hook." She laughed. "What does that even mean? Did landline phones have hooks?"

An image of a telephone in the historical museum popped into my brain. "Over a hundred years ago? Yes, they did. Stop by the museum next to Vino y Vida sometime. They have a wooden wall phone, and the part you spoke into hung from a hook on the side."

"Cool. I will."

"So, how did your dinner with Ian go?"

The smile slid off her face. "It was okay. He didn't seem angry with me, at least not Saturday evening. But he sure carries a lot of anger inside. I'm kind of worried about him, Cece."

"Life hasn't treated him well," I murmured.

"No, but he's had choices. He always seems to choose the victim role, not the one where he figures out how to improve things."

"Did he go to college?"

"He didn't. I thought community college would be a good choice for him, but by then Karl and I were divorced. The kid didn't want to hear my opinion on anything. Actually, he never did. I'm surprised the dinner on Saturday went as well as it did, frankly."

"He went straight from high school to working for Karl," I said.

"Yes. He actually began working for his uncle before he graduated. Well, getting trained, anyway."

"Karl wasn't at all gentle with him when they were in the wine bar."

"Gentle wasn't in Karl's vocabulary," she said.

Ouro wandered around the side of the building. When I held out my fist for him to sniff, he nudged his head against it. I rubbed his ears.

Without looking up, I asked, "Jo, how did you and Karl get together in the first place? I must say, I have trouble imagining what you saw in him."

"He could really turn on the charm when he wanted to. We had fun for a while, and he convinced me to marry him. Said he wanted a family. I'd wanted kids since forever. Still do." She barked out a harsh laugh. "But Karl could turn off his good side without a moment's warning. Then he was just plain mean."

"And you finally had enough."

"I decided I was done tiptoeing around, walking on eggshells, never knowing whether he'd be nice or lash out at me. The bad side was becoming the rule, not the exception. I felt bad leaving Ian with him, but I had no choice."

Car wheels crunched on pavement as a Ford with impressive fins pulled in.

"I'll let you get to work," I said. "Thanks for fixing Blue."

"You take care." Jo's attention had already moved on.

I fired up my own vintage car and let the engine warm up for a couple of minutes. Maybe one of these days I'd buy a new car. One that didn't use much gas, if any, and that could be driven as soon as it was turned on.

Except I barely drove the car I had, and I liked it that way. More exercise for me, less wear and tear on Blue. Right now? It was time to pay a visit to a winery.

# CHAPTER 32

I drove slowly along Las Marias Road, not sure exactly where the winery was. I hadn't bothered to put the Holt winery into my phone's GPS before I left. I knew it was located somewhere between Colinas and the town the road was named for.

I'd put the Mustang's top down before I left Jo's lot. It was cool out, but I loved the sun and the fresh air. I passed a few houses that grew more spaced out as I left Colinas town proper.

After a few miles, I spotted rows of bare grapevines on the left that stretched in neat rows into the distance. A sign on the fencing bore a logo comprised of a capital H nestled in an open V. These had to be some of the Holt grapes.

At the crest of a hill, several men moved down the rows wielding red-handled pruners. This was the season, while the plants were still dormant, to clip, shape, and rejuvenate the vines. One of the men straightened and lifted a hand in greeting, nudging his coworker. Blue was a popular car. Everybody seemed to love the vintage Mustang.

Around a wide bend I came upon a wide, low building set back in a parking lot. The structure, which faced to the side, featured a wraparound veranda with multicolored umbrellas to shade the tables. A big sign at the road proclaimed HOLT VINEYARDS, with a larger version of the logo I'd seen on the fence. This one had green vines twining around the arms of the V, with two full wine-glasses on either side, one red, one white.

I pulled into the lot and turned off the ignition. I sat for a moment, thinking of a plan. I came because I was curious about Wesley Holt, but I needed a plausible reason to ask to speak to him, assuming he wasn't already busy doing something as simple as conducting the wine tasting. I clapped my hand to my forehead. *Well, duh.* I had a perfect ruse. I managed a wine bar. I would ask if he'd like me to add Holt wine to our pour rotation.

Could I pull off such subterfuge? I sat another moment, reflecting on my gumption. A year and a half ago I would not have been confident enough to waltz into a place like this and tell a story in order to learn something else. But meeting that farmer from Massachusetts at Christmastime and learning some tricks from Cam Flaherty about solving a murder boosted my nerve. Investigating mostly solo last October had as well. That, combined with my success managing a popular drinking establishment, had fostered a faith in myself I hadn't had in years, if ever.

I grabbed my keys and bag and climbed out. I didn't expect to be too long here and decided to leave Blue's top down. I was due to pick up Ed at the diner at one thirty. This couldn't be a lengthy visit, and the cloudless sky meant the car's pale blue vinyl seats were in no danger of a drenching. I made my way around the side to the entrance.

On the veranda, a table of four couples sat sipping and conversing, punctuated by laughter. Three middle-aged women had an array of glasses in front of them, as well as a piece of paper with a list of something. They consulted it and a phone and sipped, taking their tasting seriously.

Before I ascended the few steps, I turned to take in the view. The winery was situated with a small valley rolling out before it, all of it covered in vines except for a pond at a low spot. The higher hills of Colinas formed the backdrop to the beautiful scene. No wonder the place had a big veranda.

I tore myself away and stepped inside through a wide entrance made by the two doors standing all the way open. A wine bar lined the opposite wall. Small tables and chairs were situated in front of big windows facing the valley, while the side walls held shelves of merchandise.

"How can we help you today?" a young man behind the bar asked. His light hair was neatly trimmed and he wore a maroon polo shirt with the Holt logo on the chest.

"I wondered if I could speak to Wesley Holt, please."

He frowned. "Do you have an appointment?"

"I'm afraid I don't." I slid a Vino y Vida business card out of my bag. "I manage a popular wine bar in Colinas. I happened to be passing by and thought I'd see if he wanted to supply one of our featured wines."

His expression lightened. "In that case, for sure. Let me see if he's available." He poked at a cell phone and stepped into a room off to the side, speaking words I couldn't make out before he returned. "He'll be here within five minutes. May I offer you a tasting on the house?"

"Why not?" As long as I didn't down a whole glass on my increasingly empty stomach, I could sample the wares while I waited. "Thanks. What are you pouring?"

We discussed a few choices. I thanked him again and carried my half pour of sauvignon blanc over to peruse the bottle openers, stopper options, and various gift items like coasters and wine tote bags that could hold one, two, or four bottles. I swirled and sniffed and tasted the wine, which featured notes of peach and almond blossom. I tasted again, enjoying the fresh energy of many sauvignon blancs. I would be happy to include this wine in the pouring rotation at Vin y Vida.

"Ms. Barton?" A man spoke from behind me.

I turned. "I'm Cece. Are you Wesley Holt?"

"I am." He held out a thick hand.

I shook it and regarded him. With neatly combed hair mostly

gray and an open-collared shirt under a tan blazer, he looked the part of an industrious winery owner. But the hand thickened by years of manual labor and his ruddy complexion showed that he might also have the background to be a successful vine grower and viticulturist. He was maybe two inches taller than me.

"How can I help you, Cece?" he asked.

"I manage the Vino y Vida wine bar in Colinas, and we feature wines from different vineyards in the valley. Holt is fairly new, isn't it?"

"Compared to some, yes." His tone shifted to wary. I wasn't sure why.

"I'm fairly new at running the bar, myself." I smiled, hoping to signal solidarity rather than criticism. "Vino y Vida is popular with locals and visitors alike," I said. "We're in one of the antique adobes next to the river."

"I've heard of it."

I handed him one of my business cards. "Do let me know if you're interested in doing business."

His already small eyes, a strange dark blue, squinted from under a heavy brow at the card. My own eyes widened. Karl's eyes had been nearly identical to Wesley's. That must have been what Allie had noticed. I reminded myself that figuring out if the two men had any connection was why I was here.

I took a sip of the wine. "This is very nice. On Thursday I was pouring a white from Kendall Jackson that was similar to this, but not as good. I'd love to include your version at the wine bar." I scrunched up my nose. "We had a slow start Thursday. I was getting some lights replaced that morning and the electrician wasn't finished by the time I needed to open the bar. Unfortunately, he was the man found murdered the next morning. Have you heard about that?" I cocked my head in all innocence while mentally crossing my fingers.

A look swept across his face. Sorrow? Or maybe a long-held grievance. Either way, it vanished almost immediately.

"Yes, I heard," he said. "It's very sad."

"I thought he mentioned he'd done work for you here."

His nostrils flared. "No, ma'am. Not for me, anyway." He narrowed his eyes at me again. "Will there be anything else?"

"No, but I'd be happy to pour some Holt varietals at Vino y Vida. Give me a call if you're interested." I made the thumb-and-pinkie gesture by my ear and smiled again.

He didn't return the smile. "Enjoy the rest of your day." He turned and disappeared through a door behind the bar.

He was about Karl's height. In addition to those eyes, they had the same kind of stocky build. I finished my glass and set it on the bar. I looked for the young pourer to thank, except he was busy with customers at the other end of the bar. I didn't see a tips container but slipped a few bucks under my glass and made my way out.

Near my car, a tabby cat sauntered up to greet me. I stooped to hold out my fist, apparently a good move, because the cat rubbed its head against my hand, and then along my leg. A kind of winery barn cat? Maybe.

Blue's lap seat belt clicked in as surely as the biological connection between Wesley and Karl. What wasn't tight and sure was exactly how they were related and why the winery owner had not liked talking about Karl. Not one bit.

# CHAPTER 33

I rounded the bend toward the field where I'd seen the workers pruning. The three guys now sat in the shade of a live oak tree taking a lunch break. Two perched atop small chest coolers and one sat on the ground, knees up, leaning against the trunk of the tree. The tree sitter waved, gesturing to me to stop.

I slowed and pulled over, smiling to see that the guys were Tom and Felipe, the workers I'd met at the wine bar. I peered at the third. Ian Meier?

Tom pushed up to standing next to the tree. "Cece, come join us for lunch." He held up a crispy rice ball wrapped in a lettuce leaf. "I have extra."

"You do?" My cavernous stomach told me to stop. My curious brain seconded that move. I checked my watch. I still had time. I turned off the engine and slid out of the car.

"Hey, Tom, Felipe. Ian, how are you?"

"I'm all right." He took another bite of a sandwich that looked like bologna on white bread.

Felipe smiled and stood from his perch. "It's not much, but you're welcome to sit." He waved his sandwich at the cooler.

"No, thanks. I have to get going in a minute." I leaned against the passenger door.

"Seriously, Cece." Tom approached, holding the rice ball in a paper napkin. "I won't eat it."

"Are you sure?" I was dying to take the lunch, but he was a wiry man who looked like he could easily scarf down four of these. It wouldn't be fair to deprive him of the second half of his midday meal.

"Please," Tom insisted.

"Is there meat in it?"

"Usually there is in Hmong cooking, but this is a fish version. And I have more. My wife sends me with too much food every day."

"All right. I have to admit I'm hungry. Thank you, Tom." I accepted and unwrapped the napkin. "This looks a bit like Japanese onigiri, which I love."

"It's sort of similar. In my country we call it *nam khao*, and it's fried."

"Where are you from originally?" I asked.

"Laos, but my parents brought me here as a tiny baby. I don't remember it at all."

"How's the vine work going?" I gazed at the group as I bit into the rice ball. I savored the flavors of curry, peanuts, lime, cilantro, and mint. The rice was crunchy on the outside and tender on the inside, and the lettuce added a fresh touch. If this wasn't the perfect lunch, I wasn't sure what was.

"It's pruning." Felipe shrugged. "It's kind of an art form. It's also hard work, but work that makes a difference for the health of the vines and the grapes. We're trying to teach Ian here what that means."

From the little pruning I'd done in my backyard both here and in Pasadena, I knew it was important work. If not in the short term, then certainly in the long run.

"How do you like working for Mr. Holt?" I asked them, not addressing a single person, although I was looking at Ian. In my peripheral vision I nearly missed a lightning-fast glance the two other men exchanged. It made me want to follow up with them later.

"Holt is fair and offers decent benefits," Felipe said.

"He's not our direct supervisor, in any case," Tom added.

*Interesting.* They were holding something back, but what? A twin of the cat back in the parking lot came around from behind the tree. Or maybe it was the same one.

"Hey, Gatito." Felipe extracted a morsel of tuna from his sandwich and fed it to the kitty.

"I saw one like him in the parking lot," I said.

"We have a whole family of them," Tom said. "They keep down the vermin."

"Nice." I gazed at Ian. "Have you been working here for a while, Ian?"

He swigged from his soda bottle and swiped his mouth with the back of his hand. "Not that long."

"We told him he didn't have to come back so quick after his uncle died," Tom murmured.

Ian stared at me through eyes like Karl's. And like Holt's, whatever kind of relation he was. "I need the money, okay?" he snapped. He jumped to his feet and strode back into the vineyard, sandwich in one hand, bottle in the other, pruners in the back pocket of his jeans.

When a morsel of sandwich meat fell to the ground, Ian kept moving. A scrub jay made a croaking sound and hopped down from the tree, gulping the meat in one bite.

Felipe watched him go. "I think he's hurting, but he doesn't know how to express it. At least not to men."

"When did he start working here?" I asked.

"About a month ago, I think," Tom said.

"It was more like the beginning of December," Felipe said. "Ian said he wanted to grab a seasonal job while he could."

"Last week he was working for Karl, his uncle, in Vino y Vida," I said.

"Did you witness how he was with the kid?" Tom asked. "May Karl Meier's soul rest with God, but seriously, the man was a brute, and toward his own flesh and blood, no less."

"We don't blame Ian for trying to get out from under that

man's abuse." Felipe finished his last bite of sandwich and picked up his cooler. "Sorry, Cece, but we need to get back to the job."

"I'm sure you do." I watched Tom also finish his lunch. "Guys, stop into my wine bar again when you get the chance, okay?

"Sure." Tom pulled a wide-brimmed straw hat firmly back onto his head. His gaze toward me was intense. "I'm thinking we might have more to talk about."

"Same here." I gave him a nod. "I'll be there tomorrow through Saturday. You can also text or email me at Vino y Vida. In case you, you know, learn anything."

Tom and Felipe exchanged a knowing look.

"We will," Felipe said.

# CHAPTER 34

I was only a couple of minutes late picking up Ed at the diner. He wore a broad smile as we drove out to Colinas Cat Rescue.

"This car is really something, Cece. My uncle, Tio Gordo, had one like it when I was a kid." He twisted to look at me. "Don't you worry about the Mustang wearing out with it being your only vehicle?"

"No." I stroked the big steering wheel. "I truly don't drive Blue that much, and otherwise she lives in my garage. Jo keeps her in good shape for me."

"Speaking of Jo, have you learned anything else about the murder?"

"Not exactly. I was out at Holt Vineyards before I picked you up. Do you know Wesley, the owner?"

"Can't say that I do," he said. "Henry and I went out there one fine day recently for some sipping."

"It's a lovely setting."

"Why do you ask about Holt?"

"Allie mentioned that he reminded her of Karl." I signaled a left turn with the blinker and also extended my arm straight out. "Ed, I think the two men are related somehow, or were. Wesley's eyes are nearly identical to Karl's, and Karl's nephew Ian's are the same."

"The men have different last names. Maybe they were cousins?"

"Could be." I pulled into the small lot next to the rescue build-ing, which appeared to be a repurposed older home.

We made our way up to the front door. A typed sign read, CAREFUL! WATCH FOR OUR DOOR DASHER. I held my bag low in my hand to shoo back any potential escapees and slid inside. Ed moved quickly behind me, but no cat was waiting, and we were in an enclosed porch. The same sign was on the interior door.

A young woman sat at the desk in the main room. Her hair was dyed bright orange. Tiny silver rings marched up the sides of both ears and decorated her eyebrow and nose, and one arm was al-most completely inked. She gave us a big smile, stroking a fat yel-low tabby who sat on the desk eying us with suspicion.

"Welcome to Colinas Cat Rescue. How can I help you?" She slid a bookmark into the book she'd been reading and closed *The Stand* by Stephen King.

The last King book I'd read had given me nightmares for weeks. This girl was made of stronger stuff than I.

"We'd like to speak with Tara Pulanski, if she's free," I said. "I'm Cecelia Barton and this is Ed Ramirez."

"I'll see if she's available." The greeter rose and headed for a door at the back.

A rectangle of stacked crates filled the middle of the room. Cats of all sizes and colors filled most of them. In one, two black kittens lay sleeping entwined. In another, a white long-hair was giving herself a good wash. A big tortoise tabby lay curled up. He peeked out at us and decided we weren't worth waking up for.

Ed nudged me. "Did you see that?" He pointed at a glass wall lining the back of the space. On the door was a sign reading, IN-FECTED AND ILL CATS. DO NOT ENTER WITHOUT PERMISSION.

"Poor things," I said. "They must have feline HIV."

The young woman emerged and headed for her desk. "Tara will be right with you."

"Thanks. I'm considering volunteering," I said to her. "But I heard there's a guy here nobody gets along with. That worries me."

Ed, who was visiting with one of the cats in the middle, gave me a sharp look. I ignored him.

"It's true." The greeter glanced around, even though the only people in here were us and her, and stroked the yellow cat as she went on. "Nobody could have been sweeter with the kitties, but he kind of had a problem with humans."

"That's too bad. Did you lose any volunteers because of him?"

"Yes, a couple." She looked straight at me. "But you don't have to worry about that. He won't be working here any longer."

Indeed. Nobody volunteered from the grave, no matter how much they loved cats.

Tara came through the door at the back and moved briskly toward us, all business, hand outstretched.

"Hi, I'm . . ." She slowed her step. "Cece?"

"Hi, Tara."

Ed moseyed over.

"I think you know my friend Ed Ramirez," I said.

"The owner of Edie's?" Tara asked. "Absolutely. How are you, Ed?"

Ed shook her hand. "I'm good, thanks."

Tara was nearly as tall as Ed, and today wore black stretch pants and a pale blue CCR hoodie with a white tee underneath.

Tara looked from him to me. "You both want to volunteer for us, I gather."

Ed nodded.

"I'm considering it," I said.

"Come with me. I'll give you the VIP CCR tour."

We followed Tara through the facility upstairs and down. She explained about the cats with feline leukemia or kitty HIV inside the glass enclosure. We saw a room in the back with really sick cats who were being treated and another room where recent rescues were treated for mites and fleas and malnutrition. Both areas had a stronger aroma of litter than the front had. We stepped into the vet room, which smelled of antiseptic.

"We're lucky to have a veterinarian volunteer once a week and at our feral clinics," Tara said. "Another offers his neutering services at no cost."

"That's wonderful. I understand Karl Meier was an active volunteer here." I hoped my tone sounded casual.

"He was." She drew out her words, folding her arms over her chest. "He had a real gift with the animals, may his soul rest in peace."

"Had you used his services as an electrician as well?" I asked. "You mentioned something about it being a good thing when I said I didn't plan to hire him again."

"I did not have him do work for pay." She gazed up at the corner of the room.

"I met him a couple of times in the diner," Ed chimed in. "Karl seemed like an okay guy. What was the problem with him?"

I could have kissed him for taking the heat off me being the only one inquiring about Karl.

Tara frowned at both of us. "The problem was that he was an awful person to his fellow humans. He berated and scolded other volunteers. Criticized their work and mine while he was at it. Made out like he was the only true cat lover in the place. Every single person who comes through these doors adores kitties and wants to do right by them. He had no place putting them down."

"Did you lose volunteers because of Karl?" I asked.

"I did, and a couple of my best ones."

"Maybe they'll come back now?" I made my thought into a question.

"Maybe."

"Why did you keep Karl on the roster?" Ed asked, his voice

curious instead of accusatory. "Couldn't you have thanked him and told him he was no longer needed?"

"Yes, except we are super short-staffed. We have litter boxes going unscooped, blankets unwashed, adoption applications un-reviewed. Karl was always willing to do the very worst of the work, litter and administering deworming pills among it."

"Sounds like he was a real mixed bag," Ed said.

"He was," Tara said. "Until that last day. If you'd only heard him. I'll tell you, I'd had it up to here." She ran the edge of her palm across her neck.

A shiver ran through me at the gesture. I was about to ask if she'd fired Karl when the receptionist appeared in the doorway.

"Tara? Excuse me, but that couple who want to adopt the FIV pair are here."

"Thanks." To us Tara said, "Sorry, tour's over. You can fill out volunteer applications on our website, and I hope you will."

She hurried away. Ed took a moment to say goodbye to the cat he'd been chatting with. We slipped out the door without a feline friend trying to dash past us.

I turned the key in the ignition and sat there, letting the car's engine warm up.

"Are you going to sign up?" Ed asked.

"What?" I'd been thinking about murder, not a volunteer gig. "I'm not sure. I'm pretty busy as it is."

"So am I, but I'm positive I can do a couple hours a week, if Henry gives a thumbs-up to the idea."

"Ed," I began. "Do you think Tara got so fed up with Karl she killed him?"

He leaned his arm on the open passenger window and drummed his fingers on the outside of the door. "I hope not. If she did and gets caught, her life is over."

"Totally." I sat up straight and fastened my seat belt. "Where to, *señor*?"

Ed launched into a stream of Spanish.

"Wait, stop," I protested. "I can't understand all that. Give me the destination. The diner or home or wherever."

"Come to *mi casa*. We'll put our heads together with my brilliant and handsome husband. Henry will know something, and we can have a little happy hour while we're there."

I smiled. "You're on, my friend."

# Chapter 35

Henry enveloped me in a hug, then kissed me on each cheek. "Come. Sit. Nosh. Sip." He took my hand and led me to the expansive living room in the back of the house he and Ed had remodeled after they moved to California.

The home sat sheltered by old trees most of the way up a ridge. The view through huge windows was of the canyon below and rolling hills beyond. It looked like nobody lived nearby. In fact, other homes were strategically tucked into adjacent lots, but nobody had cut down the trees, which provided much-needed shade during the hottest months of August and September.

I sat on the couch facing the windows. A spread of nibbles was already set out on the low table in front of me.

Ed came in carrying a bottle of sparkling wine and one of merlot.

"What's your choice, Cecelia?" Henry asked.

"The prosecco sounds perfect, thanks. I do have to drive home, so I'll sip slowly."

Ed popped the cork and poured into three flutes Henry brought in from the other room. We clinked glasses and they both sat, Ed beside me and Henry in a chair at the corner of the table.

As I sampled a tasty morsel of smoked salmon atop a small round of dark rye smeared with a soft herbed cheese, Ed filled Henry in on our visit to the shelter.

"I think Meier's behavior, while extreme, is not uncommon," Henry observed. "Those who lack skills to interact with other people, or who feel threatened by them, have no such issues with the far simpler demeanor of animals."

"I guess," I said. "Apparently Tara wasn't going to tolerate it another day, from what she said. Right, Ed?"

"That was my impression, as well." Ed took a sip from his glass. "Cece, I think there was more she didn't tell us. Do you?"

"Possibly." I sipped. "But if she killed Karl, she would have had to arrange to meet him at the garage. know how to operate the lift, be strong enough to crack him over the head, and then crush him. That's a lot."

"True," Ed said. "But you have to admit, she's tall and looked strong. Who knows, maybe her dad owned a gas station when she was young and she was comfortable with such machinery."

"Might I point out a possible flaw?" Henry asked. "Why kill the man when all she had to do was tell him his volunteer services were no longer required?" He glanced from me to Ed.

"That's the most important question," Ed said. "Why, indeed?"

I sat back, turning my glass in my fingers. "Her twin said Tara followed her here to the valley, that they'd grown up in Sebastopol but Tara had been living in Santa Rosa or somewhere like that. I don't think she mentioned when that was. Maybe Karl had been living there too, and they had some bad history together."

"How can you find out?" Henry asked.

"For starters, I'll ask Jo," I said. "She was married to him. If anyone would know, it would be her." I speared a shrimp with a toothpick and swirled it in cocktail sauce before I popped it into my mouth.

"Good plan," Ed said. "Cece, have you met this real estate guy who's been all over town this week?"

I sat up straight. "Gareth Rockwell?"

"That's him." Ed pointed at Henry. "You tell."

Henry, always impeccably dressed even at home, crossed one pressed-jeans leg over the other at the knee. He'd paired the pants with a navy crewneck sweater that hung nicely, as if it was a silk-wool blend.

"Gareth came into the gallery and insisted he and his firm had all but inked the deal to buy our adobes."

"And you told him they weren't for sale." I helped myself to another salmon appetizer. I really should have remembered to include an actual lunch in my schedule for the day.

"I certainly did."

"He pulled the same thing on me," I mumbled, covering my mouth. "I sent him to Allie as a diversion. She said when they went out looking at properties, he insisted she drive him by Karl's house. He knew the address and everything."

"Where is it?" Ed asked.

"On the other side of town from here, but in a similar location. Halfway up a hill with great views and an entire acre of gently sloping land, although the house is a plain-wrap ranch."

"Ours was a boring ranch house before we remodeled it." Henry furrowed his brow. "Can you get Allie to research the deed and see what you can find out about when Karl bought the place and such?"

"I think she's already working on it," I said. "Gareth could have been talking to Karl already about selling. If Karl was resistant and happened to die, his heir might be more willing to unload the property."

"His nephew Ian," Ed said.

"Exactly." I drained my glass.

"Eat more, Cece," Ed said.

"Everything is really good." I gestured to the spread. "You just whipped this together, Henry?" I selected a toothpick holding a cherry tomato, a tiny ball of mozzarella, and a basil leaf. "I love this. A tiny caprese on a stick."

Henry smiled. "Ed texted me a heads-up you two were on your way. We had everything in the fridge. I had merely to assemble."

Ed gave him a fond look, then focused on me. "What else can we help with, Cece? We all want this murder solved. It's a teeny bit good for business in the short run, but long-term it'll hurt if people get scared to visit Colinas."

"I hate to say it," I began. "But Dane Larsen is hiding something relating to Karl. Henry, you know her because you sell her paintings in the gallery. Does she have some proverbial skeletons in the closet that you're aware of?"

"I'm not sure," he said. "Let me see what I can find out. Subtly. Under the radar."

"I'll try to learn something as well." Ed tilted his head. "You're a hundred percent sure Jo is innocent?"

My posture slumped. "I think so. I hope so. But maybe not a hundred percent."

What if she wasn't? What if she'd been lying to me and everyone else? What then?

# CHAPTER 36

Darkness was about to fall at five twenty when I finally left Ed and Henry's. We'd left hashing through the homicide behind and segued into talking about art, with Henry telling stories about gallery openings he'd attended in New York, and Ed entertaining us with tales of exceedingly stupid query letters he'd received as a book editor. I'd enjoyed my time with these two friends so much I failed to leave as early as I'd planned. Ed made me promise to text him when I was safely home.

The temperature had dropped, and I took a moment to raise Blue's top and secure it for my drive home. I kept a scarf in the glove compartment for hair-taming. Now I wound it around my neck, since my denim jacket was too light to do much good in the warmth department. I buttoned it all the way up and turned on the car.

I knew I was blessed to have found friends like Ed and Henry. They were open and affectionate with each other and with me, and I found communication flowed easily with each. I'd made another friend since moving here. Yukiko owned the Japanese restaurant, but she was away on a winter vacation right now. While I liked Mooncat a lot, I was also her boss, which cast a different light on a friendship. I'd had hopes Jo and I could be good pals. Maybe once this case was over. Or maybe not.

Starting down hills on the curvy road, I regretted not leaving earlier. Blue's lights weren't the brightest and many stretches here had no streetlights. Good for light pollution, not as good for this driver.

I drove slowly. I tooted the horn before a hairpin turn. I sweated. And let out a long breath when the road leveled out a little. This was only the second time I'd been to my friends' house, and I didn't know the road at all. I hoped this meant I was nearing the town proper, despite no lights being visible in the distance.

Headlights turned in behind me from somewhere. Had I passed a side road? It could have been a driveway I didn't notice.

The lights grew closer. A curve to the left approached, and I couldn't see anywhere to pull over and let the speed demon pass. This driver was going to have to practice patience, like it or not.

A horn blasted from behind me like it was from a semi. I jerked, startled, and the steering wheel slipped. I got control of the wheel but not my heart rate, which was hammering in my chest.

With my low-slung car, the headlights from a higher-profile vehicle blinded me. I flipped up the rearview mirror and slowed even more, navigating the turn. The jerk with the loud horn leaned on it again. I gripped the steering wheel with all my might despite sweaty palms.

No trees lined the shoulder on the right. If the slope dropped off sharply, the road should have a sturdy guardrail. It didn't.

I kept my gaze on the center line of the road, watching out for oncoming vehicles, but I apparently shared the road only with the monster-in-a hurry to my rear. I refused to speed up, and I was terrified he'd nudge my rear bumper and I'd go over the side to my death.

Blue's convertible top was not sturdy. It didn't feature roll bars or space-age strength polymers. If this car rolled over, the top would collapse and crush me along with it, but I didn't have time to pray.

The road straightened out again. Town lights appeared in the distance. Still no cars approached from the other direction. The driver behind me gunned the engine and pulled level with me on my left. I shot a quick look in that direction, except I couldn't see the driver through the window. Was that red dot the glow of a lit cigarette? I thought I glimpsed writing on the door, but it was smudged.

Paint, cigarette, none of that mattered. I lifted my foot from the accelerator. If this jerk carried a gun of any size, I wanted to be well out of reach.

*Whew.* As I slowed, the vehicle pulled ahead by a length. I focused on my tailgater's car in the dark, hoping to identify what make or model it was. An SUV, or maybe a van? I didn't see a truck bed, and I didn't want to stay close enough to make out the license plate number, although I was pretty sure it had been issued by the California DMV. All I could tell was that the vehicle had dark paint. The color could have been blue, black, dark green. It was anybody's guess.

The driver treated me to another hugely loud blast of the horn before speeding away.

"Go, awful person," I said out loud. "Go far away and stay there. May we never meet again."

The experience was extra unsettling because I don't know if my pursuer had actually been a murderer chasing me and hoping I'd go over the edge. Alternatively, they could have merely been one of those irate people who wants to get where they're going with no obstacles and no care for safety.

Me, I drove slowly and nervously home, never more glad to see my neighbor's porch light on and hear two hungry cats happy to see me.

# CHAPTER 37

Those kitties of mine got more stroking in one half hour than they had since the last time the nephews were over. Is there anything more comforting than running your hand along the head and back of a purring feline happy to see you?

I poured a big glass of water and curled up on the sofa to try to recover from my ordeal. Instead, my thoughts roiled. The person behind me on that twisting road couldn't have been pursuing me, could they? Who would have known I'd be at Ed and Henry's? Nobody, that's who. Unless it had been one of the people I'd been poking at about the murder.

An ordeal it had been, but not one that had made me completely panic. I hadn't frozen or lost control. Blue was fine and in the garage instead of being towed out of a ditch or worse, having my crushed body extricated from a wrecked car at the bottom of a precipice. I planned to hang on to this feeling of competence and small success.

I needed to contact Benjamin and talk about the postponed dinner I'd agreed to. For now, I squinted into my memory. I thought I'd seen letters on the side of the vehicle when it had pulled up level with Blue.

On an impulse, I called Jo. It took her a while to pick up, and I was about to disconnect when she answered, breathless.

"Cece? What's up?"

"Are you okay?" I asked. "You sound out of breath." What if she'd been chased too, but on foot?

"Why wouldn't I be okay? Ouro and I got back from a run a few minutes ago."

"That's a relief. I mean, good."

The sound of running water came over the line for a moment.

"Well, have a good evening," I said.

"Um, Cece? You called me," Jo said. "Was there something you wanted? I hope Blue's running all right."

"Right. Yes, the car's fine."

"Do you have news about whoever killed Karl?" she pressed.

"Sorry, I don't. Do you?"

"Are you kidding?" Jo scoffed. "The police are going to tell me things under exactly two conditions: A, if his killer has been arrested; B, if they come to arrest me. So far neither have happened."

The latter was good. Still, I could tell she was waiting for me to ask whatever I needed to know. "Can you tell me what kind of car Karl drove?" I asked.

"Um, that's a weird question. Why do you want to know?"

I let out a noisy breath. "Somebody might have been chasing me as I drove home. I mean, like trying to run me off the road."

She snorted. "Well, it wasn't Karl."

I waited.

"Oh." She drew out the word. "You mean it might have been his vehicle."

"I have no idea, and I barely saw the side, but I thought it might have letters on it. Or letters that had been painted over to obscure them. Did he drive a dark-colored van or a work SUV?"

She let out a low whistle. "He sure did. A van, and guess who has the keys?"

"Ian."

"On the nose. The kid drove Karl's van to dinner with me the other night. He tried to pretend he hadn't, that he was going to catch a ride home. But I waited around and saw him drive away in it."

"I don't know why he'd be pursuing me, though."

"Where were you driving?"

"Home from Ed Ramirez's house on Calistoga Road. They live a little ways outside of town in the hills."

"I'm not aware of any reason Ian might be out there," Jo said. "Then again, I don't really know him anymore."

"I was surprised to see him pruning grapes out at Holt Vineyards today."

"See? Point made. I had no idea he was working there."

"Gotcha," I said. "I'll let you go, but thanks for the info. You should know that Blue held up really well today. I was going faster than I wanted around curves with some idiot on my tail. The steering was tight and the tires stayed on the road. We came out of it alive and safe."

"Glad to hear it. Take care."

"You too." I disconnected.

Yes, the car had held up, and I also had. I'd been nervous, a little scared, but I hadn't freaked out. I hadn't lost control of my beloved vehicle. I'd come through, as I told Jo, alive and safe. I could add it to my mental whiteboard labeled My Successes. They'd been few up to now in my life, but I figured focusing on them might make more happen. Self-confidence had a lot going for it.

My phone rang in my hand. I was beat, but it was Benjamin.

"Are we still on for dinner, Cece?" he asked. "I'd love to cook for you."

What I really wanted to do was veg out here alone. On the other hand, I was the one who had had to cancel out yesterday. I couldn't do it twice in a row.

"Absolutely," I said. "I had a kind of rough thing happen. Would you mind picking me up?"

"Are you all right?"

"I am. A little rattled is all."

"I can be there in five minutes," he said.

*Yikes.* "Thanks, but give me half an hour, if you don't mind."

"Not a problem. See you in thirty."

I boosted myself to stand and headed in to freshen up. This was a date, after all.

# CHAPTER 38

I leaned back in my chair at the end of a delicious dinner. A log popped in the glass-fronted fireplace, where he'd lit a fire to warm the chilly evening.

"Thank you. That was perfection." I sipped a delicate pinot noir that had been a perfect accompaniment to the tart, soup, and salad that he prepared today instead of yesterday.

"Food is always better when it's shared. I'm glad you liked my modest efforts." His smile disappeared. "I'm sorry you had to endure that hair-raising drive home."

I'd given him the thumbnail sketch of my experience on the road without getting into conjectures about the other car's driver.

"Are you sure you don't know who the tailgater was?" he asked.

"I don't, and I couldn't catch the license number either. I think it was a California plate. All I know is, the driver was some turkey with a lead foot. But I'm fine." I thought about what Zoe had dug up last night. "Remember yesterday you started telling me about Karl and those unsavory characters?"

"Yes."

"Last night, unasked, Zoe dove into the internet and dug up dirt on Karl's past. She found that he tried to buy a winery. Ridley. But he apparently had no idea what he was doing. She confirmed what you told me, that he defaulted on taxes and on a loan."

"That's it," Benjamin said. "It was the loan that got him into trouble. I haven't been able to learn how he got himself out of it." He drank from his glass. "So, you two had a good visit, I gather."

I smiled. "Yes. As it turned out, she wasn't in trouble. She simply wanted to see her mom. What a turnabout in her attitude."

"I'm pleased for you."

A shadow crossed his face and he rubbed his forehead. I imagined he was thinking about his relationship with his son, which hadn't yet had a turnabout.

"Thanks," I said. "I really appreciate your being understanding about my need to leave yesterday."

"Always. Say, did you mention a real estate developer in connection with the case or was that someone else?"

"I'm not sure if it was me." Had I spoken to him about Gareth? "There's certainly one snooping around Colinas recently. Gareth Rockwell?"

"That's the name I heard. It seems he had some history with Karl."

I sat up. "Seriously?"

"Yes." He drummed his fingers on the table. "I'm trying to remember the details. I wonder if it had to do with that private business loan Karl had taken out."

"Hmm. Gareth was pushing hard about wanting to buy the adobes in our cluster, but he seems pretty clueless about real estate. He didn't even know that those buildings sit on town-owned property." I finished my wine. "What makes you think he's connected with Karl's murder?"

"I'm not sure. Sorry, Cece. I shouldn't have brought it up without facts to back up the gossip."

"I wondered if Gareth wanted to buy Karl's house but got resistance. According to Allie, it's a boring house but sits on a beautiful plot of land that could hold at least one more home."

Benjamin gave a slow nod. "And if the nephew inherits, he might be more willing to sell?"

"Yes."

"For my part, I wonder if that fancy developer has it in him to murder for property. I mean, you know how everybody says, 'I could kill that guy.' But they don't mean it, don't follow through on it."

"Exactly. Whoever murdered Karl quite clearly followed through," I said. "You might have a point, at least for a physical death like Karl's was. Gareth strikes me as someone fastidious about his appearance. A slow-acting poison might be more his speed."

"On the other hand, he probably works out at a gym. He's a young dude and would have the strength to kill."

"Right." I suppressed a yawn.

"You had quite a day. I have dessert and an after-dinner liqueur to offer, if you're interested."

"Ice cream, cognac, and thee?" I smiled as I stood. "Sounds like a plan. Let me clear up first."

He rose. "We'll do it together."

I leaned over to kiss his cheek. "You know, I almost begged off tonight. I'm glad I didn't." I meant it. I felt relaxed and supported and well fed. If we'd moved knowledge of the case forward a bit, so much the better.

He wrapped his arms around me. "Same here."

# CHAPTER 39

After Benjamin dropped me off at home, eight thirty the next morning found me deep into my Pilates routine on the patio. I'd been neglecting my core fitness lately, and I felt it.

As I stretched and crunched and twisted, I kept thinking about my hair-raising drive home yesterday. I wished I could report the vehicle that had seemed to pursue me, but without a license plate number or any real vehicle identifier, I'd be laughed out of the police station.

Speaking of the police, I wished I knew the status of the case. How did Quan's persons of interest list compare with mine, and did he have alibis for those people? With any luck they were tailing someone suspicious, amassing evidence, interviewing witnesses. Hopefully there were witnesses of some kind.

Ed and Henry had asked if I was sure Jo was innocent. Honestly, not a hundred percent. It was to clear her name that I'd even stuck my nose into this mess. What if she was guilty?

My fingers were crossed that the detective was close to an arrest. This amateur sleuth business was getting old.

One of the acorn woodpeckers Richard loved to hate set to hammering somewhere nearby. The birds, pretty as they were, could destroy a wooden home with their ping-pong-ball–sized holes. I knew the woodpeckers only wanted to store one acorn in each cavity, but half the time the nut fell down inside the wall and the bird felt obliged to drill again. And again and again.

They were persistent, which was an admirable quality. I wouldn't bring that up with Richard, though. He wouldn't like that perspective at all. I only hoped Quan and the others investigating the murder were as persistent.

I rolled on my left side to begin leg lifts at different angles. Martin wandered up and rubbed his head against my fist.

"Not now, buddy." If I interrupted the routine to give noodgies to pets, I might never get back to the exercise.

I was only two lifts in when my phone buzzed where it lay above my head on the mat. I groaned to see Allie's ID. Abandoning my exercises, I pushed up to sitting and answered it.

"What's up, Al?"

"I'm coming over. We need to talk. See you in five." She disconnected.

*Um, okay.* So much for my fitness.

By the time she arrived, I'd put coffee on, washed my face, and thrown a sweatshirt from Pasadena Community College over my exercise shirt. Allie sat at the kitchen table.

"I don't have any pastries, but I can offer you granola and fruit," I said. "Or avocado toast."

"Just coffee is fine, Cee. Thanks." She ran a hand through her hair. While it was not as mussed as mine at the moment, my twin didn't look ready for prime time with the public in one of her usual movers-and-shakers outfits. Her tousled hair matched her yoga leggings and blue-and-gold Cal sweatshirt.

I set our mugs and the carton of half-and-half on the table and took the chair across from her.

"Remember I said I would look into the deed to Karl's house?" she began.

"Absolutely." I dosed my coffee and sipped it. When she didn't speak, I added, "And? What did you find out?"

"Kind of a lot of nothing, unfortunately." She scrunched up

her nose. "Karl owned the house, but about ten years ago he signed away forty-nine percent of it to a real estate trust. For the life of me I can't find out who owns the trust."

"What's the trust called?"

"NAR Concerns." She shook her head. "I tried, believe me. I couldn't crack it."

"We'll get Zoe onto it. She's a whiz."

"Brilliant." Allie took a big swig of coffee.

"Apart from who owns the trust, what does it mean for Karl's heir that someone has the right to nearly half the property?" I gazed at her as I mused. "It must be like a controlling share in a company. I wonder if Karl negotiated that."

"Refusing to hand over more than half? I would have held that line, for sure."

"I told you about him trying to buy the Ridley winery but bombing at it," I said. "This half-ownership deal might have been in payment of debt."

"Good thought."

"Sis, what do you know about Dane Larsen? She seems to have a long-standing beef with Karl, or maybe she's keeping a secret about him."

"Secrets are what mysteries are all about, aren't they?" She tilted her head. "Dane. Daughter is Serena. Dad is Sam the Cheese Man."

"And her ex is Nico Rispoli, former manager of our buildings. But beyond that." I knew all that stuff, and was Dane's boss, to boot.

"Hmm. Does she know more than the average bear about electricity?"

"No idea. I haven't seen her stepping up to fix broken lights or anything. Why?"

"When did you hire her?" Allie asked.

"At the start of November last year."

"I was thinking that maybe she knew Karl before she got mar-

158 / MADDIE DAY

ried and had kids. We don't really know his history before trying to buy a winery and working as an electrician, do we?"

"No." I drained my mug. "I'll see her at work later today. Maybe I can worm it out of her."

"Great. And text Zoe about looking into that trust."

"I will. Do we have more business to conduct?" I asked her.

"Can't think of a thing. Except don't forget to bring the Scotch to the boys' party."

"I won't." I smiled. "I have perfect gifts for each of them."

Allie stood. "Ooh, what?"

"No way, Ms. Snoop. I want you to be as surprised as they will be. Now, you, get out of here. I have to get on with my day."

She pushed up to standing. "Aye-aye, Captain Little Sister."

# CHAPTER 40

Allie had been gone barely five minutes when my phone rang. Had she already learned something new?

Instead, the ID read Quan. *Ugh.* Still, I connected the call.

"Good morning, Detective. How can I help you?"

"I would like to have a brief meeting with you this morning, if possible," he said. "I can come to your home or your place of work, or we can meet in town somewhere. What is your preference?"

"I can do that. How about at Vino y Vida at eleven? I have a few things to accomplish before that." Like breakfast and a shower, at a minimum. I already planned to head in early to get some ordering and bookkeeping out of the way.

"Very well. I appreciate it." He disconnected without saying goodbye.

His all-business style was abrupt. Then again, he had a murderer to find. I wasn't going to object.

I got my own business underway, and by ten o'clock I was lacing up low boots to go with my new maroon jeans and black sweater. My hair was clean, dry, and in a French braid. My stomach was satisfied with a green smoothie plus a yummy piece of whole grain avocado toast with cheese. I'd tended to the cat box, cleaned and refilled the feline water and dry food bowls, and shot Zoe a text about investigating the NAR real estate trust.

Jacket, bag, keys, and helmet, and I'd be on my way pedaling to work. A knock came at the back door simultaneously with the front doorbell ringing.

"Cece?" Richard called from the back.

"One second." Dashing to the front, I fixed my eye to the peephole and groaned at both the sight of the police chief and what a Colinas PD cruiser parked in my driveway signaled to the neighbors.

"Chief Fenner," I said after unlocking and pulling open the door. "How can I help you?"

"I'd like a few minutes of your time, if I might."

"I was about to leave for work. I only have a very few minutes. Come in, but you'll have to excuse me for a second. My neighbor is at my back door."

I hurried through the kitchen to the back door and unlocked it. Richard stood there, combed and shaved and outfitted in a dress shirt and slacks with a sport coat.

"Going to a party this morning?" I asked.

His laugh lines crinkled. "I wanted to let you know that I'm heading down to Marin for a luncheon and I won't be home until evening. I didn't want you to worry that I wasn't around."

"Sounds fun. You're not driving, are you?"

"Oh no, dear. There's a group of us old coots, and we've hired a car and driver."

"What's the occasion?"

"It's a north of the city annual meeting for Stanford alumni. Sadly, our number dwindles every year."

"Have a good time, and thanks for letting me know." I smiled, then watched to make sure he made his way safely through the gate back to his side. I heard the click as he relocked the gate with the key I had made for him.

I let out a sigh, locked the door, and returned to the head of the Colinas Police Department. He stood near the door turning his hat in his hands.

"Your neighbor is Richard Flora?" the chief asked.

"Yes. A lovely man and a good guy to have on the other side of the fence."

"I am acquainted with him as well. He is, as my wife would say, a treasure. We have had many fruitful discussions about growing and harvesting wine grapes." Fenner smiled with a closed mouth that turned down a little at the edges, but a smile it was.

I smiled in return. "I didn't know he knew about viticulture, but I'm not surprised. Richard and I often discuss gardening over morning coffee back there in our gardens. But I expect, sir, you didn't pop by to talk about Richard Flora."

"No, ma'am, I didn't." He cleared his throat. "I understand you employ a Danika Larsen at your wine bar."

Danika? Oh, right. "You mean Dane?"

"Yes, ma'am."

"Sorry, I forgot that's her formal name. Yes, she works for me."

"In what capacity?" He clasped his hat behind his back.

"We all mostly do the same job. Take wine orders, pour, refill glasses, take money, clean up. Rinse and repeat."

"Is she a reliable employee? On time and trustworthy?"

"Why, is she applying to be a patrol officer?" I knew I was making light of something serious, but I couldn't help myself.

He gave me a stern look from under those severe eyebrows. "No, but Ms. Larsen might have had disturbing past experiences with the recent murder victim which could have a bearing on the case."

"If she did have those experiences, she hasn't talked about them at work." *Oops.* With the possible exception of a vague comment she'd made about Karl one evening. That surely didn't count.

"When will she be on the job today?" he asked.

"Dane is due in at one o'clock." And she'd better be on time. "Are you working with Quan on the homicide?"

"This is a murder investigation, Ms. Barton. For your information, homicide refers to any death judged to have been caused by another person, but it isn't necessarily a crime. Murder is."

"Thanks for straightening me out on that." Despite him not answering my question. I didn't mind, and I didn't need to know. Their areas of responsibility weren't my problem.

I glanced at my grandmother's clock on the mantel. It was already ten thirty. Not getting my work done, however, was totally my problem.

"Will that be all, Chief?" I asked.

"Yes. Thank you. Please let me know if you happen to learn anything new about Ms. Larsen's past, particularly as it pertains to Karl Meier."

"I promise." I locked the door after him.

Dane and Karl had had clashes in the past. Did it have to do with electrical jobs or some other conflict or disagreement? Now I had yet another reason to weasel information out of her. And maybe out of Quan too, regarding his work relationship with Paul Fenner.

None of that would happen if I didn't hop on my green pony and ride.

# CHAPTER 41

I barely had time to open the door and turn on the back room lights before Detective Quan rapped at the front door of Vino y Vida. My wristwatch read ten forty-five.

"You're early," I said as I let him in. I relocked the door and led him to our workroom. "I actually walked in only a couple of minutes ago. We can talk here in the back so the general public won't think we're open."

"Good idea," he said. "I'm sure you don't want to be seen putting your head together with a police officer."

I glanced over at him and thought I caught a glimmer of a smile.

"My reputation at home is already shot," I said. "Chief Fenner was at my house a little while ago and parked his big honking Colinas PD cruiser in the driveway."

He pressed his lips together. He looked displeased, but he kept quiet.

"At least you're not in uniform," I went on. "Do you drive a sheriff's SUV?"

"No. I have an official car, but it's unmarked." He pushed his glasses back up the bridge of his nose.

He'd gotten out of a county SUV at Jo's that morning. Now that I thought about it, he'd climbed out of the passenger side.

Going incognito made sense for a detective. "Are you working with the local police on the case?"

"We are coordinating efforts, which I'd like to get on with, if you're done with your questions."

*Oops.* I gestured at the table. "Please have a seat."

He sat and folded his hands on the table. "As you might have gathered, we have not yet made an arrest in the murder of Karl Meier."

"I did notice."

"Did you ever know him as Charlie?"

I frowned and wrinkled my nose. "No. But I haven't lived in Colinas even a full year. You should ask Allie, Mooncat, or any other longtime resident of the town."

"So noted. Meier seems to have gone by the name of Charlie while he trained to become an electrician."

"Where was that?" I remembered Mooncat addressing Karl as Charlie.

"In Sonoma, at the technical college."

"You know, Detective, Chief Fenner has lived here a long time, as far as I know. Why don't you ask him?"

He gave me a tight smile. "Thank you." He tapped his pen on the table but didn't say anything else.

I jumped into the void. "What do you know about the relationship of Karl and Wesley Holt of Holt Vineyards?"

"Not a thing. Why do you ask?"

"They look like they're related," I said. "Wesley Holt's eyes are almost identical to Karl's. I happened to stop by the Holt winery yesterday and had a chat with him."

"You happened to?" Quan held his forehead in his hand.

"Yes. As I'm sure you've already learned, Karl tried to buy the vineyard when it was called Ridley."

"And enmeshed himself in considerable financial jeopardy as a result. Yes, we know that much."

"Don't you think it complicates things that some dude who

looks like Karl bought the vineyard and is making a go of it? The Holt tasting room is lovely, and they have a wraparound veranda with a view of the vineyards in the valley. It's really nice." I heard myself rambling but couldn't seem to stop. On the other hand, Quan said he didn't drink wine. He'd surely never been out there for a tasting.

"Thank you for that information," he said. "Have you noticed anyone else who looks mysteriously like Meier?"

I cocked my head and stared at him. "You can be as snide as you want, but I think you shouldn't ignore whatever must have tied Wesley, Karl, and Ian. They all have the same eyes."

"So noted. What else?"

"Do you know about this Gareth Rockwell guy? He's been cruising around town trying to buy up properties, including these antique adobes. He asked my sister to drive him by Karl's house when she was showing him other places for sale. Gareth knew the address but said he hadn't seen it while Karl was alive. Allie found out the house and acreage are half owned by some real estate trust. NAR Concerns is what it's called." I had rattled off a slew of odd bits of information and hoped at least one would be useful to the investigation.

"You're being particularly forthcoming," he said. "I appreciate it."

I shrugged. "It's merely stuff I've heard. And I want Karl's killer caught as much as you do. All of us businesspeople do, including Jo Jarvin."

"I'm glad to hear it."

"So, I understand Ian is driving Karl's van around."

"Is that so?"

*Oops.* Now I would have to identify Jo as the person who told me, which I really didn't want to do. Or . . . maybe not. "When I drove by Holt Vineyards yesterday, I stopped to chat with two customers of mine who do vine pruning for Holt. It turns out Ian also works there."

"And you saw Karl Meier's vehicle there?" Quan pressed.

"No." Darn, I had to do it. "Actually, Jo Jarvin told me she saw Ian driving it. But is there something wrong with that, Detective? Ian had lived with his uncle. Maybe he still did. The keys were probably right there on whatever key rack they used or the dish by the door." Most people had some kind of system for depositing their keys when they came inside so they could find them when they left.

"Have you seen young Meier driving this van?"

I blew out a breath. "Maybe."

"Maybe?"

"Yeah." At his stormy expression, I held up a palm. "Hear me out, okay? Let me tell you what happened last evening." I relayed my drive home in Blue, in the dark, from Ed and Henry's. "I never saw the driver's face clearly. I did see the tip of a lit cigarette, and I know Ian smokes. The vehicle was a dark-colored van and seemed eager to intimidate me or maybe run me off the road."

"But it didn't."

"No. The road is two-lane and has curves around the hills. It could have simply been a driver in a hurry. But the way the vehicle pulled up next to me on a straight portion and blasted its horn multiple times felt aggressive."

"Why didn't you call it in?" He kept his voice curious. He wasn't accusing me.

"I didn't think anybody would give me the time of day. I didn't catch the plate number or the car's make. It was a dark van, which Jo said Karl drove. It might have had writing on the passenger door that had been painted over."

Quan stood. "I appreciate you telling me, Ms. Barton. It's one more data point."

"Detective, I would be fine with you calling me Cece since we're talking so much. I mean, this Ms. stuff gets old, don't you think?"

He smiled. "Agreed and please call me Jim."

I gave him a thumbs-up as I stood. "One more question. Were you able to find any evidence at the garage? Have any witnesses come forward? Somebody who might have seen the killer drive away or anything like that?"

"That's two questions. We might have evidence. We're still working on identifying it."

"You mean DNA."

"That and other markers. Witnesses so far have been unreliable, but the call is still out there and is repeated at every press conference."

I hadn't thought about the police continuing to deliver reports to the press. I should look for those.

"I have to go," he said. "Thank you for the information."

"Good luck." I held out my hand. Too bad it was clammy from nerves at being questioned.

"I appreciate that." He shook with a cool, smooth-skinned palm. "I'll be in touch," he said, and slipped out the back door, which clicked shut behind him.

I hoped he would be in touch. Preferably with news of an arrest.

# CHAPTER 42

By noon I'd put in orders for wines from three of our usual vineyards and tallied my employees' hours. I had great payroll software that calculated the various deductions every employer needed to take out. Today was January fifteenth, so I hit Send on their direct deposit paychecks for the first half of the month. The money would show up in their accounts at a little after midnight tonight.

Dane was on the schedule to work again today, and Mooncat would hopefully be back tomorrow. I poured myself a glass of water, settling back at the worktable to text Mooncat. Her referring to Karl as Charlie had been knocking at my brain in the background. Nobody else had called him that. Karl and Charles were the same name in different languages, but why would Meier have changed his name?

**Hope you're feeling better. Tell me more about when Karl went by Charlie? Thx, and see you tomorrow.**

She didn't immediately reply to my text. I could ask her tomorrow, her health permitting. I sat back to poke around the internet a bit before I had to begin setting up the bar. I found a local press conference from last night and tapped Play.

Quan stood next to Fenner. Quan, wearing a tie with his blazer for the occasion, was dwarfed by the much taller chief. The cur-

DEADLY CRUSH / 169

rent mayor, a curvy woman in a red dress named Malia Guttierez, opened the meeting, standing behind a chest-high lectern.

"We'd like to thank our capable law enforcement agencies. They are working diligently to put a suspect behind bars and close this tragic chapter in Colinas's history. Deputy Detective Sergeant Quan with the Sonoma County Sheriff's Department will deliver an update." She took a step back.

The detective moved up to the microphone. "Thank you, Mayor Guttierez. The process of gathering evidence and interviewing witnesses is never a speedy one. My team members, operating in coordination with the Colinas police, are working around the clock to apprehend the perpetrator. Chief Fenner?"

Quan retreated, letting Fenner take his place. The chief raised the angle of the microphone as high as it would go but he still had to lean over to speak into it.

"Thank you. We appreciate the cooperation of the county officers and are lending our support wherever possible. We continue to request the assistance of all residents of the area. If you viewed any activity at all on the night of January eleventh or the early morning hours of the following day at or near the JJ Automotive shop on Dry Creek Road, please call or text the following number." He rattled off a toll-free number, which also appeared on the screen. "Or stop into the police station. Thank you." He moved away from the mike.

"Many thanks to both of you," the mayor said. "Colinas residents, rest assured you are in good hands. It's always prudent to be careful and lock doors, but do not be afraid. Thank you."

Several reporters called out questions, but the trio moved off-screen and the piece ended. I clicked away when the station's reporter came on repeating the number to call. This was the fourth day after the murder. It wasn't looking good for a resolution anytime soon.

I thought about my conversation with Quan an hour ago. I'd almost seen a hint of humor in the detective. I entered a search on

Jim Quan. When there were too many people by that name to wade through, I switched it to "James Quan detective." There he was. His profile on the Sonoma County Sheriff's page. Highlights included his promotion to detective a few years earlier, a charity project the department had done at a local food bank, and receiving a commendation for service after what the press had dubbed the Bocce Ball Murder.

I kept digging until I found Quan's bachelor's degree from UC Berkeley—aka Cal—in criminal justice, with a music minor. After the University of California founded other campuses, many began referring to the flagship school as UC Berkeley. My parents always called it by its original nickname of Cal. So did I.

Either way, no state college for the detective. And a minor in music? Following that rabbit hole led me to an image that made my eyes fly open. Jimmy Quan played bass in a rock band called Jimmy and the Queue Tips, a groaner of a name if ever there was one.

The picture showed him in tight leather pants and a silk shirt with the sleeves turned up above the elbow twisting over his guitar with a flair that reminded me of Bootsy Collins in Parliament Funkadelic. Just . . . wow. Buttoned-down Detective Quan and his wild and crazy alter-ego. I was so asking him about the group next time I saw him.

# CHAPTER 43

A rapping came from the front door. We weren't open until one o'clock, but it was twelve thirty and time for me to stop hiding out back here. I stuck my phone in my rear pocket and still smiling from seeing Quan in a radically different persona, I headed into the front. Peering through the glass door was a man . . . was that Wesley Holt? I drew closer. Indeed it was.

I unlocked the door. "Good afternoon, Wesley. Come in. We don't open until one, but . . ." I didn't want to come out and ask if he was here on business or to sip from our selection.

"Thank you." He took several steps inside carrying a four-bottle wine tote. "This is very nice, what you've done with the place."

"I appreciate that, especially coming from a professional."

"I'm afraid I was a bit short with you yesterday," he said. "I'd like to apologize."

I blinked. "That's not necessary but thank you. I know you're a busy man. Do you have a minute?"

He nodded and I caught a whiff of cigarette smoke. For a serious wine taster, being a smoker would be an impediment. For a business owner, I supposed not.

"Please come sit at the bar." I relocked the door and gestured at one of the stools. I moved around behind the bar.

He set the bag atop the redwood. "I brought a sampling of our best vintages. Please keep the bag, as well."

A deep green, the tote had the Holt Vineyards logo and name on the side in white, plus their website in small letters along the bottom.

"Thank you so much," I said. "Would you like to taste one of today's wines? On the house, of course."

"I'd be delighted to. What do you have?"

After he said he'd prefer a red, I poured him a glass of Alexander Valley pinot and added an inch to a glass for myself.

"What are your business arrangements for a participating winery?" He swirled and sipped.

I explained the financial terms and that I needed the wine delivered. "We also have a resale agreement with a select few wineries." I picked a bottle off the shelf at the end of the bar with our "Tasted at Vino y Vida" sticker on it and showed him. "You can think about if you'd also like to be part of that program. It's popular with customers."

"All very interesting." He tapped a finger on the bar. "You mentioned the recent murder when you were out at my winery. Sounds like the police aren't too effective finding the killer. It's going to be bad for business soon."

Not a speck of sympathy for the victim or his family. "I'm sure the authorities are doing their best. Speaking of the murder, I noticed the victim's nephew is working at Holt. I saw him pruning when I drove away from speaking with you."

"What's his name?" Wesley didn't meet my gaze.

"Ian. Ian Meier. Are you involved in hiring?"

"Not at the level of field workers, no. I leave that to the vineyard manager."

"Well, it's great your winery is giving him a chance. He had a rough upbringing." I remembered the cats I'd seen. "I met a couple of your barn cats when I was out there. I bet they love roaming free. Mine only get to go outside in the backyard, and only during the daytime."

Wesley's shoulders relaxed. "We love having them. It's quite a family of hunters, which keeps rats and other vermin away from the vines and the grapes once picked. A dog could be destructive, but not the cats. They're fun to have around."

"You have a soft spot in your heart for felines. I approve."

"I confess I do." He smiled, which lightened that heavy brow.

More rapping came at the front door. A group of young people milled around. One, peering in, waved when she saw me looking at her.

"You'll have to excuse me," I said. "We open in ten minutes, and I'm not completely ready."

"Certainly." He drained his glass and slid off the stool. "I've taken up your precious time. I'll be in touch."

He extended his work-thickened hand, and I shook it.

"Thanks again for the wine and the bag." For a moment I considered handing him one of our branded two-bottle tote bags, but I decided against it. If he set up a tasting relationship with us, that would be the time for a thank-you gift.

I escorted him to the door and let him out, then turned the sign to OPEN. I smiled at the group but also assessed if they were likely all over twenty-one. "Come on in. You're a little early and I'm still setting up, but you're welcome to have a seat and take a look at our list of tastings."

All ten burbled in, exclaiming, pointing, and generally excited to be there. I was definitely checking IDs for every single one.

I glanced down the walkway toward the bookstore and Henry's gallery. Wesley stood at the bocce court, shifting one of the heavy balls from one hand to the other, back and forth. I turned away as a chill ran through me.

I forced myself to focus on the job at hand. The murder involving a bocce ball had been the first case I'd been involved in. It wasn't anything I wanted to dwell on with a bunch of happy tasters eager and waiting.

But before I began to work, I took an untouched paper napkin and carefully wrapped Wesley's glass. Quan might laugh at me, or he might be interested in the DNA of a man who looked related to Karl Meier.

Dane showed up for work at a quarter past one o'clock. She was getting closer to being on time and had the grace to simply apologize and not make excuses for her tardiness.

The weather was milder today and had already hit sixty degrees. Customers happily sipped at several small tables inside, and the first group clustered around two high-top tables out on the patio. Business wasn't crazy busy yet, which was fine. I might be able to have a quiet chat with Dane if things stayed low-key.

"You can take the patio and these tables and I'll handle the bar," I told her.

"Sure thing." She tied on an apron and headed outside.

Things did not stay low-key. Customers flooded in. I had to reject two who were underage.

"We'll just sit and sip water," one fellow protested.

"Sorry. It's posted on the door. We don't serve meals, which makes us a bona fide bar. State law says nobody under twenty-one."

I liked that law. I couldn't police if folks were sharing wineglasses with their younger friends when I wasn't looking. This wasn't a family establishment. Last fall I hadn't been totally up on the regulations, and Allie had brought the boys in one afternoon. Later, bike cop Lee Norsegian had slipped me a word that kids and underage adults weren't allowed, and if he saw it again, he'd have to do something official about it. I promised him he wouldn't have to.

So much for having time to delve into Dane's past. If I was lucky, a lull would open up later in the day. Mooncat would be back on the job tomorrow, and Dane didn't work again until Saturday.

At three thirty I glanced around and realized all but one table was empty, and that was an older couple who sat by the window, both reading books. I scooped a handful of pretzels onto a napkin and sat on a stool to munch. Breakfast seemed a long time ago, but I didn't usually take a dinner break until five. Dane came in from outside with a full tray of empties.

"That last big party left." She set down the tray and began to load the glasses into the dishwasher. "The tables are clean and ready for more."

"Thanks. Take a load off if you want."

"I might. This is full. Want me to run it?"

"Please."

The machine was blessedly a super-quiet model. After it was humming, Dane headed to the back for a facilities break. When she returned, the two readers had packed up and left.

"Want a splash?" I lifted a half-full bottle of chardonnay.

She tilted her head. "I guess so. Thanks."

I pulled out one of the opaque cups and poured in an inch of wine. I slid it across the bar to her.

"Cheers." I lifted my cup.

"That was quite a rush of customers," Dane said.

"I'll say." I nibbled on a pretzel. "How did you come to be an artist, Dane? Did you always do art?"

"I loved it as a child and through high school. But then my parents split up. Mom was in terrible shape, my dad disappeared somewhere to wrestle his own demons, and I thought I'd better find a career that I could make actual money at." She made a wry smile. "Even now I need a job to support my art habit."

"What did you do back then?"

"I dropped out of college and found an electrician training program."

I forced my ears not to perk up. "Around here?" Allie had wondered about exactly that.

"No, down Sonoma way."

"I'm happy to know I can call on you if something shorts out or I need a fixture swapped out."

"No, actually you can't." She traced a line in the wood of the bar. "I never finished the training."

"Why not?"

"Mostly because of a guy named Charlie." She blew out a long, noisy breath. "He sabotaged me six ways to Sunday, Cece. He made my work look shoddy, got all the best assignments for himself, and bad-mouthed me to the teacher."

"That's horrible," I said. And it was, whether he was Karl or someone else. "Why would he do that?"

"I'm not positive, but I was the only girl in this group of twenty guys who were always trying to out-macho each other. Charlie wasn't very good at that stuff, and it felt like he decided to out-macho me instead."

"Speaking to the teacher didn't do any good, I suppose."

"No." She stood and tossed back the rest of her wine. "Then I met Nico and got pregnant. I dropped out of the training to get married, and we moved to Colinas. Story over, chapter closed." She grabbed a rag and headed to the vacated table.

I followed her over and picked up the glasses. "I'm really sorry, Dane. Truly."

"It's okay. Water under the bridge and all that. It was a long time ago."

"Did you ever see him again?" I asked.

The look she gave me was cold, piercing. "Why do you ask?"

I didn't get a chance to answer. The door opened to let in four couples. Our window for talking was closed. Judging from the look she gave me, I didn't mind.

I had to wonder, though, as I went about my business, if her well-founded resentment had finally simmered long enough to boil over. If Charlie was Karl, Dane would have recognized him when she hired him to do work in her house. She was plenty tall enough to cosh him over the head in the garage, and I'd seen her strong artist's arms. I now had a seed of doubt about my wisdom in hiring Dane Larsen.

I hoped Karl's murderer hadn't been her. I hoped even more for a quick apprehension of the killer, whoever it had been.

# CHAPTER 44

After Dane returned from her dinner break at four thirty, I took off my apron and said I'd be back. I'd remembered to bring a sandwich, and I could have sat in the back and eaten, but I had other plans. I buttoned up my purple coat and headed out the back door.

I pointedly did not look at the heavy bocce balls in their rack when I passed them on my way to Acorn Gallery. I wanted to grab a word with Henry.

The windows were dark. I did a little forehead smack. It was Tuesday, and the gallery was open Wednesday through Sunday. I knew that. As an alternate plan, I headed for the bench overlooking the river. Dark was falling, but a light illuminated this path beyond the bocce court and one end of the bench. I sat and pulled out my phone.

I poked Quan's number. He needed to know what Dane told me about her past with an electrician named Charlie. Alas, he didn't pick up. Instead of leaving a message, I dictated a text.

**Talked with Dane Larsen at wine bar. She went to electrician school near Sonoma with man named Charlie. Karl? He maligned and undermined her. She dropped out. Still sounds resentful. FYI.**

I remembered the wineglass and thumbed out another message.

**Wesley Holt came in to talk business. He sampled wine. I wrapped glass in napkin. DNA?**

I sent that and opened my sandwich container. A new text pinged in, but it wasn't from Quan. Benjamin had written.

**Thinking of you. XXOO**

That was it, but it was enough to make me smile. I wrote back.

**Back atcha. OOXX**

*Geez.* I was falling hard for that man. Up to now, I hadn't come across any reason not to. I took another bite of my hummus and sharp cheddar sandwich. I'd layered in sliced red pepper for some crunch, plus a smear of avocado mayonnaise on the top slab of sourdough. It made a delicious and portable dinner for a vegetarian.

Benjamin sent back another message.

**Remember I'll be in SF until Thurs midday. Will miss you.**

**Got it. Text me when you get in Thurs. Will miss you too.**

**He had an on-site work meeting going on, which he'd told me about but I'd forgotten.**

I sniffed, smelling cigarette smoke, and then heard voices. Men's voices. I slid down to the other end of the bench, which was less well lit by the lamp, and muted my phone. The voices grew closer, as did the smell of smoke. Wesley Holt had smelled of smoke. Maybe he was back.

"Come in with us," one man urged.

Did his voice sound familiar?

"It's a cool joint," another man spoke. "Sip a little wine, have a visit. The lady who runs it is cool as well. The one who stopped by when we were eating lunch yesterday, remember?"

"What if I don't want to drink wine?" A third man spoke, making the word "wine" sound like it meant spoiled milk. His voice was reedy, almost raspy. That voice I recognized. It was Ian Meier's.

*Aha.* The two must be Tom and Felipe. The click of a lighter sounded. Soon more smoke drifted my way. Dissipated in the fresh air as it was, I didn't find the odor offensive. Indoor smoking was a different story, not that anyone did that anymore.

"Well, we're going in, bro," Felipe said.

"Finish your smoke and join us, man," Tom added.

I kept eating my sandwich. I had to get inside myself soon.

"Catch ya later," Ian muttered.

The door closed. I gave a quick glance down toward my building. Ian leaned his back against it, ankles crossed, smoking. He looked straight ahead, not to the side. I was safe. But why had he come here if he hadn't planned to sample wine with his work buddies?

I frowned at my sandwich. He must have driven from the vineyard separately from the other guys, which would mean Karl's vehicle might be parked nearby, unless Ian had his own car. My frown deepened as I realized he stood between me and the wine bar, and it was fully dark now.

I swallowed. Was he a threat? Possibly. Or the danger might be all in my imagination. Either way, I wasn't hungry any longer.

At least I had a working, charged phone. I set my sandwich container on the bench without making a sound and picked up my cell. A phone rang, startling me. But it wasn't mine.

"Yeah?" Ian spoke. "What do you want?"

A bat beat by on silent wings. It nailed a bug in the lamplight and disappeared.

"No, I ain't doing that," Ian barked. "No way."

I waited, barely breathing.

"Listen. Get outta my hair. Outta my life. Nobody asked for you." He muttered something under his breath. "No. You can go stuff it."

I dared a glance to see him rub his hair with one hand as he flicked the cigarette butt onto the ground with the other. He left it smoldering and slipped into Vino y Vida.

I needed to go in too, but not before I mulled over what I'd heard. I was dying to know who had phoned Ian. Whoever it was, he hadn't been happy with them. The caller wanted Ian to do something. Ian refused. It was the "outta my life; nobody asked for you" that bothered me.

Had Jo been the caller? They'd apparently had a congenial dinner together Saturday. Ian could still be resentful she had been part of the family after his mom died.

Maybe Wesley had lied to me and had been responsible for hiring Ian. The two men appeared to be blood relations of some kind. And now Ian didn't want this mysterious relation to be in his life?

My appetite returned, and I scarfed down the rest of the sandwich. Time to head back inside and see what new surprises awaited. I pulled on my leather gloves.

When I got to the door, I spied the butt, now no longer aflame. I scrabbled in my deep pocket for the little packet of tissues I kept in there. I extracted one as carefully as I could, shook it out, and lifted the butt with the part I hadn't touched. I wrapped it, also carefully, and held it with thumb and one finger.

If the police could use something with Ian's DNA on it, this might help.

# CHAPTER 45

I entered through the wine bar's back door. Before I removed my gloves, I slid the tissue holding the butt into a new envelope and sealed it, then stashed it back in my coat pocket. Gloves off, coat hung, and facilities visited, I headed back to work.

Tom, Felipe, and Ian occupied barstools with wineglasses in front of them. I greeted the men, then rewashed my hands and donned an apron. Dane approached, and we confirmed that she'd work the tables and I'd take the bar.

She cast a funny look at Ian but turned away without saying anything. Maybe she recognized his uncle's eyes.

"I'm glad to see you two back, and welcome, Ian," I said. "All those new lights are due to his handiwork," I told the guys, gesturing at the pendants.

"Yeah, not really," Ian mumbled into his glass.

"Nice job, buddy." Felipe twisted to look at the lights.

"It couldn't have happened without you, Ian," I insisted. "So, how'd the pruning go today?"

"Good," Tom said. "Our new guy is getting the hang of it." He gave Ian a friendly elbow. "Finally."

Ian sat up straight as if shaking off his hangdog attitude. "I kind of think I am. You dudes are good teachers."

I liked the sight of that, of him gaining self-confidence. I knew the feeling from years of not having any myself. The dishwasher signaled the cycle was finished. I opened it to let the air cool the glasses for a minute before I touched them.

Tom and Felipe exchanged a high five.

"You have to sort of read the plant, right?" Ian asked.

"On the nose, man." Felipe nodded. "You have to take it back, but not too far. Find the node. Snip and move on."

"Good sharp pruners really help." Tom looked at me. "Mr. Holt insists we keep them sharp."

"The right tool for the right job is important no matter what kind of work you do," I said. "You know, Wesley Holt was in here this afternoon."

Ian's face went a shade paler.

"He doesn't get enough of his own wine?" Tom asked. "Or he's checking out the competition, maybe."

"It was actually neither of those," I said. "When I spoke to him at the Holt tasting bar, I mentioned that Vino y Vida has relationships with a number of vineyards. I suggested he might want to have us pour his vintages here. He stopped by today to follow up on that idea."

"That would be cool," Felipe said.

"Question for you," I began. "You mentioned Mr. Holt insists on sharp pruners. Does he involve himself directly in your work? I know you said he's not your immediate supervisor."

Again Tom and Felipe exchanged a glance. Tom spoke up. "He's not, but he does swoop in from time to time to check things."

"He's the owner," Ian said. "He can do whatever he . . . wants."

Why did I have the feeling he'd bitten back an expletive?

Ian swirled the red in his glass, as one does, but the swig he took was more suited to a glass of beer.

"Easy, man." Tom used a gentle voice. "You're supposed to sip the wine and taste it. Right, Cece?"

"In general, yes. Do you like it, Ian?"

He blinked. "Do I like it? Um, sure. It's kind of, like, smooth. Or soft. Like velvet or something."

Felipe nodded approvingly. "I also find that."

These guys were acting like the supportive big brothers Ian never had. I was glad to see it.

When a phone buzzed, Ian glanced at his. He swiped, read, and grimaced. And stood.

"Sorry, I gotta go." He lifted his glass but this time took a sip and savored it for a moment. He set it down and reached for his wallet.

"Put that away, bro. We got it," Tom said.

"Thanks. See you tomorrow." He glanced up at me. "Thank you, Cece. Sorry if I was rude earlier."

"No worries," I said. "Drive safely."

"Will do." He shrugged into a lined camo jacket that had seen better days and headed out.

Four newcomers perched on stools next to Felipe. I chatted with them, explained today's offerings, and poured. I took our card reader over to a couple near the door and closed out their tab, then wiped off their table and brought their glasses back to the bar.

Tom gestured for me to come closer. "Got a minute?"

"Yes, I think so."

"We think you should know something. We heard you are a kind of detective."

"I'm actually not, but please go ahead."

"With Ian's uncle being murdered, this might be important." Tom pointed at Felipe.

"Holt has some kind of hold over Ian," Felipe began in a low voice. "We don't know what it is, but we try to take care of the kid, you know?"

"I noticed," I said. "And I think it's great that you do. What do you mean by a 'hold'?"

"I'm not sure," Tom said. "He's kind of been around a lot more since Ian came on board. And have you noticed their eyes? It's like they're related."

"I have noticed, yes." I waited.

"But we're pretty sure Ian didn't know Holt before he was hired," Felipe said.

"Interesting." Not thinking, I picked up Ian's glass. *Oops.* Too late to save it for DNA evidence. I hoped the cigarette butt would suffice, although maybe none of it would.

"Is that Dane Larsen, the artist?" Tom asked in a murmur as Dane filled a tray with empties over near the door.

"It is," I said. "She works here part-time. Do you know her work?"

"I sure do," Tom said. "She came out and painted the vineyard a couple of times in the fall."

"She set up her easel and a stool at the edge of the field and painted. I can't afford her pieces, but they really capture the feeling of being out there." Felipe stood when Dane approached. "Hello, Ms. Larsen."

She carried her tray around behind the bar looking puzzled. "Hi. Have we met?"

Felipe gestured to Tom and himself. "We work in the field at Holt Vineyards. We met you in October."

"That's right." Her face lit up. "How are you guys? Enjoying the fruits of your own labor?"

"You bet," Tom said. "Or somebody's."

I left them to catch up and grabbed a rag. I cleared and cleaned vacated tables before another big rush of customers came in, and I thought about Wesley taking a special interest in Ian well before Karl was murdered. That was something I'd like to know more about. A lot more.

# CHAPTER 46

By eight o'clock, we were nearly full again. Who'd have thought a Tuesday night would be this busy?

Ed and Henry had come in half an hour earlier wanting after-dinner drinks. Sitting at the bar, Ed nursed a port, while Henry sipped a vintage that was lightly sweet but not cloying.

As during a previous shift, Dane seemed absorbed in her phone. I'd had to nudge her a few times to help customers in need of attention. With darkness, the temperature had dropped to the mid-forties, which meant nobody wanted to be out on the patio.

"Henry, you'll find this funny," I said during a moment when everyone at the bar was served and seemed happy. "During my dinner break, I went over to the gallery to chat with you, but all the windows were dark. I know full well you aren't open today." Smiling, I shook my head.

He arched his eyebrows, which were always so well shaped I wonder if he waxed them.

"Was it a social call, my dear, or something perhaps more . . ." He glanced right and left and lowered his voice. "More serious?"

"On the serious end of the spectrum, as you might imagine. I—" I shut my mouth when I saw Gareth push through the door. "Speaking of serious, we need to find out more about him. His history, his family, whatever," I whispered.

"Leave it to us, *mija*," Ed said.

Henry gave me a knowing nod. As smooth as silk, he turned when Gareth approached the bar.

"Good evening, young man." Henry smiled. "Please sit with us."

Gareth's eyes widened in surprise until he recognized Henry. "Ah, yes, the curator of Colinas. Thank you, sir, I'd love to join you." Gareth removed a new-looking gray fedora and laid it on the bar.

"Welcome back, Gareth," I said politely but not with as much enthusiasm as I might have offered to a different customer. "What can I pour for you tonight?"

"I'd like something in a big red, Cece," he said. "I just came from an Italian dinner and I want to continue the theme."

"This cab sauv is as close as I can get." I held up the open bottle.

"Hit me."

*Rude much?* Despite the lack of a "please," I poured him a glass. I kept it on the scant side of the imaginary pour line.

He leaned over to Ed and extended his hand. "Hi, I'm Gareth Rockwell. You own the diner in town, right?"

"I do." Ed shook his hand. "Ed Ramirez. I saw you in the restaurant the other day but didn't get a chance to greet you."

Yeah, the day Gareth said he'd like to drink wine in the morning with me. Now I wanted to go wash my hands again.

"I'm sure you've learned by now that these adobes aren't on the market," Henry said. "How is your search going?"

Gareth took as big of a swig as Ian had earlier. "It's looking pretty good for a certain property. Fingers crossed and all that."

How I wished Zoe had responded about NAR Concerns. Who they were, what their concerns were, and why they owned nearly half of Karl's real estate holdings. Alas, she hadn't, and I didn't want to push her.

"What property would that be, Gareth?" Henry asked with a sweet, innocent smile.

It was a look completely out of character for suave Henry, and a smile that made me want to either snort or break out in a giggle. I did neither and instead moved down to the three women at the other end of the bar, which was still within earshot. It didn't matter if I heard. Henry would fill me in on Gareth's response at the next possible opportunity.

The women seemed to be in about my mid-forties age range.

"This white is very nice," one said, swirling the last inch in her glass. "What was it again?"

I pointed to the varietal printed on the board behind me. "I'm glad you like it. We sell bottles to take home if you're interested."

"I'm planning for my son's rehearsal dinner." She made a face. "I mean, the welcome dinner. These days the groom's parents have to throw a party for half the invitees."

"Right?" One of her friends leaned in, a woman pushing fifty but working hard to appear forty. "The rehearsal used to be only family and the various attendants. And they actually rehearsed the ceremony."

"Get out of the dark ages, you two," the dark-haired third one said. "Or the nineties, more like it. I think a welcome dinner is a great idea. It can be super casual, and it accommodates everybody who comes in from out of town. Don't complain. It's a lot more low-budget than the actual wedding reception." She raised her hand. "Says a mother of three girls."

The champion of the old ways sniffed.

The first woman nodded. "You're completely right. I get off easy with two sons, and this is the second one." She eyed my name tag. "Anyway, Cece, I think I'd like to buy a case of this white. If they don't drink it all at the dinner, then I'll have some nice bottles at home."

"Would you like to take the case with you tonight?" I asked.

"Why not? It's one thing I can cross off my infinitely long to-do list."

"I'll get that ready for you." I hoped I had a full case in the back. I'd need to slap stickers on each bottle and write up the invoice, but a case was a good sale and easy money. I'd make it work.

I was about to let Dane know I'd be in the back for a little while when Gareth jumped to his feet. He nearly knocked over his barstool.

"That's an outrageous accusation." He set fists on hips, glaring down at Henry. "I won't stand for it."

Ed rose. I slid down to that end of the bar. Henry, looking saintly, sat with hands folded in front of him.

"Sit down, amigo," Ed urged in the softest of voices. "Nobody accused you of anything."

"He did." Gareth, now red of face, pointed a shaking finger at Henry.

Henry gave me a "What can ya do?" look and a quick shrug.

"May I help?" I asked, and hoped the kind of help I could offer would defuse the situation, ASAP. Other customers were beginning to stare.

"I doubt it. For the record, I didn't kill anyone," Gareth said in a low tone that felt menacing despite his words.

The room fell quiet, as customers strained to hear the words, to understand the cause of the spat. To discern whether Gareth was dangerous.

The developer laid a twenty on the counter. "Keep the change. I won't be back." Chin high, Gareth stalked out.

Conversation inside resumed. Henry pointed to Gareth's hat.

I picked it up. I gazed at the door and stayed put. "He'll be back if he wants it." I set the hat on a shelf behind the bar. "Okay, who's going to tell me what happened?"

# CHAPTER 47

As soon as Gareth left, and after notifying Dane I'd be absent for a few, I adjourned to the back room. Ed and Henry came with me.

A few moments later, we had an efficient circular assembly line set up. Ed lifted out a bottle of the wine the customer wanted to buy from one side of the case and wiped a section with a dry cloth to make sure the Vino y Vida sticker would adhere. I peeled a sticker from the sheet and stuck it on the bottle, checking that the words were level. Henry slotted the bottle back into the other side of the case.

Henry slowed. "Seriously, Cecelia, I didn't accuse Gareth of murder."

"I believe you. But what *did* you say?"

Henry picked up the next bottle and slid it into the box. "I might have alluded to what seems to be his desperation to acquire Karl's property."

Ed snorted. "He asked Rockwell how far he would go to get hold of that house and land. Dude didn't like the insinuation."

"I didn't insinuate anything," Henry protested. "It was a simple question. If he interpreted it that way, it's not my problem."

Ed sidled over and kissed the top of Henry's head. "I'm glad you weren't alone with him in a dark alley, *querido*."

Henry scoffed. "We don't have alleys in Colinas. You know that."

Ed rolled his eyes. "You know what I mean. Face it, he's younger and more fit than you. Wouldn't you agree, Cece?"

"I don't want to think about that. Let's all make sure it doesn't come to a physical face-off between Gareth and Henry, okay?" I held out my hand for the next bottle. "Come on. I want to finish up. I appreciate your help, but it's almost closing time, and Dane shouldn't have to do it by herself."

A couple of minutes later, Ed carried the full box of wine to the woman's car after she put the case and the tasting for three on her credit card.

For the first time, I got an uneasy feeling that I probably should be saving money for Zoe's wedding, whenever that happened. I doubted she was going to want a big expensive do, but with her, you never knew. She might prefer a barefoot beach ceremony with a potluck supper after, or she could opt for white and lace with a sit-down meal for two hundred. We'd cross that crazy bridge when we came to it.

"Thank you, ladies," I called after them. "Come back any time and have a lovely wedding."

The mother of the groom waved and called back her thanks. Ed and Henry resumed their seats and their sipping.

At nine o'clock, I raised my voice and addressed the room. "Drink up, please. We close in thirty minutes."

A group of three youngish women with three others who might have been their mothers or aunts asked for one more pour. "Don't worry, we have a driver picking us up," one in the older generation assured me.

I poured. It would be a fast tasting, but hey, the customer was—almost—always right. I checked the patio. It was still empty, so I locked that door.

Back at the bar, Ed asked, "Did you walk over, Cece?"

"No, I rode my bike."

Henry inhaled sharply, hand over his mouth. "Oh, honey, you don't want to be riding home alone in the dark." He leaned closer. "Not with a killer running free."

"And it's cold," Ed added. "Let us give you a ride."

"Can you fit my bicycle?" I loaded the dishwasher.

"Sure. We drove Big Dog," Ed said.

I'd never had occasion to ride with either of them. "Big Dog?"

"It's his name for my vehicle." Henry shot Ed a fond look. "It happens to be a ridiculously large car, but I sometimes need to transport large works of art, paintings and sculptures. I'd rather drive the seventy-two Carrera, but needs must."

"Wait." I stared at him. "You drive a vintage Porsche? Henry, how in the entire universe did I not know this?"

He blushed and looked abashed. "I'm sorry. I know how much you love your Mustang." He glanced around and spoke so softly I could barely hear him. "Thing is, it's in mint original condition, and the car is worth rather a lot. That's why I don't talk about it much and only take it out for a drive under pristine conditions."

I shook my head marveling. In the years after Greg's death, a friend I met at line dancing was also a vintage car enthusiast and owned a 1970 Porsche Carrera. We'd swapped taking each other for spins for a few years. Hers was a sweet ride.

"Well, next time the conditions are pristine, I'll never forgive you if you don't come take me for a drive."

"It's a deal, sweetheart. As long as you reciprocate by driving me somewhere in your Blue."

My expression darkened. "OMG, I didn't tell you what happened on the way home from your house yesterday."

Ed touched my arm. "You must."

The last customers were cashing out with Dane. It was after nine.

"How about I tell you while you drive me home, or you can come in for a nightcap once we're there?" I asked.

"Deal," Ed said. "What can I do to help close? Sweep the floor?"

I smiled. "Deal."

# CHAPTER 48

"This is nice." Henry sipped his herbal tea as he sat on my couch. He opted for the addition of a shot of cognac.

Ed had chosen straight tea. "I've had quite enough to drink this evening. Morning comes early when you run a breakfast diner."

"I don't want to even contemplate getting up early enough to have breakfast ready for customers at six in the freaking morning," I said.

Ed laughed. "You get used to it." He gave Henry a glance. "But we can't stay long."

After I fed the cats, I joined Henry in a splash of cognac with my chamomile and settled into the cushioned armchair next to the couch. Both men looked expectantly at me.

"Well? Dish, honey." Henry stroked Mittens, who had adopted his lap for the duration. Her purr was audible.

"All right." I retold the tale of the dark car pursuing me down the hill too fast and too close.

"It was scary, but Blue did really well." I took a sip of tea. "Thanks largely to Jo."

"That's a blessing," Ed said. "You have no idea whose car was behind you?"

"No. I couldn't see the driver's face. All I know is that they were smoking. The whole thing went too fast to grab a plate number. I told the police. I can't do anything else about it." Martin jumped up on the wide padded arm of my chair. I scooted over to make room for him next to me, but he chose to stay on the arm. He assumed a resting Sphinx pose, his long paws stretched out in front, his head up but eyes closed.

"We'll be on the lookout for big black vehicles," Ed said.

"Like mine?" Henry asked, his eyes twinkling.

"Silly man." Ed gave him a sweet smile. "Now, Cece, I found out something about Tara. She seems to have had a possibly illicit affair in her past when she lived in Sonoma."

"Does this relate to Karl's murder?"

"The affair might have been with Karl, himself."

My eyebrows shot up. "Wow. It was illicit how?"

"Well, she was married to someone else at the time," Ed said. "Kind of the definition of illicit, don't you think?"

"Do you think Karl was threatening to make that public after all this time?" Henry asked.

"Dunno." Ed shook his head.

"How did you find out about it?" I asked him.

"I grew up here in Colinas. My good childhood friend was the mayor of Sonoma for a few years. She knew everyone and everything that transpired down there. Still does. Thing is, she said Karl went by Charlie Meyer during that time. Spelled M-E-Y-E-R."

Dane's Charlie, no doubt. "And he changed his name to a German spelling when he moved up here?" I mused. "Sounds like he was trying to escape his past."

"It does," Ed said.

"Eduardo, why did you say her affair 'might have been' with Karl?" Henry asked.

Good question. I sipped my tea, waiting for the answer.

"My friend thought it might have been with Charlie Meyer, but there was another man who was a possibility. Someone with unusual eyes, is what she said." Ed covered a yawn with his hand.

Henry stood. "Forgive us, Cece, but I have to get this big guy home."

"No worries." I followed them to the door. "Who's driving?"

Ed raised his hand.

"Good. Careful on those dark curves, amigo." I gave them each a kiss on the cheek and locked the door behind them.

Well, well. I had more to think about now. What if the affair hadn't been with Karl, aka Charlie, but with Wesley Holt, another man with most unusual eyes? He could have lived in Sonoma before here, too. He was older than Karl. His age would fit better with Tara's than hers would have with Karl's. The mayor might have mixed up the two men who shared those unusual eyes.

My phone dinged with a text from Zoe.

**NAR Concerns is a cover for Norman Arthur Rockwell, some kind of real estate tycoon. Can you even the name? Gotta be fake . . . but maybe not?**

*Wow*. I dictated a reply.

**Thx, honey. Gareth's last name is Rockwell. Could be real. His father? Uncle?**

I waited, but another text didn't come in right away. I forwarded Zoe's message to Allie, adding the same response and questions to my twin. It was nearly ten, but she was usually still up at this hour. If she wasn't, she'd answer in the morning.

While I waited to see if either Allie or Zoe would reply, I got up and added another glug of cognac to my tea mug. As I was pouring, my phone rang with a call from Allie.

"Cee, I've heard of Art Rockwell. His full name is Norman Arthur."

"Okay," I said. "What else about him? Zoe said he's a real estate tycoon, whatever that means."

"It means he buys and develops and sells a lot of property, mostly high-end stuff," she said. "My guess would be he's a relative and is trying Gareth out on some low-level properties to see if he can operate on the family model."

"Would that include murdering the owner of a much-desired property?" I asked.

"Ick. But I suppose. Rockwell is known to be ruthless. I don't know why I didn't think of him in the first place."

"Is he Gareth's father? Or his uncle?" I sipped from my mug.

"Hmm. That I don't know. Very likely the next generation up, though. Or it could be a much older brother." She yawned unabashedly, loudly.

"Sorry, am I boring you?"

"Hey, sis. That school bus comes early."

"Then go get your beauty sleep. Breakfast at Edie's tomorrow?" I asked.

"Ooh, good idea. See you at eight?"

"Um, how about nine? You know eight is way too early for me to be up and presentable to the public at large."

"Yes, I do know. It's a date. Sweet dreams."

I disconnected, smiling. Life with a twin wasn't always smooth sailing, but we had each other's backs, forever. That I knew.

# CHAPTER 49

"Looks like we'll be getting rain by late afternoon." Richard gestured at the sky at eight the next morning.

I heard him whistling in his garden as I wandered around mine, coffee in hand, and he invited me through the gate. We sat under the roofed section of his patio.

"Feels like rain too." I pulled my fleece closer around my neck against the raw air. "How was your outing yesterday?"

"Full of nostalgia among geezers, mostly." He stretched out his legs and smiled. "I engaged a couple of them in discussions about current topics, thank goodness. One can't dwell solely in the past. It's an occupational hazard of being a VOM."

I loved that he referred to himself as a Very Old Man. "You make it sound like you only went to school with other males. Were there no women at Stanford then?"

"There certainly were, and some good-looking ones." He winked. "Why, that's where my beloved wife and I met."

"Was Cal always co-ed?"

"It has been since 1870, only two years after the founding." He stroked his chin. "Now then, neighbor. Fill me in on the news. I want to know all the developments in this homicide business."

"I wish there were some news or developments. I've been doing what I can, but it's limited." I took a swig of my coffee, which was cooling despite being in a lidded travel mug. I tilted my head. "What do you know about Tara Pulanski?"

"The cat rescue woman. You think she murdered Meier?" He sat back, frowning, as if considering the idea.

"I really don't know. It seems she had a romantic connection in her past, maybe with Wesley Holt or it might have been with Karl Meier. Either way, she was married to someone else and lived in Sonoma."

"You're talking about the owner of Holt Vineyards."

"Yes," I said.

"It's well-known about town that he and Tara Pulanski are a couple these days, no matter how much they try to keep it under wraps."

"That's interesting," I said. "Why would they want to have a clandestine relationship? Are either married?"

"He isn't. Never has been, far's I know. I couldn't say about her." Richard tented his fingers. "I'm curious how you think all this pertains to Meier's murder."

"I think Wesley and Karl were related. Wesley appears to be doing well financially. Maybe Karl uncovered their blood tie, whatever it is, and was hitting Wesley up for money. Or he could have been threatening to reveal a secret from Wesley's past."

"If Holt killed Karl, you're thinking Tara must have been in on the plan?" he asked.

"Or at least known about it if she and Wesley are a couple as you say."

"Or vice versa, I suppose. But would Tara have a motive?"

"Hmm," I said. "Maybe it was Karl she had the affair with in Sonoma, and he was threatening her with exposure."

"Would that be ruinous to her?"

"Maybe not ruinous but certainly embarrassing."

"Say, neighbor." He pointed to the hexagonal shed in the back corner of his garden, the one with a small brass plaque on the door reading JOURNALISTE. "How's that book of yours coming?"

I tried to hide my grimace. "I'm afraid I haven't been making time for it."

"The door is unlocked and it's at your service. My house-cleaner keeps the spiderwebs at bay, too." He gave me an encouraging smile. "You will find time if you want to."

"I know. I really appreciate the offer of the space." I'd had an idea for a novel for several years. After I confessed it to this life-long journalist and author, he'd offered me free use of the writing shed he no longer used. But my ingrained fear of failure had kept me from typing the first sentence.

"Try it one morning. You don't need to let me know. Wander over with your laptop or a pad of paper and take the plunge. It might surprise you."

"I'm sure it would." I checked the time on my phone. "I have to run, Richard. I'm meeting Allie for breakfast at nine."

"Have fun."

An acorn woodpecker set to hammering into the fence at the far end of Richard's garden.

"Cursed bird," he yelled, rising. "Shoo! Out!" He waved his arms. "Off with your bloody beak." He grabbed a small stone from the basket he kept on his patio and lobbed it at the pest, missing wildly.

The woodpecker ignored him and continued with its destruction. I made my way into my own garden. Something more ominous hammered at my brain. I was as unable to identify it as Richard was at hitting that destructive bird.

# CHAPTER 50

Ed set down a platter of Huevos Californios at the table in the back booth Allie and I had snagged. He also delivered her western omelet with bacon and hash browns.

"*Gracias*, Ed." Allie beamed at him. "This looks beyond yummy."

"*De nada*," he said. "You both all set?"

"For sure." I picked up my knife and fork and spread my napkin in my lap. "Thanks. I hope you guys got home okay last night."

"Without a snag—or a tailgater." He smoothed down his apron and headed off to the next order, the next customer, the next smile.

"He's a natural at this kind of business," Allie murmured.

I nodded, my mouth full of corn tortilla, refried beans, fried eggs, and sliced avocado, all topped by sour cream and salsa.

"Were he and Henry at the wine bar last night?" Allie asked.

"Yes, and they drove me home. Ed had a couple of interesting tidbits to share."

"Ooh, do tell."

I was facing the rest of the diner, while Allie had her back to the other tables and the counter. The booth behind her had been empty when Ed seated us, but three college-age women in winter biking togs had now claimed the banquettes. Today being a Wednesday, I assumed they were tourists and didn't know any of the people I was about to name. I hoped so, anyway.

Still, I kept my voice barely above a whisper. "Someone Ed knows in Sonoma told him Tara Pulanski had an affair with a man she thought might have been Karl. This was while Tara was married and living down there."

Allie whistled softly.

"But what Ed's friend actually said was that it was a man with unusual eyes. You noticed the similarity between Wesley Holt and Karl. I think it's their eyes and that they are somehow related. Maybe the affair had been with Holt."

"His winery seems to be doing quite well." Allie also kept her voice down.

"Yes. I drove out there recently. Did you know they have a family of friendly free-range cats? He said they keep the rats and mice away."

"I hope they don't lose too many to coyotes and bobcats."

"I hope not too," I said. "Wesley seemed to be a real softie about the cats when he came into the wine bar yesterday."

"Are you going to start pouring Holt wines? By the way?" She pointed at my plate. "Your breakfast is getting cold."

"Yes, Mom." I enjoyed a couple of bites, then continued. "I might include Holt. Wesley and I haven't inked a deal, but I told him how I usually run the arrangements and he said he'd get back to me. Shoot. He gave me a selection of Holt wines in a tote and I meant to bring them home to share with you."

"Always happy to help when it comes to wine tasting." She grinned.

"You were right about something else, Al," I said. "Yesterday Dane said she had begun training to become an electrician years ago, but a dude named Charlie—which apparently is the name Karl went by at the time—really shafted her in the program. She finally dropped out."

Allie shuddered. "Electricity is dangerous. I could never do that job. What if I got electrocuted? Or worse, was responsible for someone else being hurt by a bad connection I'd made. I wouldn't be able to forgive myself."

"I'm sure electricians have ways of being careful." A woman began making her way down the aisle in our direction. *Uh-oh.* "Don't look now," I murmured. "But here comes one of the people we've been talking about."

Tara stopped at the booth before ours. She didn't seem to have seen me.

"Hi, sweetheart," she said to one of the cyclists in the booth. "Did you girls have a nice ride?"

*Sweetheart?*

"Hi, Mom," came a voice from behind Allie.

One of those young women was Tara's daughter? *Yikes.* If she'd heard Allie and me speaking, we could be in big trouble.

"What's that?" Tara asked, leaning down to hear what her daughter was saying. "Really?" She straightened.

Head down, I focused on my food. I glanced up when Allie kicked me under the table. Tara stood beside us, arms folded.

"Good morning, Tara," I said with my hand over my mouth to cover the food still in there.

"I hear you've been talking about me." She didn't smile.

I swallowed. By a stroke of luck, or maybe it was a strategic move on his part, Ed materialized next to her. She ignored him.

"Yes, I was telling my sister here about the great cat rescue program you run," I said. "Do you know Allie Halstead?"

She glanced down at Allie. "Yes, we've met."

"Hello, Tara," Allie said.

I forged on quickly. "I told her I'd seen some cats recently out at Holt Vineyards. I understand you're close to Wesley Holt. He's quite the cat lover, isn't he?"

Tara's mouth dropped open for a second, and then she seemed to steel herself. "I don't know what you're talking about."

"Cats. Vineyards. Holt?" I asked sweetly.

She glared at me.

"Tara, would you like to dine this morning?" Ed asked.

"What?" She finally registered his presence. "Yes. I can slide in with the girls here." She shot me one more look and then joined the daughter and the others.

"Excellent. I'll bring coffee right away." Ed kept his voice level and addressed Allie and me. "Anything else for you two?"

Allie smiled up at him. "No, thank you. We're almost done."

"*Bueno.*" Silently, staring at me, he made a "call me" gesture next to his ear and mouth.

I nodded. Allie and I switched to discussing birthday cake and the guest list for Saturday.

"Mom said she's coming," Allie said.

"Seriously?"

"Yep. She and Zoe both."

"That's fabulous," I said. "Zoe didn't tell me."

Allie covered her mouth. "Oh. Maybe they were going to surprise you. Sorry, sis."

"That's okay. I can fake a surprise as well as the next person." *Oops.* Maybe I shouldn't have said that out loud with Tara in the next booth. Tara, to whom I had just faked an entire situation. I couldn't take back the words now. I'd live with the consequences.

We paid and made our way out without another word exchanged with Tara. I was pretty sure that the jabs I felt in my back as I made my way down the aisle toward the door were daggers she was shooting at me with her eyes.

# CHAPTER 51

Allie and I stood next to her car outside the diner. I snugged my coat collar around my neck against the damp, raw wind and stuck each hand in the other sleeve.

"I can't believe how totally bold you were with Tara," Allie said. "You sat there and lied to her, cool as a cucumber compress. Nice job. Very nice."

"Well, I had to say something. Honestly, I can't believe I pulled it off. That I, like, had the nerve."

"Keep it up, Cee. You're on a roll. Just, you know, don't even attempt lying to me."

"Ha. Not a chance." I wanted to glance at the windows at the end of the diner where Tara sat with the girls. I restrained myself. "Earlier Richard told me she and Holt are well known to be a couple. What I don't know is whether they've rekindled an old flame."

"If it was him and not Karl back then, you mean."

"Yes," I said. "It was pretty dumb of me in there to talk out loud in a public place about Tara."

"You kept your voice super low. I doubt the daughter heard more than her mom's name."

"Hope not."

Allie checked her phone. "I have to run to a private showing."

I somehow hadn't noticed she was in full real estate agent regalia of cream-colored slacks, a tasteful navy cashmere sweater with a string of chunky beads, and flats. Her carefully coiffed hair matched the rest of the outfit.

"Of course." I made a shooing gesture. "Go."

"Keep me in the loop, okay?" she asked, beeping open the car.

"I promise. Hey, if you get a chance after your showing, see if you can dig into the Rockwell dude."

"I will."

"Good luck at the showing, Allie. Hope you make a million."

"Or my percentage of it, which would still be pretty great. Love you." She slid in and drove away.

Allie dealt in all kinds of properties but particularly high-end homes, which made her the most money. California real estate prices being what they were, she'd been socking away sizable savings. Her husband, Fuller, made a decent living as a financial adviser. Those kids of theirs weren't going to have to go into debt for college, which was a real gift.

As for me, I had a couple of hours before I had to open the wine bar for the day. It was too cold to sit on a park bench. I could head over to Vino y Vida super early or stroll home and hang out. Or I could see what other kinds of trouble I could get into.

I pulled on my gloves and meandered along Las Marias Road, hands in pockets. Here it was a residential street, but it was the same thoroughfare that headed out of town to the Holt holdings. I turned left on Manzanita and strolled until it bisected Palito Street. The public library was not far ahead on Palito. I could perch there and do some digging, or maybe I'd read a magazine until I had to get over to Vino y Vida.

I moseyed up the ramp to the building. It was only ten years old but had been built in the Old California style with curved red terracotta roof tiles and a stuccoed exterior. Native palm trees in various heights lined the walkways, which had benches posi-

tioned in shady spots. Outside and in, the library was fully acces-
sible for anyone with an impairment, be it mobility, sight, or hearing. I approved.

A library computer was available, and I checked in for half an
hour. A bigger screen and a keyboard always felt more comfortable to use than a phone, although I knew that dated me.

I went to work on Wesley Holt first. I paired his name with
words like "wedding" and "divorce" and got zip for results.
Never married? That was what Richard had thought. I tried
adding "Sonoma" to his name. That yielded something. Wesley
Holt had been on the rugby team at Sonoma State. A photo of
him dated a few years later appeared in a *Sonoma Index-Tribune*
article about a winery in the same area. Holt was the field crew
manager.

Wesley had learned vineyard work in Sonoma. How did he
come to buy Ridley in the Alexander Valley, and where had he
gotten the start-up money to make Holt Vineyards a success?
When my next queries hit dead ends, I decided to shift focus to
Tara Pulanski.

I didn't remember if either Tara or Zara wore wedding rings,
but according to Ed's friend, Tara had been married, at least for a
time. Choate was Zara's last name. Was Choate their family
name? If so, Zara had either not married or hadn't changed her
name when she'd wed.

Off a-searching I went. *Bingo.* A Tara Choate had graduated
from high school quite a few years ago with honors and a scholar-
ship to Sonoma State College. She had to be our Colinas Tara.
How many Tara Choates could there be?

I sat back. She and Wesley had gone to the same college and
were more or less the same age. They could have fallen in love
then. But something had interfered. A something with the last
name of Pulanski.

"Pulanski Sonoma" was the next phrase I entered. *Whoa.* I
stared at what I saw. The earliest link was a notice on the society

page about a gala wedding between Tara Choate and Chip Pulanski thirty years ago. I didn't think newspapers had society pages these days. Photos showed a high-necked frothy wedding gown and a dashing groom in a cutaway tuxedo. They apparently were off to honeymoon in Tahiti.

The next reference to handsome Chip was him in handcuffs a decade later, having been busted for serious drug offenses, including running a smuggling ring that imported unusual breeds of cats with opioids attached to or inside their bodies. And worse.

No wonder Tara became an advocate of abandoned and mistreated kitties. I followed a thread to read that she'd filed for divorce soon after her husband's conviction. Since good old Chip was in federal prison for the foreseeable future, and because the couple had apparently hammered out a prenuptial agreement that ended up favorable to Tara, she came out ahead. What Chip had brought to the marriage went to her and their daughter. What he made after the wedding but before being incarcerated went straight back to the government because of his crimes. It seemed like a kind of backward arrangement, but I obviously didn't know the details nor the motivation behind it.

That must have been when Tara moved to Colinas, to get herself and her daughter out of surroundings with bad memories attached, the daughter at Edie's who now liked to ride a bike in cold weather and was possibly about Zoe's age. She and her mom were on at least superficially good terms, with Tara calling her an endearment and being welcome to share a breakfast booth with the girl and her friends.

All that aside, I still didn't know for sure if Tara and Wesley had rekindled their love during the time when Tara was married. Or if they found each other after she moved north to Colinas. Or both. It seemed neither was married now. Nothing wrong in my book with two consenting adults enjoying themselves at any age.

I flipped back to the question of Holt Vineyards and did my best to dig deeper. Wesley bought Ridley from the bank four years ago after Karl had failed at the enterprise. That much was public record. But who had financed the sale and the renovations? Maybe Wesley came from a family with money or he'd inherited a chunk.

Or . . . I sat back, thinking. What if Tara's family had money? She'd certainly had a fancy wedding. Inherited wealth could be how she came out of her divorce with enough funds to start over up here. She could have loaned Wesley the money or become a silent investor.

Zara would know. I'd have to figure out some excuse to see her and ask, but I would need to phrase the question as casually as possible.

The library director, a handsome, dark-haired man about my age, rolled up in his wheelchair next to me and flashed me a white-toothed smile in a clean-shaven face.

"Good morning, Cece. Catching up on some archives?"

"Hey. Yes, kind of. Trying to run down someone I used to know." Should I ask him how to look up personal finances? No way. I'd have to reveal way too much, although I was sure he could help. He didn't have the use of his legs for reasons unknown to me, but his brain was sharper than most, and he had the legendary research skills of any experienced librarian.

"I'm afraid your time is up on this machine." He gestured behind him at the desk. "A couple of people are waiting for it."

"My bad." Sure enough, the timer on the screen was at zero. I closed the browser windows I'd opened and stood. "I'm sorry. I'll get out of the way."

"No worries. Come back any time. And if you need help, I'm always here."

"Thanks." I gathered my coat and bag and headed out. To find Zara? Could happen.

# CHAPTER 52

Even though I was not a bit hungry right now, I knew I would be later, and I hadn't brought anything to eat on my work break. The Exchange Bakery and Gourmet Provisions could solve that in a flash for me. I wandered in to survey the list of made-to-order sandwiches and inhaled some yummy smells.

It was already eleven o'clock. The line at the deli counter seemed split between people still ordering coffee and a pastry for breakfast and those looking, as I was, for lunch. Despite three people behind the counter working as fast as they could, I was number twelve in the queue.

I perused the menu on the board above and behind the deli workers. I thought I might go with the Pesto Panini, which included Bastardo del Grappa cheese, sliced tomato and pepper, and a generous layer of traditional basil pesto, all grilled in a panini press.

When the door opened behind me, I turned and cringed a little. A hatless Gareth hovered in the entrance, his gaze boring into me. He'd been angry when he left the wine bar last night. It hadn't been my fault, but still. I mustered what I hoped looked like a friendly smile.

"Join the crowd, Gareth. Best lunch in town, right?"

He kept hold of the open door as if deciding if he was going to turn around and leave. Cold air streamed in with him.

"Door, please?" one of the workers called, pointing.

Gareth glanced at his hand and let the door shut behind him. He stepped up to join the line behind me.

"I believe I left my hat in your little wine bar yesterday," he said without a word of greeting.

My "little" wine bar? "You did. We'll be open at one today. You're welcome to pick it up any time before nine tonight." I let my smile slip away.

"Well, if I stop by, I hope I don't run into the same rude customer as last evening." He crossed his arms and planted his feet shoulder-width apart.

"I'm sorry you had a bad experience." I was, but no way was I apologizing for Henry's remark. The bad experience was totally on Gareth and his reaction.

The door opened again, this time admitting Lee Norsegian in his CPD uniform jacket, his bicycle shoes clomping on the floor. The dark cargo pants must be a bike-friendly version, since he also carried a helmet by the chin strap. He surveyed the store, his gaze passing over Gareth as if casually, but I was pretty sure Lee came in only because Gareth had preceded him.

This was interesting in the extreme. Police surveillance via bike? Could happen.

"Hey, Lee." I smiled at him, this time genuinely.

"Hi, Cece."

Gareth turned.

"Good morning, Mr. Rockwell," Lee said.

Gareth's lip curled. "Do I know you?"

Lee clasped his hands behind his back. "Patrol officer Lee Norsegian with the Colinas Police Department."

Gareth swallowed and put on his own version of a polite smile. "Officer." He stuck his hands in his high-end lined jacket and turned back to the front, except that put him face-to-face with me.

He turned again, taking a step around Lee. "If you'll excuse me, I think I'll find my lunch elsewhere."

Lee shot me the faintest of smiles, then focused on Gareth. "I'll walk with you a few steps, Mr. Rockwell. I have a couple of things to ask you, if you have a minute."

Gareth blinked. "I don't, actually."

"After you, sir." Lee, unfazed, gestured at the door.

They left. I gazed at the door, dying to follow and listen in. Except I was more than sure I wouldn't be welcome by either of them, especially Gareth. The last thing I wanted to do was jeopardize the police investigation.

# CHAPTER 53

I was about to unlock the back door of Vino y Vida at about noon when I glanced over to Henry's art gallery. The lights were on, so I headed there first.

Except the door was locked. Was he here or not? I held my hand to the glass in the door to reduce the reflection. I couldn't see him. I knocked. Waited. Knocked. Had something happened to my gentle, dapper friend?

I breathed more easily as he emerged from the back, waving and hurrying toward the door.

"Sorry, Cecelia. I was finishing up a frame in my workroom. Do come in." He held the door open for me.

"I won't take up a lot of your time. I've got to get the wine bar ready to open soon."

"It's fine. What's up?" He peered at my face. "Everything okay?"

"Yes. I'm fine."

"Come, sit for a minute." He led me to the bench in the middle of the room, the only thing that wasn't for sale. As in a museum, it let people sit and contemplate the art on the wall.

"I've been thinking about this murder, a lot," I began. "and Dane Larsen is one of the people on my list to think about. At your house you said you might be able to look into her a bit more."

"I'm afraid I haven't been able to find anything new. She has expressed a dislike for Karl Meier on more than one occasion."

"How did his name come up?" I asked.

"I was musing about changing some of the lighting in here, and I asked her if she knew a good electrician. Basically, she warned me off hiring Meier."

"That fits."

"Doesn't make her a killer, though."

"No, it doesn't."

The small bell on the door jingled. Henry stood, and I gazed that way. Zara Choate stood in the entry holding a large flat portfolio case. *Oho.* Another person I'd been wanting to talk with. I also rose.

"Ah, Zara." Henry beamed at her. "Come in, my dear."

She came in, letting the door shut behind her.

"Do you know my good friend Cece Barton?" he asked.

"We've met several times." Zara sounded tentative.

"We attend the same church, Henry." I smiled at her. "Hello, Zara."

"Hi, Cece. Sorry if I'm interrupting something."

"You're not," I said.

Henry rubbed his palms together. "Let's see what you brought me. Bring your case over to the table." An empty table sat behind the counter where Henry rang up sales. To me he said, "She's going to show me some of her work."

"Okay if I stick around and see?" I asked.

"That's . . . fine," Zara said. It didn't sound fine.

I took her words at face value.

She pulled out a half dozen large black-and-white photographs. They were striking and artistic. One was a close-up of a bicycle taken from a foot off the ground, with only the wheels showing. Other sets of wheels were lined up behind, as at a bike rack.

None of the pictures showed people, although one was of

214 / MADDIE DAY

weather-roughened hands wielding pruners on a grapevine. Any of them were pictures I'd love to have on my walls.

"Did you take this out at Holt Vineyards?" I pointed to the one with pruners.

She shot me a sharp glance. "No."

Henry gave me an inquiring look but didn't say anything.

The last photograph was of a kitten fast asleep and splayed on its back. The light and shadows slanting over the little creature were stunning.

"I love this," I said.

Henry jumped in. "I bet you took that at Colinas Cat Rescue, Zara. Am I right?"

"I did," she said. "The kittens presented an overload of cuteness, but the light in this shot was the best."

"It's really lovely, Zara," I said.

"Thanks very much."

"I need to get back to Tara about volunteering there," I continued. "I saw her this morning but didn't get a chance. She was at the diner with a young woman who called her Mom. You have a niece?"

"Yes, Isabelle."

"Does Tara have other children?" I asked.

"No."

I thought I probably shouldn't ask one more question, but I did. "What does Tara's husband do?"

"She doesn't have one." She folded her arms.

"Great to see you Cece," Henry said, giving me a "get out of here" look. "I'll stop in for a glass later after I close." He turned his back on me. "These are perfect, Zara, and I'd love to work out a showing for you. Come back to my office and we'll talk terms, all right?"

"Bye, all," I said, but they were already heading to the back. I didn't think I'd been overly nosy. Still, from the time she came in, Zara seemed to be uncomfortable I was there. Why?

# CHAPTER 54

By the time I got to Vino y Vida at half past twelve, Mooncat had let herself in. She had the music cranked up and was dancing to a rocking Linda Ronstadt song as she unloaded the dishwasher and filled baskets with pretzels. She always brightened the spirit of a room.

"Thanks for getting here early," I said. "Are you all better?"

"I'm good, thanks. Sorry for leaving you in the lurch." She turned down the volume so we didn't have to shout.

"Between Dane and me, we managed," I said. "Your health has to come first."

"I appreciate that. So, what do we have today?"

I went through what we'd be pouring, which was the same as yesterday. I often kept the same wines going for a week. Most people didn't come in to taste more than once a week. Even if they did, we always offered a choice of reds and whites.

"You heard about Karl being murdered, I assume?" I asked.

"Yes, but not until I emerged from the darkened room. Tough thing for Jo, right?"

"Very. Mooncat, when he was in here working on the lights that day, you called him Charlie and asked him to stay away from your niece. When did he go by Charlie?"

She looked at me over the top of her granny glasses. "You're working this case. I can tell."

"I'm trying, yes. Nobody's getting very far at solving it, especially not the police and the sheriff's department. At least not that they've told me."

"To get back to your question, Charlie was the name Meier went by when he moved up here from Sonoma ten or fifteen years ago."

"Do you know why he changed his name?" I asked.

She made a dismissive noise. "Probably trying to escape debts or scorned lovers. I don't actually know. But after the pass he made at my niece, I don't care what name he went by. He was serious bad news under any name."

"How old was your niece at the time? She must be my age, more or less?"

"She is." Mooncat's smile was a sad one. "She's a sweet young-minded woman and always will be. And I mean that literally, Cece. She has Down syndrome."

"Karl tried to take advantage of her? That's awful." And disgusting and unseemly and a whole string of negatives.

"Yeah, well. You better believe I straightened him out on that score, big-time."

I smiled to myself as I tied on an apron and set up a row of wineglasses. Mooncat could be a fierce champion. Her niece was lucky to have an aunt like that on her side.

"You should see what a brilliant reader she is," Mooncat continued. "A lot of people still think of Down syndrome as the old stereotype of someone stupid and incapable. But my brother's girl loves, loves, loves books. She especially reads mystery series, the ones on the gentler side. She, like, eats books. It's the best."

"You're right. I wouldn't have expected her to be an avid reader. Thank you for expanding the walls of my universe."

"Anytime, hon."

"Dane mentioned a guy named Charlie." I relayed Dane's experience in the training program. "I'm pretty sure that was Karl, especially since the Charlie and Karl you know were the same person."

"Poor thing. Dane would have made a crack electrician. And then painted cool pictures of wires and connections. I can imagine it, but I have zero skills in the fine arts area."

"I find that hard to believe. You've been an astrophysicist, grew organic veggies on a commune, you can crochet entire pieces of clothing, and you both belly dance and fly a private plane. Plus, you know your wines. Are you sure you can't paint?"

"Hundred percent positive. Believe me. My art looks worse than toddler finger painting."

"Okay, here's a question for you. I've been trying to find out how Wesley Holt came to acquire the Ridley Vineyards. He renamed it Holt and seems to be making a go of it. In fact, he and I are talking about us also pouring Holt wines." I swiped a rag along a part of the counter that didn't need it.

"But? And?" she asked.

"And I can't find any information on where he got the funds to buy the property and upgrade it enough to turn out drinkable wines. An angel investor, personal savings, an inheritance, all of it's possible. I can't seem to turn over the truth from whatever dark rock it's hiding under."

"I might have an idea or two." She glanced at the analog wall clock, which showed a skinny white wine bottle pointing at a vat of pressed grapes and the shorter red wine bottle aimed at a cluster of pale green grapes, which meant it was one o'clock. "Time to open. Let's talk more when we get a lull."

"Sounds good."

"And you can tell me who you think killed him." She headed over to shut off the music.

I unlocked the door and turned the sign to OPEN. "Deal."

# CHAPTER 55

The afternoon in Vino y Vida wasn't overly subscribed, maybe because the raw air of earlier had condensed into rain. Tasters who did come in wore rain jackets or sported wet hair. Still, Mooncat and I kept busy pouring and explaining and refilling both snacks and wine.

At about five thirty, Jo hurried in. *Good.* I'd called her earlier but she hadn't picked up. I left a text saying I'd love to talk with her if she got a chance.

She slipped out of her hooded jacket and shook it. She hung it on one of the hooks I provided in the short hall where the restrooms were and slid onto a barstool.

"Pretty bad out there?" I asked after greeting her.

"It's raining. What can you do?" She ran a hand through her short hair. "But it's not a deluge. Could be worse, and we always need rain. Sorry I didn't answer your call earlier. I was slammed with work."

"I figured as much. What would you like to drink?" I asked.

She surveyed the list on the whiteboard. "Whatever the heartiest red is. It's too cold for white wine."

I laughed. "Agree. This Russian River Valley pinot noir from Twomey isn't as big as some, but it should do the trick."

I did have electric heat in here for the few cool months of the year. We four business managers—the bookstore owner, the historical museum director, Henry, and me—had convinced the city to spring for solar panels. They were on the back side of the two adobes with newer shingled roofs. That way the panels didn't spoil the historic look of the cluster of buildings, and we all benefited.

I waited until Jo had tasted the wine before speaking. "Jo, I've been hearing about a time when Karl went by Charlie, possibly also with a different spelling of his last name. Did you know that?"

"Unfortunately, I did." She leaned closer across the bar. "That was one reason for our divorce. He had this whole identity thing from before I met him. He'd hidden it from me on purpose, Cece. That's not what a marriage, an intimate relationship, is supposed to be about."

"I couldn't agree with you more." I swiped at the redwood with a rag, even though it didn't need it. "My late husband kept some pretty heavy secrets from me. I wanted to divorce him, but he died before I could." Putting it that way implied I would have actually taken the steps to get free of him, which is something I hadn't done. Greg's had been a convenient death, for sure.

"Seriously?" She glanced around. "You weren't responsible for that death, I hope."

"Jo! Of course I wasn't."

"I'm kidding." She shrugged. "But they're still looking at me for Karl's, and we split up years ago."

"Do you know why he changed his name?" I might as well ask everyone I could.

"I found out he borrowed money to attend an electrician training program. Not from a bank, either."

"Who lent it to him? Family?"

"No. I'm not totally sure, but it seemed like some total bad guys. Who knew they had people like that in Sonoma? Anyway, when he bombed out on the repayment, he had to leave town in a hurry."

"Colinas isn't very far from Sonoma," I said.

"Yeah, well, Karl wasn't the liveliest wire in the circuit box. Apparently, neither were his creditors. The move and name change seemed to throw them off his trail."

"What do you know about his failed attempt to buy the winery?"

"The one that's now Holt?" She took a hearty sip of wine. "That also happened before I met him. I don't really know about that, Cece, sorry. It apparently was another one of his many secrets."

"Have you met Wesley Holt?"

"Nope."

"Their eyes are really similar," I said. "You know how Ian has those intense blue eyes that aren't that big?"

"He does. Exactly like Karl's." She grimaced. "Like Karl's were."

"Wesley's eyes are nearly identical."

Jo's own eyes widened. "And you think they were related?"

"Seems like they have to be. But I can't find out what the relationship was."

"I know exactly what you need." She whipped out her phone and began madly swiping and thumbing it.

A trio of customers signaled for my attention. "Be right back," I murmured.

She waved me away without glancing up.

It took me fifteen minutes to get back to her.

"You won't believe this, Cece," Jo said. "Holt was Karl's half brother."

I stared at her. "Seriously?"

She nodded, pointing at her phone on the bar.

"Did Karl know?" I asked.

"Not that he ever said. He never mentioned a brother, half or otherwise, while we were together. I thought his only sibling was the sister who died."

"Ian's mother?"

"Right." Jo tapped the phone. "This genealogy site pegs Karl and Wesley as having different fathers but the same mother."

"Thus the different last names."

"Exactly." She sipped her wine, which she seemed to have ignored while doing her search since it was still mostly full. "The thing is, if one of the two had seen the match, they probably sent the other one a message about it, which you can do through these sites."

"I wonder if Ian knows. Even if he doesn't, maybe Wesley got him the job at the winery."

"Could be," Jo said.

"Sounds like you're into all that DNA stuff."

"I've been digging around in my own family. It's kind of fun, although it's an infinitely deep rabbit hole once you fall in." She lifted a shoulder. "What else do I have to do in the evenings? Streaming shows and reading only go so far when you live by yourself."

I didn't have that problem, despite living alone. I was here working in Vino y Vida most evenings.

"If Wesley knew they were related, that gives him less of a reason to kill Karl, not more," Jo said.

"One would hope so. Killing your brother? That's too horrible to think about."

# CHAPTER 56

I locked the front door at nine thirty that night. My brain had been busy with the genealogical news, but Vino y Vida had been even busier with sippers. I hadn't had much of a chance to dwell on what Jo had told me.

"Mooncat," I began. "Jo discovered something interesting when she was in here."

"Dish, hon." She loaded her hands with dirty glasses from a couple of tables and brought them to the bar.

"It turns out Wesley Holt and Karl Meier are half brothers, or were."

She whistled. "That's pretty interesting. With different fathers?"

"Right. Jo found the information on a DNA site." I loaded the glasses into the dishwasher. "But she didn't think Karl knew about Wesley during the time she was married to Karl."

Mooncat grabbed a rag and headed to the nearest table to wipe it down. "Can you think of why those two being related would matter to the murder?"

"I'm thinking aloud here. Wesley seems to be doing pretty well with the winery and all. Maybe Karl began hitting him up for money because they were brothers."

"Was Karl in bad shape financially?"

"I don't know," I said. "Ian might."

"Karl was a bad businessman in several ways. I can't imagine his bottom line was thriving, no matter how good an electrician he was."

"Right." I polished the top of the bar, thinking.

She pointed at the door to the patio. "Nobody sat outside today, right? It was either too cold or too rainy."

"Right. You don't have to wipe down those tables. They'll be wet now anyway." I slowed my hand. "Some guys who work with Ian in the Holt fields came in yesterday. They told me Wesley has been taking a special interest in Ian since he was hired, but they didn't think Ian knew the boss before he began working there."

"Holt could have told Ian he was his uncle."

"Maybe he said he'd take care of Ian, which could have put the idea of getting rid of Karl in his head."

"Or they did it together." Mooncat gave a knowing look as she emptied the baskets of any remaining pretzels or crackers and began rinsing out the plastic shells we offered the munchies in.

"Also possible." I emptied the tips jar and handed the cash to Mooncat. Later I would calculate the total of any tips left on credit card purchases and add it to her paycheck.

"Thanks, but you don't have to do that. I wouldn't care if you'd rather plow it back into the business."

"No, you should have it. Listen, earlier you said you might have an idea about who might have invested in the Holt winery purchase and renovation. Can you elaborate on that?"

"I'm pretty sure it was Holt's honey, Tara Pulanski," Mooncat said. "She totally cleaned out her ex-husband, and he had considerable funds to clean out. Her family had money as well."

"My neighbor said it's well known in town that Tara and Wesley are a couple."

"He's correct. She's also his angel investor, as far as I know." She set her hands on her hips and gazed around the room. "I think we're done in here, yeah?"

"Pretty much. Do you want any of these partials to take home?" I gestured to the several bottles less than half full.

She leaned over and peered at the labels. "I'll take the petite syrah, thanks. It'll go perfect with my leftover peanut stew." She corked it and slid it into her very large handbag.

"You didn't ride your motorcycle today, I hope."

"Not in the rain, ever."

"Good," I said. Riding a motorcycle was dangerous enough. In the rain, amidst California drivers who weren't used to wet pavement, it could be fatal.

"Do you want a ride home?" she asked.

I thought for a moment. "You know what? I'd love one. I should have brought my car today, but instead I came on foot." The idea of walking home in the dark with at least one murderer at large was a distinctly bad one. "Give me a minute to deal with these." I picked up the rest of the partials.

"I'll start the dishwasher and turn off the lights out here."

In the back, I preserved the wine in the bottles that were more than half full, then slipped on my coat and looped my bag across my chest. Mooncat came through and we made our way out. I checked the back door twice to ensure it was closed and locked. The rain had stopped but the air was chilly, as befit the season.

Mooncat tucked the bottle of wine into a plastic storage bin secured to the bed of her older-model Toyota truck. "Can't have an open bottle in the cab."

I slid onto the bench seat. My door creaked mightily as I pulled it shut. Mooncat's did the same.

"Sorry about the noise. There isn't enough oil in the world to quiet those hinges." She patted the dashboard. "This truck's an old girl, but she's reliable and I love her."

"I hear you. I hope I never have to trade in Blue for something modern."

"Totally."

She'd driven me home before, so I didn't have to give her directions. I thought about unmuting my phone to catch up on whatever had been going on while I was working. It stayed in my bag. I could do that at home.

We turned onto Rivera, the street where I lived most of the way down at the other end. Even from here I could see blue police lights strobing.

"I hope Richard is okay," I said.

"He's a great guy. I'm with you on hoping he's all right."

"Yes." I pulled out my phone. Had he written asking for my help and I hadn't responded? My breath rushed in. He'd written—but not to ask for help. I muttered a choice swear word.

"Whoa." Mooncat pointed as we drew close. "That cruiser's in your driveway, Cece."

"Richard texted that somebody tried to break into my garage."

"Seriously?" She glanced over.

I nodded.

"That's awful." She pulled up in front of my house. "Probably to steal Blue."

Or worse.

# CHAPTER 57

A spotlight from the cruiser parked in the driveway lit up the garage door as if it was a stage set. An officer squatted in front of the door, inspecting it. Lee Norsegian stood guard at the end of the driveway. The cruiser with the strobing lights was parked crosswise on the road.

Richard, wearing his wool cap and wrapped in a heavy sweater, stood conferring with Chief Fenner. I hurried up to them.

"Richard, are you all right?" I asked, breathless with worry.

"I'm glad you're here, Cece," he said. "Yes, I am fine, thank you."

"I'm glad. My phone was on mute at work. I saw your message only now as I was coming home." I turned to Fenner. "Chief?"

"Mr. Flora noticed suspicious movement from his side window."

"I most certainly did," Richard said.

"You didn't go outside, I hope." I gazed at him.

"Good heavens, no, dear." He chuckled. "I have more sense than that. No, I got on the horn with Colinas's finest. They arrived remarkably fast. I didn't leave the safety of my home until they were in full force here."

*Whew.* Mooncat joined me. She nodded at Chief Fenner and Richard but stayed quiet, a tall presence lending me her support.

"What did you see, Richard?" I asked.

"Someone in a dark hooded sweatshirt or jacket appeared to be trying to force open your garage door. It was a fairly tall figure.

Not Chief Fenner's height, but taller than you, Cece. The person didn't have an overly bulky profile, either."

That could describe Ian, Wesley, or Gareth. Or Tara Pulanski, for that matter, but thankfully not Jo. She was a couple of inches shorter than me.

"Very observant, sir," Fenner said.

Richard gave him a slightly pitying smile. "I wouldn't have been much of a journalist if I didn't notice details, would I?"

Fenner made a noise in his throat. "Do you happen to have a front door cam, Ms. Barton?"

"No. I might rethink that after tonight."

"I would advise it," the chief said. "I do commend you for your garage security."

"It's a garden-variety remote opener. I'm glad it held tight to-night." I watched the officer still inspecting the door, now joined by another. "Did the person have a tool to force open the door?"

"We'll let you know if we find marks and what they indicate." Fenner focused on Richard. "Please repeat what you saw after you called in the intruder."

"The scoundrel kept at the door until the sirens started up. He or she glanced around as if alarmed, then took off down the street away from here." He pointed in the direction Mooncat and I had arrived from. "I'm afraid it was too dark to tell if a vehicle was parked nearby or if the person continued on foot."

"You said 'he or she.' You couldn't tell if it was a man or a woman?" Mooncat's tone as she questioned Richard was curious, not accusing.

"No, Martha."

So Richard was a member of the small circle who had known Mooncat forever, since before she'd changed her name, one of the few she allowed to still call her Martha. Of course he was. Richard knew everyone in town.

"The figure might have been a male, but it could have been a woman as tall as yourself," Richard continued.

Like Tara, who was at least five foot ten.

"And you are, ma'am?" Fenner asked Mooncat.

"Mooncat Smith. I work for Cece."

"She gave me a ride home," I told him, surprised he didn't **know her.**

"I see." Fenner pursed his lips. "What kind of vehicle do you keep in your garage, Ms. Barton? Do you own a car?"

"I do, a 1966 convertible Mustang. It's in good shape and runs like a charm, thanks to Jo Jarvin."

"Is it valuable?" Fenner asked.

"To me it is," I said. "I doubt it's worth more than a few thousand dollars on the open market. But I would think the only purpose in forcing open my garage would be to gain access to my house."

"I agree," Richard said. "I imagine whoever was trying to get into Cece's property wasn't doing it to make off with her vintage automobile. Or if they were, it was to hurt her, not to make money from selling it."

"Sir?" One of the officers in the spotlight motioned to Fenner.

"Thank you, Mr. Flora," the chief began. "We have your contact information. You may retire to your home, as may you, Ms. Barton. We'll be on-site for another few hours. Officer Norsegian will contact you tomorrow after we are finished with the scene."

"Thanks."

"We'll have someone patrol the street every hour, so you'll have a police presence," he added.

"I appreciate that."

I didn't care if the garage was off-limits until late morning. I didn't need my car until it was time to go to work. There would be no more walking home in the dark for me, at least not while this case was active. Somebody wanted to get to me, which gave me an uneasy feeling in the extreme.

# CHAPTER 58

I tried to get comfortable on my couch. Fleece throw across my lap, check. One cat on the back of the couch and one next to me, check. A plate of cheese and grapes to nibble on, check. My favorite cognac in a small snifter and an entertaining novel about three generations of women on a wacky road trip to Graceland, check.

But the bright police lights intruding through my front windows jarred the cozy scene. Figures of officers and their shadows moved about, doing all the police things.

I was more than grateful the intruder had failed to break in. Except if it was someone connected with Karl's murder, that meant they knew my address, which was bad. It also meant they thought I knew they might have committed the crime, or I was at least getting close, which was also bad.

These thoughts weren't remotely relaxing. With any luck, all the police presence would keep bad guys away from my home, my sanctuary, until tomorrow. But I had to figure out what else I could do to ensure said bad guy was arrested and put away for a long time ASAP.

Ian. Wesley. Tara. Gareth. I ticked the persons of interest off on my fingers and then remembered Dane. I'd kind of forgotten about her. Did she fit the tallish, not bulky profile Richard had

230 / MADDIE DAY

described? Maybe. I didn't think she was much taller than me, but Richard admitted he hadn't gotten a close look at the person because he'd wisely stayed indoors and safe.

I had all tomorrow morning to do some sleuthing. It was the where and why I wasn't sure of. I sipped. I stroked Mittens's long, silky fur, which produced a satisfied purring. I gazed at the moving shadows and heard the muted voices outside.

*Huh.* I wondered if Karl's home was a possibility for a place to check out. Gareth was too interested in it. Ian lived there, according to Jo. The killer must have picked Karl up at his house and driven him to Jo's garage. Maybe I could poke around the property and find a clue the authorities had missed.

Every good amateur sleuth—something I seemed to have become—had a sidekick, and mine had a plausible reason to check out a property that might be coming on the market soon. I texted Allie, not sure if she'd still be up and willing to talk on the phone.

**Want to do some sleuthing together in the morning?**

**Yaass! Pick you up at 9?**

**Perfect. Thx. Sweet dreams.**

All right. Maybe now I could relax. I nibbled and sipped and let the delightful book take me out of my nerve-wracking world for a little while. My heart rate returned to normal. The tension in my face and shoulders slid away.

I slipped into bed an hour later with heavy limbs and multiple yawns. I couldn't see the police lights from the back of the house, although I knew they continued out front. I plugged my phone in to charge and was about to switch off the bedside lamp when the phone rang.

Eleven o'clock was too late for anybody I knew to call, but it might be Allie with an emergency. Or Benjamin.

I peered at the number. Not Allie. Not someone in my contacts list. I almost muted the ringer, but instead I connected with trepidation. I didn't speak, hoping it was nothing more than a random robocall trying to sell me a timeshare or trick me into revealing personal information.

"Lay off your snooping, Barton," a muffled voice said. "We're watching you." The call disconnected without as much as a click.

My heart pounded. I couldn't tell if it had been a man's or a woman's voice. I sat up. I had to let the police know about this. Throw on a robe and go outside to tell those guys? Call Fenner? No. The garage attacker could have been anyone, but this call had to be related to Karl's death.

I copied the unfamiliar number and texted Quan.

**Got a threatening call from unfamiliar number a minute ago. Muffled voice told me by name to lay off my snooping, then hung up. Did you hear about attempted break-in on my garage? CPD are here. Here's the caller's number.**

I added the number and sent the message. I waited, but he didn't write back immediately. For all I knew, the guy had the evening off and was relaxing watching the news or a movie. He could be busy reading or sleeping or consoling a child after a nightmare. I knew nothing about his personal life except his alter-ego as a rock bassist.

As for me, I was no longer relaxed and ready to sleep, but I knew I should try. An ill-intentioned person out there had my cell number and was very likely the same scoundrel, as Richard put it, who tried to get inside my home.

The urgency to solve this had notched up a thousand percent.

# CHAPTER 59

"You don't look that great, Cee," Allie said the next morning after I climbed into her car.

"Why, thank you, and how are you today, dear sister?" I couldn't hold back the snark. I knew my lack of sleep showed. I'd showered and done my best to get presentable for our excursion and for the rest of the day, but still.

"Sorry. You know I love you, sis, and you know what I mean." She put the car in gear, or whatever it's called in an electric vehicle, and pulled away. "But first, where to?"

"I thought we could poke around Karl's house. Maybe we can learn something." I sketched out my thoughts from last night about the possibilities. The rain had moved through and today was a crisp winter's day, all the better.

"Ooh, I like how you think," she said. "Now, tell me what's going on."

"I know I'm a wreck, but I barely slept." I let out a deep breath. "Two things happened last night." I told her about the break-in attempt.

"What?" She turned to stare at me. "You should have called me."

"Watch where you're going," I urged, as the car in front of us slowed for a stop sign.

She faced front. "I wish you'd called."

"I texted you, okay? Al, I really didn't want to go into it. I was trying to relax after it happened. It was pretty shocking to come home to a swarm of blue uniforms and bright lights aimed at my garage door. But the police had everything under control, and I was safe. There was nothing either of us could have done last night."

"True. I guess."

"But then I got this phone call. I had just gone to bed." I relayed what the voice had said.

"Yikes."

"Exactly. And yes, I immediately let the detective know." My sleeplessness had been from worry that another call would come in, plus half waiting for Quan to get back to me. The muted sounds of the police moving around out front didn't help. Whatever the cause, I tossed back and forth trying to get comfortable until my sheets were scrambled. When I did sleep, the dreams were vivid and scary and seemed way too real.

"What did Quan say?" she asked.

"He never got back to me. Not this morning, either. Come to think of it, I told him I had a wineglass with Wesley's DNA on it, and he didn't respond about that, either." I'd been busy getting my day underway and hadn't reflected on his lack of response. Yesterday morning I'd moved the envelope with Ian's cigarette butt on it out of my coat pocket, but now realized I'd never told Quan about it. "Maybe he has the day off."

"While a homicide remains unsolved?" She frowned. "That doesn't sound right, unless they assigned someone else to cover for him, which would be nice to know."

"Right. I'd better let Chief Fenner know about the call." I found the number for the police station and asked to speak to Chief Fenner.

"He's unavailable," the person said. "Would you like to leave a message, ma'am, or shall I put you through to his voice mail?"

"Voice mail, I guess. Thank you." I found the caller's number and copied it, then left the same message I had for Quan last night. I added, "I let Detective Quan know right after the call last night but haven't heard back from him." I included my number and disconnected.

"Good," Allie said. "I hope he gets right on it."

"You and me both. Getting that call was part of the reason I slept badly."

"You were afraid they would call back."

"I was, or that someone would try to get into my house again, despite the cops keeping a close eye on the house. I still don't know if whoever called was the person who tried to break into the garage or if that was unrelated to the homicide."

"Like a kid or a burglar," she said.

"Yes." We were passing through the outskirts of town now, and I spied a FOR SALE sign from Allie's agency on a house. I turned to gaze at her. "Hey, Al. Today is Thursday. Don't ou have your meet-and-greet thing this morning?"

"Yes, but I got one of the other agents to run it. It's fine."

That weekly open house was important to her, and she'd come with me instead. "Thank you, sis."

"What's your plan when we get to the house?" she asked.

"Ugh. It's underformulated." I picked a piece of lint off the knee of my jeans. "Maybe we'll find a clue somewhere around the house. Like something the murderer dropped when they picked up Karl, or another piece of evidence."

"WWNDD?" She shot me a wicked glance.

"I have no idea what you're talking about."

"What Would Nancy Drew Do?" Allie gave a little snort. "But seriously, she was always looking for clues. Like Sherlock Holmes."

"And Kinsey Millhone and Gamache."

"Let's not forget Miss Marple and Poirot."

"Or Vera," I added.

"Did you bring a magnifying glass?"

"I did not." The road now wended through vineyards, the long lines of bare vines scraggly but full of promise. I gazed into the side mirror. "Al, that black truck has been behind us for a while. Do you think it's following us?"

She took a look in the rearview mirror. "This is a two-lane road. They kind of have to follow us. Anyway, we'll be turning off in a mile. I'd pull over and let them pass, but the shoulder along here looks too squishy from the rain."

"I'm probably still freaked out by my experience driving home from Ed and Henry's."

"What experience?" Her voice rose. "When was it? Cee, are you making a habit of not telling me bad things that happen to you?"

"Didn't I tell you?" I thought back. "Maybe not. I'm sorry. So much has happened this week. I was tailgated by some speed maniac, but it turned out to be nothing. They finally passed me. I was fine. End of story."

Allie glanced in the rearview mirror again. "That dude is end of story, too. He—she, they, it, whatever—turned off. We're good."

My shoulders relaxed as I let out a noisy exhale. "That's a relief."

When a text dinged, I clutched my phone. It could be from Zoe, my mom, or Benjamin, or it might be from Mooncat with an emergency I needed to know about. It ended up being a trivial thing from one of my suppliers. I sniffed and glanced up. The small valley we'd entered was filled with smoke.

"Allie, is that a wildfire? I haven't heard of one. We should turn around." My voice held an urgency bordering on panic. "If it's fast moving, we could get trapped on the road."

"Calm down, sis. While you were being Text Queen, we passed a big orange sign telling us they're doing a controlled burn today. They were quite clear that people are not to report the fire."

"Seriously?"

"Yes, seriously."

*Whew.*

After another minute or two, Allie swung right. As the black truck had done, she pulled the car onto a smaller road. We ascended several hills with houses dotting both sides of the road, which was beginning to curve like the one leading to Ed and Henry's home.

After we crested the hill, she pulled over at a slightly wider spot in the road and pointed.

"That's the place."

The ranch house was nestled under several large trees and had an attached garage on the right side.

She twisted to look at me. "Do you think Ian will be home?"

"I doubt it. Ed told me Ian moved out to live with friends, but Jo thought he was still here. Whether he has a key or not, he should be at work in the Holt vineyards, especially with this clear weather." I freed my seat belt. "Shall we?" I swallowed, knowing I sounded calmer than I felt.

My fear of failure rose up once again. Surely Quan and his team had gone over the property. How could we find what they hadn't? What if the black truck figured out where we were going and sped here by a different back road? Allie and I might not make it out alive.

*No.* I'd made it through dangerous situations before. I wouldn't let my former fear destroy my resolve now.

# CHAPTER 60

I slid my phone into the pocket of my purple coat and climbed out. Allie got out and locked the car.

Here up on the hill the wind blew strong and cold. It shushed through the leaves, both dry and green, on the scrub oaks, black oaks, and olive trees, and rattled the branches of cedars and the terribly fire-prone eucalyptus.

"I'll check the front door area," I said. "Do you want to inspect around the garage?"

"I'm on it, but I'm still not clear about what I'm looking for."

"Anything that doesn't belong there? I don't really know. Maybe something the person dropped, the dude who convinced Karl to leave here in the middle of the night."

"Dude or woman, you mean," Allie said.

"Yes." Was coming here a stupid, illogical move on my part? We probably wouldn't find anything. I gave my head a shake and again scolded my defeatist self. What was the harm in our excursion? My twin and I had gone for a drive, and we'd be back. "Plus, you've been here before, right?"

"Yes, but I didn't go over it with a fine-toothed comb."

"That doesn't matter. You might notice if something is different."

"True. Okay." She angled for the garage.

I made my way to the start of a flagstone path that led to the front door. The yard was unkempt, littered with unraked leaves and fallen branches. Moss grew between the stones but not in that landscaped way that made it look planted on purpose. The paint on the siding was a faded green, with a few cracked clapboards near the foundation, and the windows bore a dirty film.

Karl's property might be worth a lot of bucks to someone like Gareth, but it didn't look like much from this vantage point.

I moved slowly down the walk and focused on the ground. I got excited when something white barely showed under a leaf, but when I picked it up, it was only the torn corner of an envelope with nothing written on it.

A movement caught my attention. I glanced up at the house. Had a curtain stirred behind one of those dirty windows? I'd better go to the door and make sure nobody was home. Ian could have taken the day off from his vineyard work or not be feeling well.

I pressed the doorbell, hearing a jarring buzz from within as if the chime was broken. After a minute of no one appearing, I knocked a few times, despite a case of the nerves that made my knock weaker than I intended.

Silence and a still-closed door were the results. Allie and I seemed to be alone on the property. I swallowed and got to work, searching all around the door. I knelt on the stoop and felt the sides and into the crevices. Standing, I turned to gaze down the path the way I came, in case a change of perspective helped. I made my way back toward the street, one step at a time, searching for an unknown object.

My efforts yielded exactly nothing. *Oh, well.* I glanced at the garage. Allie had disappeared around the far corner. I could meet her at the back. I began to sweep my eyes back and forth on the ground as I skirted the periphery of the house.

I crunched over leaves and nearly turned my ankle on a pile of oblong acorns. Staring at the ground as I walked turned out to be a bad idea. A low-hanging branch swiped through my hair and caught on my hair clip, jerking me back. I extricated myself, then stooped to pick up a fallen branch the size of a baseball bat so I wouldn't trip over it.

I was about to round the corner to the rear of the house when Allie called to me.

"Cece, come see." Her voice sounded like it came from the back.

"Coming."

Had her voice sounded quavery? I flashed back to Friday morning. Jo sounded shaky when she telephoned and asked me to come over. I hoped Allie hadn't come across something as awful as a corpse. I stopped searching the ground and hurried on.

A head-high wooden deck as run-down as the rest of the house stuck out from the back side of the ranch. The view of the valley spreading out in front of me was stunning. This property had a lot of potential, and I could understand why Gareth wanted it. I only hoped he hadn't murdered Karl to get it.

Where was my sister?

"Al?" I called, making my way around the deck and the steps leading down from it. Maybe she was headed back to the front looking for me.

I stepped past the corner of the deck, my eyes on the garage ahead. At a muffled sound from my right, I whipped my head that way. My breath rushed in with a rasping sound.

Wesley Holt had Allie's hands tied behind her with what looked like narrow dark green tape. He gripped her right upper arm with his left hand, on which a curved blade like a mini-sickle stuck up from a thick band on his ring finger. His eyes glittering, he held an open pair of red-handled pruners in his meaty right hand with the razor-sharp blades at her neck.

Her eyes were wide with terror.

# CHAPTER 61

"Wesley, what are you doing?" I asked, my voice both urgent and shaky. I took a step toward them, my heart racing as fast as my mind.

"Stay where you are," he growled.

"Lower those pruners, would you please?" How was I going to get him away from her? I couldn't let him hurt my Allie.

"No. You wouldn't back off, and now your twinnie here is going to pay for it. Nobody's getting in the way of my dream."

"Is that what your half brother was doing, interfering with your ambitions?" I still gripped the limb I'd picked up, and my phone was in the right pocket of my coat. I needed both weapons while desperately trying to keep him from hurting her. But I'd have to drop one to use the other.

"How'd you know about that?" he asked.

"Your relationship with Karl isn't a secret anymore," I said. "You killed him because he wanted part of your business, right?"

He stared at me. "None of it is any of your concern." He brought the gaping maw of the pruners closer to Allie's pale skin, exactly where her pulse beat visibly.

*No!*

"I mean, I don't blame you." I swore silently. Accusing him of the murder had been a strategic error. Could I course-correct? I swallowed and tried to keep my voice casual. "What is your dream?"

"You've seen my vineyard." He puffed up in pride. "Our pinot has already won awards."

Did his grip on the pruners loosen ever so slightly? I hoped it had.

"I'm already making a success of it," he went on. "I've started young Ian's training. I plan to pass the business along to him."

As he spoke, I slid my right hand casually into my coat pocket and felt my phone. I knew I had an emergency button on it, but I'd never tried it and had no idea if it made noise or not. I couldn't risk angering Wesley, not with Allie's life on the line. I swore, but only in my head.

"You have a lovely tasting room out there," I said, as if talking about his winery facility at a time like this was totally normal. "The wines are both well balanced and well made. The business will be a nice inheritance for Ian."

Wesley puffed up a little more. I would do whatever it took to take his attention away from his anger and his weapon on Allie's neck.

"I have years of experience as a viticulturalist," he boasted.

"You're quite accomplished." I felt nauseated at having to compliment a man who clearly had murdered once and wouldn't stop at doing it again. If stroking his ego kept my twin alive, I'd do it all day—or at least until he let his guard down further. "I bet you're great at training your workers."

I wondered how he figured he would get away with this attack. He must not have thought things through. I could run around to the front and call the police. He'd be caught in a few minutes. Unless . . . I swallowed. He might have a gun in his pocket. He could shoot me in the back. I'd be dead, and I would have failed at saving my twin. I was sure he was betting on my highest priority being keeping Allie safe. He was right.

As I gazed at her, Allie's expression changed in the subtlest of ways. Her face conveyed less alarm and fear and more a message. What was she trying to tell me?

Wesley had his back to the garage at the end of the house. Allie faced it, and I kind of did. Without turning my head, I spied the movement she must have been alerting me to.

A man in a dark watch cap stood at the back corner, staring at us. The cap made him look different, but I was sure that was Gareth. Was he friend or foe? He pointed at Allie, made the thumb-and-pinkie phone gesture, and disappeared again. That had to be friendly. I hoped.

"What's going on?" Wesley's tone changed back to arctic. He whipped his head around toward the garage, but there was nothing to see.

I gave Allie a nod. She twisted away from his hold, ducking and pivoting to her right.

"Hey!" Wesley yelled in a rage.

I stepped forward, tightening my core. With both hands, I swung the thick branch sharply up against his elbow, which made the pruners fly out of his hand. He cried out in pain. I leaned to my right, then batted a home run against the side of his head. Wesley crumpled to the ground.

I squatted in front of my sister, this person I had known since before forever. "Al, you okay?"

She had pushed up to sitting, her back against the latticework under the deck. "Yes." A roll of the tape that had secured her hands lay on the ground nearby.

Gareth ran up. "I called the police. They're on their way."

"Awesome. Grab those pruners." I stood and pointed. "Help Allie up and cut her hands loose. Make sure you give this jerk a wide berth." I picked up the tape.

He hurried to comply, skirting Wesley's hands and feet as much as he could.

I peered at Wesley. Was he faking being unconscious? He could try to kick out or launch another attack. That sharp ring attachment could be lethal. I glanced at the deck. After Allie was standing and rubbing her wrists, I held out my hand for the pruners.

"Bring down the heaviest chair off the deck, Gareth. I'll let you have the job of sitting on a murderer."

His eyes widened and he swallowed, but he trotted up the steps and back down, carrying a wooden chair with a slanted back. He positioned it over Wesley and sat forward in the seat, pressing his feet firmly on the bad guy's torso.

"Gareth weighs more than either of us, but here's some insurance." I unwound a few lengths of the flexible non-sticky tape. I wrapped it around Holt's ankles several times, then cut the tape with the pruners. I tied a tight double knot, then sidled up to Allie and slid my arm around her shoulders.

She curled her arm around my waist and leaned her head on my shoulder. She might be six minutes older, but I'd been taller since we turned fourteen.

"You saved my life, Cee," she murmured.

"Hey, it was a team effort." I squeezed her arm. "Gareth, how did you know to show up?"

He had the decency to look chagrined. "You don't want to know. But when I saw what was going down, I knew what I had to do."

The undulating of sirens were faint in the distance. They grew louder and louder every second.

"We're glad you did," I said.

"Thank you, Gareth," Allie said. "After this is all over, let's talk real estate. Sustainable, kind, positive real estate. I could mentor you, if you're interested."

"Would you?" His voice rose, but it was tentative.

"For someone who helped save my life? Always." She sounded shaky despite managing a smile.

I kept my eye on the guy now starting to moan and stir. I hadn't killed him. *Thank goodness.* I was feeling shaky too, but I needed to make sure Wesley Holt never hurt anyone again.

# CHAPTER 62

The police still hadn't arrived when the sliding glass door on the deck shooshed open.

"Wes, where are you?" Tara stepped out. "We're late for—" She broke off, staring down at us, and gaped.

*Great.* This was precisely what we didn't need. If she was Wesley's partner in crime, she might be the one with the gun. I once again girded myself. This was no time to be wobbly.

"Tara?" Allie asked. "Why are you here?"

I thought I might know the answer to that question, but I kept it to myself.

"What's happened?" Tara cried. "What in heaven's name have you done to my Wes?" She ran down the steps and knelt at his side. "Wes, sweetie, wake up. It's Tarrie, your sweet baboo." She touched his cheek, then patted it.

Her "sweetie" didn't respond, but his chest moved with his breath.

She glared up at Gareth. "Get off him, you monster. Don't you know he has a heart condition?"

Gareth checked with me. I shook my head.

"Ma'am, he tried to kill Ms. Halstead," he told Tara. "I'm staying put."

"The police are on their way, Tara," I said.

"The police?" Her voice rose into a shriek.

"I'm sure they'll have EMTs following shortly," I said. "Wesley's not dead."

"But you can't . . . they can't . . ." She glanced around like a rat caught in a trap.

The sirens blared closer, louder. Tara jumped up and started to run toward the garage. I tightened my abs and stuck out my foot, managing to hook it under her ankle. She crashed to the ground with a cry. The sirens went silent.

"Sorry," I said. *Not sorry.* "The police are going to want to speak with you. And, look. Here they are."

Lee Norsegian and another Colinas PD officer rounded the deck. Two county deputy sheriffs appeared from the far side of the garage, with Detective Quan right behind them. All wore thick vests and had weapons drawn except Quan, who strode toward us.

Tara pushed up to sitting with a groan, resting her head on her arms atop her bent knees.

"Lee or somebody, make sure this one doesn't try to get away, okay?" I asked.

"Yes, ma'am." Lee stood over Tara, at the ready in case she pulled a move.

"Cece, are you and your sister unharmed?" Quan asked.

"We're fine, as is Gareth. I'm pretty sure Tara Pulanski was in on whatever Wesley did."

Quan gave a single nod.

"Wesley had his pruners open on Allie's neck," I continued. When Allie shuddered, I draped my arm over her shoulder and squeezed her in close to me. "Gareth used the pruners to cut Allie loose. His prints will also be on the handles." Maybe that hadn't been the best choice of a cutting object, but I'd wanted her hands freed. I pointed to where I'd laid the pruners on the edge of the deck.

"Very well," the detective said.

"Be careful with Wesley's hand," I cautioned Quan. "He's wearing a ring with a sharp blade on it."

"Thank you."

"His elbow might be hurt, and I whacked him pretty hard on his head with . . ." I glanced around, then gestured with my chin. "With that thick branch."

"Which you happened to have in your hand?" he asked.

"Actually, yes. I . . . never mind." Now was not the time to explain.

"Did you also happen to whack her?" Quan asked, pointing to Tara.

"I didn't."

"But Cece tripped Tara as she was trying to run away," Allie said with pride in her voice.

The detective smiled a little.

"Tara said Wesley has a heart condition, but I'm not sure if she was telling the truth," I added.

"I was," Tara insisted, but her voice was listless, as if she knew no one would believe her.

"Got it." He shook his head, addressing me. "We were very close to apprehending Mr. Holt and Ms. Pulanski. I'm not sure why you thought coming out here was a good idea, but what's done is done. You and Allie can wait on the deck, if you don't mind. Mr. Rockwell, please join them. I'll need detailed reports from all of you."

Two EMTs jogged up carrying their big red bags. Quan turned aside to speak with them. I helped Allie up the stairs, and Gareth joined us. Allie sat but began to shiver.

Gareth looked at her. "Hey, that's no good." He shrugged out of his wool coat and draped it over her. "It's your adrenaline wearing off."

"Thank you." She shot him a grateful smile.

I shivered a bit, as well, but leaned my elbows on the deck railing and watched as Wesley, now fully awake and struggling to get away, was checked out by the EMTs.

"I'm fine," he snarled. "You can't do this to me."

They loaded him onto a wheeled stretcher, strapping down his hands and arms.

"Wesley Holt," Quan began. "You are under arrest for the murder of Karl Meier." He listed a few more charges and went through the right to remain silent.

The accused didn't seem to hear that part. "Charlie was going to ruin my life." Wes's glance shifted to Tara. "Our lives. He was demanding part of my profits, just because we had the same mother. A mother who deserted me, by the way." The corners of his mouth turned down, as if even the thought of his mother pained him.

"So you killed him." Quan crossed his arms and looked at Wesley over the top of his glasses.

"You better believe it. He had it coming to him." Wesley caught sight of me and cursed me up and down. "You're nothing but a fraud, Cece Barton," he spit out. "Should have kept your nose to yourself."

"That's enough of that," a CPD officer said. "Let's get him out of here." He strode by the side of the stretcher as they wheeled Wesley away.

"I want to go with him," Tara wailed. "We're a pair."

"You'll be going with him, ma'am," Quan said. "No worries about that. I assume you know what the words 'aid and abet' mean?"

She swore under her breath but didn't answer.

Paul Fenner appeared from near the garage and made his way toward us. "Nice job, Quan." He held out his hand.

*Wow.* The chief was complimenting the man he'd seemed to regard as a competitor. I liked the look.

Instead of shaking hands, Quan cleared his throat and gestured toward the deck. "It was those three, as a matter of fact, who secured both criminals. Cece and her little gang were unauthorized but ultimately effective."

I smiled and waggled my fingers at the chief.

"Why am I not surprised?" Fenner turned his smile on me.

# CHAPTER 63

Ten minutes later Tara had also been taken away. Both Quan and Fenner had joined us on the deck while a crime scene team worked on the ground where Wesley had attacked Allie.

"Let me begin by saying I'm glad you three ended up alive and unharmed." The detective cleared his throat. "That said, I would appreciate an explanation from each of you about what you hoped to accomplish here."

Fenner nodded. He looked relaxed in the deck chair, his long legs stretched out in front of him, but Quan stayed on his feet.

"Let's begin with you, Mr. Rockwell." Quan gestured toward Gareth.

Gareth's eyebrows gathered in the center as he scrubbed a hand over his face. "I've been working for my uncle in the family business."

Quan raised an eyebrow.

"Real estate development," Gareth continued. "They own a share in this property. My uncle wanted me to come over and check it out. See if there was a way we could reduce the value before it sold."

"You mean sabotage the place to get a cheaper price." Chief Fenner didn't look surprised.

"Yes. Believe me, I was a reluctant player." Gareth blew out a breath and squared his shoulders. "As of this morning, I plan to cut my ties with them and their unscrupulous practices."

Allie gave him an encouraging smile.

Could he pull off separating from his family's borderline illicit enterprise? I hoped so.

"I'd recommend that course of action." Quan turned his focus on Allie and me. Mostly me. "What about you two?"

Allie rightly pointed at me.

"I know our excursion out here was ill-advised." I flipped open my hands. "I hoped to find some clue or bit of evidence you all might have overlooked. I dragged my sister along with me."

"Did you uncover anything of the sort?" Fenner asked, his tone mild and curious, not accusatory.

"Only a murderer and his accomplice." Allie came to my defense. "She didn't drag me here. I wanted to help."

I shot her a grateful look. A gust of the chilly breeze rattled dry leaves. A murder of a half dozen noisy crows flew in, landing on the branches of an old oak in the yard. Gareth, who stood leaning against the deck railing, snugged his scarf around his neck and tucked his hands in his pockets, apparently trying not to shiver. Allie still wore his coat. I rose.

"It's cold. Are you done with us?" I asked Quan.

The sliding door to the house opened. "What are you all doing here?" Ian asked. "What's going on?"

"Ah, Mr. Meier," Quan said. "Glad you could join us."

"What?" Ian didn't look a bit glad. "This isn't a freaking tea party. I get a text at work telling me to get over to my uncle's house, and I pass a quiet ambulance and a cruiser going the other way. Like I said, what's going on?"

"Are you currently living in this house?" Fenner asked.

"Pretty much." Ian pulled his mouth to one side. "It, like, didn't work out with my buddies, and I moved back before Uncle Karl died."

"Did anyone else have a key to the house?" Quan asked.

"I don't know. It doesn't matter, though. We never . . ." His face fell as his voice trailed off. "I mean, I don't lock it."

"Would Wesley Holt have any reason to be here?"

Ian gaped. "What? Why?" He shook his head, hard. "No. No, he wouldn't."

"You work for him, is that correct?" Quan gazed at him.

"Yes," Ian said. "But he had no business here."

"Were you aware of a family connection between Mr. Holt and your uncle Karl?"

Ian's shoulders slumped. "That's what Holt claimed. He said he wanted to take care of me, to be my new uncle."

"And?" Quan asked.

"I told him it was the first I'd heard of it." Ian straightened his spine. "I said he was my employer, and that was all. Uncle Karl had some issues, but he was good to me. I didn't need another one butting into my life like some savior." He gazed down at the team collecting evidence from where Allie had been attacked. "Hey, dude, hold up that tape."

The officer raised the flat roll of half-inch green tape.

"Detective? We use that tie-tape on Holt's vines." Ian looked at Fenner and back at Quan. "What's it doing here? Tell me what happened."

When neither the chief nor the detective spoke, I jumped in. Ian deserved to know.

"Wesley Holt attacked Allie," I began.

Allie held out her wrists. "He tied my hands with the vineyard tape."

Ian sucked in a breath.

"Holt threatened her life and mine," I went on. "We managed to overpower him and his friend Tara Pulanski. Gareth called the police." I pointed my chin at Gareth. "Wesley and Tara were in the ambulance and the police car you saw driving up here. It seems clear that they killed Karl."

Ian's eyes went wide with horror. "Holt murdered his half brother?"

"Looks like it," I murmured. "Now can we leave, Detective?"

"Yes. I'll be in touch." Quan cleared his throat. "For future reference, we prefer to ask questions of and reveal information to persons related to a case in our own way and on our own time."

"I hear you. Did you get my messages yesterday, by the way?"

"Yes. I appreciate you collecting DNA for us, but it wouldn't be admissible in a trial. We believe it was Ms. Pulanski who both made that call to you and attempted to enter your home through the garage."

I shivered. "Come on, Al. Give Gareth his coat and let's get out of here." I faced Quan. "Say, Jimmy, when's your next gig with the Queue Tips?"

His jaw dropped. Gareth and Ian stared at him. Fenner gave a satisfied nod.

I tucked my arm through Allie's, and we trotted down the deck stairs.

"What was that about a gig?" she whispered after we were around the corner of the house.

"Tell ya later."

# CHAPTER 64

The morning's tumultuous excursion notwithstanding, I still had a wine bar to run. I filled in Mooncat on the events of the morning as we prepared. We opened on time at one o'clock.

Now at five thirty, I sat in the back room for a minute, savoring a takeout container of sushi I'd grabbed from my favorite Japanese restaurant.

I thought as I ate. About twins, for starters. Allie and I were so close. I couldn't imagine what Zara must be feeling today, assuming she'd heard about Tara's arrest. Had she had an inkling that her wombmate was capable of abetting a murderer? The sisters seemed reasonably close when they came into Vino y Vida that first time. Maybe their twin connection was weak or had been damaged.

Or . . . I set down my chopsticks. What if they had a tight bond and Zara was also involved in killing Karl or at least covering up the murder? I shivered involuntarily, then shook it off. Investigating her was Quan's domain, not mine. He'd probably already established the facts about Zara.

I resumed eating, popping in a bite of tuna *norimaki*. I was more than glad Ian was innocent. That young man had been through enough. He would inherit Karl's house and property and at least have a place to live, if not an electrician business to take over. Maybe Gareth could help him get free of the share owned by the development company. I wondered what would happen to the Holt wine enterprise after Wesley was sent to prison. Wesley might have already listed Ian as a co-owner.

Mooncat popped her head in. "We're getting busy, and there are a few folks out there who want to see you."

"On my way." I scarfed down two more pieces of sushi and stashed the container in the mini-fridge.

The sight of a row of friends seated up and down the bar made me smile. Josie chatted with Henry, Dane and Tom Phang laughed at something, while Ed schmoozed away with Felipe Diaz. *Wow*.

"What is this, a party?" I smiled. "It's not my birthday, you know."

"Here's to Cece." Ed raised his glass.

The others followed suit.

"To your continued success in all things." Mooncat held up her water.

"You guys." I blushed. "Stop it."

"Hey, it isn't every day you put away a couple of bad guys," Josie said.

"It was a joint effort," I protested. "Seriously."

"Well, we're proud of you." Henry beamed.

Ed nodded his agreement. Dane began a slow, rhythmic clapping. The others took it up, and soon random customers had joined the clapping.

"Thank you." I held up both palms. "Thank you. Enjoy your wine, everyone." To Dane, I muttered, "You're embarrassing me."

"You can handle it, Cece," she said. "I can't tell you how glad I am to be off that detective's radar."

"I can't believe I had such a villain for an employer." Tom lowered his voice. "Then he tried to make it worse by attacking you and your sister?" He shook his head.

"He did," I said.

"I wonder what's going to happen with the winery," Tom said.

"I don't know." I wondered the same thing. I regarded him. "Maybe the employees can buy it and run it as a cooperative."

Felipe leaned in. "I like the sound of that. We have a good product, and putting together what we all know, I bet we could make it work."

If Wesley had legalized his intentions toward Ian, the nephew might already own a share of the business. Ian might welcome the participation of employees who knew a lot more about the business than he did.

"Cece, I need to apologize for being distracted this week," Dane said. "I've been in negotiations for a major commission."

"That sounds interesting." I leaned on the bar. "Did you land it?"

"I did." Her cheeks pinkened. "It's going to give my artistic career a real boost."

"Congratulations. But wait." I frowned. "Are you still going to be able to work for me?"

She laughed. "Absolutely. Don't worry."

"Whew. I'm relieved and glad."

I glanced up when the door opened. My smile split my face when I saw Benjamin's handsome face. I hurried over to greet him.

"You're back." I laid my palm on his cheek.

He took my hand and kissed it, then closed my fingers around the kiss. "That's a promise for later," he whispered.

I blushed. "Deal. Glass of wine on me?"

"I'd love to, but I'll take a rain check. I just got in and traffic on the 101 was brutal. I need to get home and recover for a bit." He cleared his throat. "I did hear that a couple of bad guys were put behind bars this morning."

"They were."

"Your doing?" He raised his eyebrows.

"Allie helped. But we're both fine."

"For which I am infinitely grateful." He leaned over and kissed my forehead. "Pick you up at nine thirty?"

"Please." I kept smiling as he sauntered out.

A group of senior citizen couples poured through the door he held open for them. They kept coming. I counted fourteen people by the time the door closed. Right now, I had a business to run. I was grateful to be alive and safe, with a satisfactory end to the week of turbulence and a lovely evening to come. With any luck, Friday might turn out to be a normal day.

I turned toward the newcomers and smiled. "Welcome to Vino y Vida."

# CHAPTER 65

I sat at Allie's kitchen table with my mom, my twin, and my daughter at three thirty on Saturday afternoon. After cake, ice cream, a piñata, and presents, Allie shooed the eleven boys and girls outside to run off the sugar high. They didn't care how chilly it was. Good-natured Fuller volunteered to watch over the kiddos and try to forestall visits to the hospital's emergency department. Benjamin went along to help.

For now, the women of the family had a few minutes of peace to sip an adult beverage and catch up with each other. Mom and Zoe had driven over from Davis this morning, and Allie and I had given them a quick summary of the week's events. Now the bookends of the family wanted more.

"That Holt dude sounds awful." The two small silver eyebrow rings Zoe had added since the holidays moved with her frown. "He was going to slash your throat, Auntie Allie?"

"Sure looked like it." Allie swallowed and rubbed her neck. "But between your mom and me, we put an end to that."

"In the end, what was Holt's motivation?" Mom—otherwise known as Professor Wilhelmina Flaherty Van Ness—gazed from Allie to me, our mother's eyes the same gray green as mine.

"He had a vineyard and winery business that was just getting off the ground," I said. "He must have had a lot of debt, even if

Tara was his financial backer. I think Karl discovered they were half brothers and wanted in on the deal."

"What kind of hold would Karl have over Wesley?" Mom ran a hand through her no-nonsense short do, her formerly dark hair now an attractive salt and pepper.

"I'm pretty sure Wes and Tara began their relationship down in the Sonoma area while she was still married to her rich former husband, or maybe when they attended the same college." I glanced at Zoe to see how she was taking this.

My girl didn't seem fazed or upset. *Good.* That meant the mention of someone having an extramarital relationship didn't remind her of what I'd said about her father. If it did, she was mature enough to handle it.

"Wesley didn't want his reputation smeared," Allie chimed in. "Now that he was becoming a player on the wine scene."

"Plus, he never had kids of his own," I said. "He seemed to want to get close to Ian, his half nephew, and bring him into the business."

"It's all a bit sordid, don't you think?" my mom asked. "Murder being a far leap beyond sordid, of course."

I nodded and sipped my single malt Scotch. Allie had served the drinks in small, elegant stemmed glasses. Scotch for us, sherry for Mom and Zoe.

"Who else were the cops looking at?" Zoe asked. "They must have had a list of suspects."

I told her about Gareth, Jo, and Dane. "I'm relieved I haven't been employing a killer in the wine bar, and I never thought Jo had done it."

"I'm glad Gareth is in the clear," Allie said. "I'd love to get him in on the honest side of real estate dealing."

"Were the police close to arresting the two guilty parties?" Mom asked.

"Quan said he was, at least about Wesley Holt."

"He mentioned Tara, too," Allie added.

"Right." I flipped my hands open. "But how close? We don't know."

"Well, I certainly am glad you girls didn't come to harm in the end." Mom smiled. "Despite the bit of a close call on the way."

Zoe gave her grandmother a side-eye. "Gran, they're not—"

Mom cut her off. "Yes, Zoe, I'm aware they are grown women and not girls. But they'll always be my girls, so get used to it."

The door from the outside burst open, bringing in Arthur and Franklin along with a burst of cool air.

"Everybody's gone," Franklin said.

"Can we open our presents from you now?" Arthur's cheeks were pink from running around outdoors.

"I hope you thanked each of your friends for what they gave you," Allie said.

Fuller and Benjamin joined us.

"They did and were thoroughly polite about it," Benjamin said.

I smiled up at this man who seemed to fit easily into our family, the one I'd referred to as Handsome the first time I saw him in Vino y Vida last fall. It was still true. I thought I might finally be getting over my distrust of men, or at least my hesitation at getting involved in an intimate relationship. Zoe wasn't the only one to overcome a deep wound from the past.

"Yes, you may open your family gifts now," Allie said.

A moment later, after ripping open the paper, Arthur flung himself at me. "I love it, Auntie Cee. Thank you!"

"Let's see, kiddo," Zoe said.

Arthur held up the framed photo. He loved my cats with a passion and was always disappointed he couldn't have one at home. I'd taken a great picture of him snuggled on the couch with both Mittens and Martin.

"That's sweet, Mom," Zoe said to me.

I smiled at her.

"Thank you, Auntie Cee." Also a cat lover, my more scholarly nephew's eyes gleamed as he gazed at the book about the history and science of domesticated cats I'd found for him.

"You both are very welcome." I ruffled Franklin's dark brown curls.

His expression suddenly somber, he turned toward Allie. "Mama, one of the kids said you and Auntie Cee almost got killed by a criminal. That's not true, is it?"

"Well, sweetheart, we did find ourselves in a tricky situation." Allie shot me a desperate glance.

"We sure did," I told the twins, since Arthur was now all ears, too. "An ill-intentioned man threatened your mom two days ago."

"What's ill-intentioned?" Arthur asked.

"It means a bad guy," Franklin told him. "Let Auntie Cee finish."

"It does," I said. "Anyway, we rescued ourselves and managed to keep that bad guy from hurting anyone until the police arrived."

Arthur's face lit up. "Twins save the day!" He shot both fists in the air.

That pretty much summed it up, I thought, as Mom laughed. Allie smiled. The boys moved on to opening other family gifts. Fuller opened beers for himself and Benjamin.

Me? I gazed around at these people of my heart, grateful to be safe. Zoe was opening up to me. Benjamin was a good man. And I knew if trouble arose again, I could always count on Allie. Twins saved the day, every single time.